About the Author

Victoria Jane is a fresh and vibrant new voice that started her first book at the age of sixteen, finishing her novel as a university student at Royal Holloway. As a girl she grew up with her nose in a book and always wished to have her own book on the shelves next to her favourite authors.

That Summertime Feeling

Victoria Jane

The Summertime Feeling

Vanguard Press

VANGUARD PAPERBACK

© Copyright 2024
Victoria Jane

The right of Victoria Jane to be identified as author of
this work has been asserted by her in accordance with the
Copyright, Designs and Patents Act 1988.

All Rights Reserved

No reproduction, copy or transmission of this publication
may be made without written permission.
No paragraph of this publication may be reproduced,
copied or transmitted save with the written permission of the
publisher, or in accordance with the provisions
of the Copyright Act 1956 (as amended).

Any person who commits any unauthorised act in relation to
this publication may be liable to criminal
prosecution and civil claims for damages.

A CIP catalogue record for this title is
available from the British Library.

ISBN 978 1 80016 847 3

This is a work of fiction. Names, characters, businesses, places, events and
incidents are either the product of the author's imagination or used in a
fictitious manner. Any resemblance to actual persons, living or dead, or
actual events is purely coincidental.

Vanguard Press is an imprint of
Pegasus Elliot Mackenzie Publishers Ltd.
www.pegasuspublishers.com

First Published in 2024

Vanguard Press
Sheraton House Castle Park
Cambridge England

Printed & Bound in Great Britain

Dedication

This book is dedicated to my brother. While I might have gotten annoyed at your constant questions, you never gave up on me.

Prologue

Life can be dull, right? Boring, tiresome, monotony. It's exhausting sometimes! Well, that's what my life has become, a constant cycle of the same day – school, work, home, school, work, home. A broken record! Sure, I occasionally went out with friends, but nothing ever truly happened. Plus, I only had three close friends and we were all pretty much the kind that kept in a group and didn't do a whole lot. My life was boring. I was too used to being in my own comfort zone and never moving. Everything had become tedious and I was tired of it. I needed change and I was going to make it happen – starting that summer! It was time for some spontaneity...

I was taking charge! I had sat around for too long and now was my time! Mum had signed me up for this random summer camp thing and I would be stuck there... for a month! I wasn't happy about it – but at least it was something new.

From the moment I set foot on the campsite I felt like something was going to happen. You know how it always does in the movies. At first, I was worried, but as soon as I arrived, I knew it would be fine. I'd make this summer the greatest, no matter what. I could feel something in the air telling me that everything was going to change – and from that moment I knew it would be true.

It wasn't until days after I arrived, though, that my life *really* changed – when disaster, in the shape of a very cute guy with delicious, chocolate wavy hair, drove into camp in a silver Volvo. I couldn't even see his face but I knew he'd be my undoing. His shoulders were broad and I could see tense muscles underneath his white cotton shirt. My breath caught just from the sight of his hand running through that luscious mop of hair. I saw him standing with Dan, laughing about something, and I immediately wanted to know what he was saying. I was desperate to know who he was!

But let's not get ahead of ourselves. That isn't a good start to the story. There's still a lot you should know. We need to go back to where it began. You need to know everything – start to finish, first day to last. Those hot days full of sunshine and nights filled with a tense chill – in the summer I'll never forget…

Chapter 1

Of course, you're eager to get to the really interesting part, the main story, but they do say that greatness can't be rushed. So, first, here's a bit about me. My name is Cassandra Bailey, Cassie to my friends. I just turned eighteen and I'm eager to finally gain my independence so my life can truly begin. I've been stuck for too long!

Now, I know some things are just meant to be. Like getting into that school you've desperately wanted to go to for years. Or scoring the winning goal for your football team. Or meeting that one person you were destined to find, the one who completes you. Knowing at that point those things were right and meant to happen – and you felt happy. One inevitable moment, whatever it was, that would change your life forever. Well that's what I hoped anyway. Maybe I sat at home watching way too many movies where everything worked out perfectly, conditioning me to believe it could all come true. But a girl could hope!

When I look back, I couldn't really complain. I had been pretty lucky. Yes, there have been ups and downs (definitely a lot of them), but overall I've been so thankful in life, even with its tedious moments. To start, I have the greatest friends in the world. I apologise, dear reader, if you'd argue that your friends are better, but I must regret to inform you that it can't be true, although if you ever met them you probably wouldn't know whether to run for the hills or laugh along with their twisted sense of humour. I definitely chose to laugh, and since then I haven't been able to get rid of my friends, who've managed to make life a fraction less mind-numbingly boring. My little group – Connie, Lexi, Lottie (except for Connie, we all had shortened names and for some reason I liked it), and me.

I have no complaints when it comes to my family, either. I know I could've done much worse. My parents are still married – I hesitate to say happily, but you know how it can be with families sometimes. With mine, it was just getting exhausting – the arguing and yelling was all too much at times. The saving grace were my siblings. You see, I'm the middle child – an older brother, Jake, and a younger brother, Bradley, then a younger sister, Hailey, too. Jake was twenty-one, Hailey was ten and Bradley was six. While we weren't perfect in the slightest, I loved them unconditionally – they were amazing!

But, something was missing. I know I should be grateful with what I have and focus on the good but I still felt like something should be there, something I couldn't quite explain but was desperate to find. And I couldn't wait for the day I'd find it.

So let's get one last thing straight before we start the story. I wasn't the kind of girl that guys noticed; not one of those beautiful skinny types with long, slender legs and golden, cascading curls that could make a guy fall in love from just a glance. I wasn't the kind of girl that guys chased after – and definitely not one who left a trail of broken-hearted boys in her wake. I knew for sure that I wasn't the girl a guy would notice in the street and still be thinking about a week later. I didn't look like that. I had straight, medium-length brown hair that just kind of flopped on my back, and my eyes were the stereotypical brown, the colour of mud after a big downpour – real attractive. I wasn't unique, different or special. I was me. My body was far from runway ready. I was short, with no killer legs or graceful arms. I didn't think a guy would ever look at me the way I always longed for. I just wasn't that kind of girl. Don't get me wrong – I'm not saying this to gain sympathy or attention. I was simply aware of who I was and what my – rather minor – impact was.

Now I'll confess it from the start… I'm a hopeless romantic, searching for that 'meet cute' moment, where eyes lock across a room, the room melts away, time stops and nothing else matters. A cheesy film, a good romantic book and I'm gone. I've always loved reading about great romances. I'd dive into a book and be lost in a whole different universe. But there's something in me that wishes, just for once, I could experience the same kind of true love story. Maybe *I* could be the main character, like at the end of a film when the man comes swooping in, confessing his love, and then everything works out. Like in *Sixteen Candles* when the guy is waiting outside the church for the girl, or in *It's a Boy Girl Thing* when the super-hot athlete gets with the brainy nerd that everyone made fun of. You know all those books where the dream boy comes out of nowhere and is completely perfect for the main girl with the quirky best friend? Well, I always seem to be the quirky best friend, the one on the sidelines who helps the main one get with the guy she was meant to be with and just stands there in the background, forgotten. That was me. But I wanted something different – to be the main character in my own story, not just watching everyone else get what I want. That desire to just meet the guy that would sweep me off my feet. Crazy, right? Well, like I said – I'm a hopeless romantic!

But no more pity, I know what you're all here for...

I'd made it to the end of the school year... finally. I'd suffered through the endless days of working, sitting and listening to dull, repetitive lessons, filled with the need to be somewhere else – anywhere else! I would sit and stare out the window, seeing the glorious sun gazing down, filling my face with warmth, and be consumed with this desperate desire to go out and enjoy it. As I sat there, I felt mocked by the sun, stuck, sweating in my uniform and dreaming of the days when I could soak in the sunny rays, in the park, on the beach... any place!

As I sat with my eyes glued to the clock, watching each minute inch by, seconds closer to my freedom, I just thought of the final hours I had left that day, knowing that I'd be finished in school for six weeks! The things I could do in my summer, the adventures, the excitement, the change! I sat hunched over my desk, my best friend Lexi next to me, looking equally exhausted, as my science teacher droned on and on about nonsense – something to do with particles or movement or some kind of ridiculous theory. I'd zoned out a long time ago and had no intention of zoning back in to hear what he had to say. I mean, who really cared? In a few hours I'd be gone from here!

The bell rang, like angel trumpets singing from the heavens, to signal the end of the lesson and save me from death by boredom. I sped to pack up all my stuff and rushed to leave with an overwhelming need to escape the classroom.

"Well, that was a waste of time," Lexi said, walking next to me and linking arms as we made our way to the food hall for lunch.

"Ugh, tell me about it", I groaned in response "I mean, come on – we have like three hours left of the whole school year and Mr Callahan was still standing there droning on with some nonsense about molecules."

"I'm impressed you got that much. I couldn't even listen to what he was saying. It was just an unbearable droning! I swear, the relief when I heard that bell go. Never has that chiming sounded so heavenly."

"Ha! You just read my mind Lex. Well, it's finally over now!" I celebrated.

Lexi nodded in agreement. We walked over to the food hall and met Connie and Lottie, who were already sitting at our table, Connie scrolling on her phone while Lottie had her nose in a book. You see, Lottie was very shy and silent and much preferred the fantasy of a book over reality – not that I could blame her. Connie was the artsy, creative type and I have no doubt that she was flipping through Pinterest looking for more inspiration. Lexi was very much the louder one and the one I was closest to. She was never afraid to speak her mind and would fight anyone that crossed her friends in a heartbeat. Then there was me. I was definitely the mother of the group, keeping Lexi in line and making sure Lottie got her head out of her book once in a while. Connie had been my best friend since nursery. We had grown up together. She was medium height but was still pretty tall compared to me. Lottie and Lexi we had met in secondary school, but they had become just as close to me. It was the four of us all the time. Lottie was similar to Connie, but whereas Connie had long wavy black hair, Lottie's was a much lighter brown. And Lexi? Well, to put it simply, she was basically a blond beauty. She wore glasses that somehow highlighted her washy green eyes, and she was composed of this effortless confidence. Yes, there had been some others in our group but they had been and gone. These three friends were my foundations. Whatever happened in life, they were the people I knew I could always go to; and I knew they were dependable. I slumped into my seat and pulled out my lunch, diving into a pasta salad.

"Man, I need coffee if I'm going to get through the rest of the day", I told my friends.

"No way! You're addicted to that stuff." Connie replied.

"Pleaseeeeee, I mean come on! If I don't get my dose of caffeine I may not make it through the rest of the day! I could die Connie, die! Do you want my death on your hands", I stuck my bottom lip out at her and she rolled her eyes.

"All right, come on then, I could do with a coffee too", Connie sighed in defeat as she rose from her seat. I leapt up with new-found energy and chased after Connie.

"I knew you couldn't resist it for very long", I grinned at her.

"Yeah, yeah." Connie sounded annoyed but I could see the smile creeping over her face as we made our way to the queue.

Within five minutes I was savouring my iced coffee. I always got it with a drizzle of caramel, and I tell you, there's no better way to have coffee in the summer. With coffee in hand, the condensation dripping over my knuckles, we started back to the table and sat down. I enjoyed these moments with my friends. They were awesome and made school just slightly more bearable.

With only a few hours left of school, excited chatter quickly broke out around the table as summer plans were discussed.

"I'll be soaking up the sun and doing nothing every day", Lexi boasted, "maybe chilling round the local pool. I've got some really nice new bikinis and I know I could land myself a new man, or", she paused, "even just some company for the summer".

"Well I think my mum wants to go on holiday somewhere", Connie said. "She just doesn't know where yet. She thinks that since dad is gone and she's finally divorced she can do everything she always wanted to – and rub it in his face". Connie sighed and rolled her eyes.

"Well, I would much rather chill round the pool or go on holiday instead of this weird summer camping thing I've been signed up for by my mum – for the whole month!" I grumbled. "She thinks it will do me good. Apparently, I don't get out much and need to *broaden my horizons* and do something different – or something stupid like that. *Her* words, not mine".

"Ah come on, I'm sure it won't be that bad", Connie said, sensing my unhappiness with the situation, "maybe she's right and it will help you".

"Why do I need to broaden my horizons? It's not like I don't have *any* friends", I argued, waving my hand across the group at the table. "I'm just... selective."

"Oh, don't be like that", Lottie chimed in quickly, then immediately went back to her book.

"Yea, maybe you'll find someone", added Lexi, raising her eyebrows at me.

"Oh, come on Lex, be serious, no guys give me the time of day. Remember when I was crushing hard on Mason and he didn't even know my name? It's just going to be a month of me being the lonely weirdo at this summer camp – and please never do that with your eyes again. That was just weird", I grumbled as I sunk down into my seat. "Plus, I'm sure the only reason mum signed me up for it was to get me out the house."

"Your parents still bad?" Lexi asked. I nodded. Lottie looked up at that point too with a weak smile, obviously trying to give me a sense of comfort. I returned the smile and she settled into her book again.

"Honestly," I told them, "it's just every single day they argue about anything. It's like they *want* to argue. I don't know what I'm supposed to do!"

"Do you think they'll get divorced?" asked Connie. She knew what it was like. Her parents had been divorced for a year now and she knew that the whole parents splitting thing can be hard. I noticed Lexi elbow her, trying to keep it out of my eyeline. "What? I was just asking!"

"Ugh, I don't know, I almost wish they would", I confessed. "I just think if they stopped being so goddamn stubborn then they could sort out whatever this mess was. We were so happy, and I don't know what happened!"

Lexi gave me a sympathetic look.

"You never know, they might not even get divorced", she said.

"They could work it out", Connie added reassuringly, shooting a glance at Lottie, who looked up from her book and nodded vigorously in agreement.

"Well maybe this camp is what I need then", I said trying to be positive, "but I'm going to be abandoned and alone *all* summer."

"Dude, come on!" said Connie. "If you have this idea, then there's no way you'll have a good time and no way anything is going to happen. You've got to *do* something, otherwise you'll be stuck in this mood the whole time and you'll be right – nothing will happen. Maybe a fresh group of people will be good", Connie added, wiggling her eyebrows. "Maybe wherever it is will have some nice new guys."

"Snap out of it!" Lexi shot at me sharply.

I knew she was right. It was just annoying. I mean I wanted it to be a good time but I was just so sure that it wouldn't. Lexi let it slide and we continued with lunch.

Soon lunch was over, and I was walking to my very last lesson of the school year. Me and Connie had English – my favourite! It wasn't so bad – Miss Walker was a great teacher, and I was with Connie, so I would get through it. We sat together as Miss Walker talked about the final parts of the play we'd been studying, *Romeo and Juliet*. I just didn't get it. I mean, I'm a romantic, don't get me wrong, but the whole idea of Juliet murdering herself so quickly just seemed a little excessive.

After a class discussion we were officially finished. My last lesson, done. I was free, and with that me and Connie raced out of the class to join our friends waiting outside. Summer was beginning, and I knew it was going to be great!

With Lexi's words ringing in my head, I was desperate to make this summer worthwhile. This was the first time I was really free – no schoolwork and old enough to do my own thing. I was so excited; days on end hanging out with my best friends and nothing to worry about, which was much needed after all the work at school.

Me and my friends went out almost every day – to the park, to museums, to the beach. We drank, we laughed, we smiled. Life was good. I was going to live this summer like I meant it! And two days from now I will be driving off to summer camp. I honestly didn't really have much of an idea about it. Like I said, my mum had signed me up for it and I really was dreading it. I would be alone with none of my best friends, hours away from everything I knew. Questions flooded my mind. What if I make no friends? What if I end up being a sad loner? What if there are no hot guys? amongst many others. as you can tell, really freaking out.

I had one day left before I had to leave, which meant the dreaded bag packing. I had tried to put it off for so long, but now it was unavoidable. I had been trying to stay out of the house as much as possible. Luckily, mum and dad were still at work, but the times they were home were just filled with arguments and shouting. My only form of self-preservation had been to put up camp at Lexi's house for the days mum and dad were around. I had done a pretty good job of it so far, but I could hardly do my packing at Lexi's house, which meant I was stuck at home packing my bag. I had begged my friends to come over, but Connie was already off on a plane for her holiday and Lexi and Lottie were both busy with family stuff.

I yanked my suitcase out from under my bed and placed it on top, and I looked around my room realising I wouldn't be sleeping in it for a whole month. The room was a pretty good size. It was painted white with one pale pink wall, which my bed was pushed against. The wall was covered in pictures of me and my friends, decorated with twinkling fairy lights. I had a double bed and it sat in the middle of the wall. On the opposite side I had a built-in wardrobe with a set of drawers underneath. I didn't have a whole lot of furniture because I didn't want my room to be too cluttered. Apart from a reading chair in the corner and two bedside tables the room was rather empty. I had wooden flooring with a soft grey rug and I liked it. I wasn't a fan of too much, so I made sure the room was just right for me.

I could hear shouting from downstairs. I couldn't make out what it was about this time – I just heard the muffled raised voices of my parents. With a sigh, I walked over to my speaker and connected it to my phone, letting my music fill the room and hopefully drown out the noises. This had become a common occurrence – me finding ways to drown out the shouting to keep me from losing my mind.

I shook myself from staring around the room and started gathering my clothes. First, I packed my favourite shorts – light blue denim, baggier around the legs and high waisted – along with some jeans, just in case there were some cold days. Once those were in, I started with some cute tops, crop tops and bodysuits. I wanted to make sure I was prepared, so I included long-sleeved and short-sleeved, plain colours, either white, pink or blue. I chucked in a couple dresses and skirts too, just to be sure. After I'd sorted that, I grabbed all the other stuff I'd need along with a few nice swimsuits – two bikinis and a one-piece just for options. One bikini had black and white stripes while the other was a sweet pale blue. The one-piece was a pale pink with added detail around the top and braided straps. I shoved it all in my suitcase and grabbed some shoes. Of course my Converses would be coming with me – white ankle boots that I practically wore *everywhere* – but I grabbed a couple of other pairs, too.

As my head was in my wardrobe getting the shoes, I heard a gentle knock at my door.

"How's it going in here?" My mum said as she peeped her head in the door.

"Yea, it's good," I smiled at her half-heartedly.

"Do you think you have everything you need?" she asked.

"I think so. I mean I just need to get my toiletries and wash things but I think I've got everything else," I assured her.

"Oh, right. Well, that's good," she replied.

I looked back down to my suitcase and shifted things around, feeling the need to do something. My mum was standing awkwardly in the door frame watching me.

"Are you OK?" I inquired with a worried glance at my mother, who was standing there glancing down at my bag.

"Yeah, yeah," she answered absent-mindedly, "just going to be weird without you around the house for so long."

"Well, I'd happily not go – you signed me up for it!" I said, hoping I could change her mind. But she just looked at me and shook her head.

"No, no, this will do you good. You could do with this break. It'll be fine here. I just want you to have a good time," she assured me. "It will just be a little weird without you."

"Well, it won't be long and I'll be back before you know it," I told her, with a small smile, although part of me wished that this month would go nice and slowly. There was part of me desperate to enjoy the time I'd have away from home – no arguments, no complications, just a whole month of enjoying the sun. Or that's what I hoped…

Chapter 2

It was the day. Saying goodbye to my home. I don't mean to sound dramatic and, to be honest, I was actually quite looking forward to it. I thought this might be the chance I need. All new people, and maybe I'd meet the one, my one. It might have been high hopes, but my friends' words stuck in my head and I wanted to make this holiday worthwhile. I've lived my life being far too safe and careful – now it was time to explore.

Me and mum set off early in the morning. My bags were loaded into the back of the car and we made our way to the camp. It was a two-hour journey and I didn't want to get there too late in the day, so we set off early and made it to the campsite at twelve. I was worried that it was going to be weird being stuck with my mum for that long. We hadn't spent a lot of time together recently, but with the radio playing and my mum's chatter, the journey passed in no time. It was crowded and hectic when we arrived. I said goodbye to my mum in the car and assured her that I'd be fine on my own. I jumped out and grabbed my bags. With a wave, my mum turned around and was out of the campsite.

Once she had left, I turned around and faced the chaos before me. It was a nightmare. I had no idea what I was supposed to do, where I was supposed to go *and* I knew no one. Perfect right? Anyways, I was going to try and make the best of a bad situation. As I arrived, I decided to scope out the area. It wasn't what I was expecting really. It was much bigger. I didn't realise just how many people were actually doing it, and here I was standing alone awkwardly, unsure about what to do. As I looked around, I spied at least a hundred campers, plus a fair amount of camp leaders and helpers. Did I just go and talk to someone? Or wait for someone to come and talk to me? I can't have done a good job of hiding my confusion and worry because the next time I looked up, there was already someone in front of me. I glanced up and I was standing face to face with a girl, seemingly the same age as me.

"Hi, I saw you here on your own and thought you looked as lost as me so I thought I'd come over so we could save each other.'' Her voice was sweet. She had long wavy blonde hair, both slimmer and taller than me (which wasn't a surprise, really). I wasn't too sure of her to be honest; she seemed like the kind of girl that I'd mock. She was tall, skinny, blonde, beautiful – no one was going to look at me twice when I was standing next to her. She was one of those girls… you know? A knockout beauty. It was at this moment I realised I'd just been standing and staring – and I knew I didn't want to scare off the one person brave enough to talk to me. So I began the conversation. Even though I felt uneasy, I wanted to try. I mean she seemed nice enough, so why not, right?

"Oh… er sorry, hi, yea my name's Cassandra. Everyone calls me Cassie though. What about you, what's your name?"

"Oh, what a cute name! Hi, I'm Emma." Oh great, even her name was pretty. "So, are you as awkward as I am?"

"Totally! I had no idea what I was meant to be doing – thanks for saving me."

"Don't worry we're in the same boat," said Emma. "It looks like we saved each other."

I was so surprised at how easily the conversation flowed between us, and I was so happy that this girl decided to come and talk to me. We continued chatting and I soon found out that she was an only child, her parents were together and she had come to this camp before – twice. It was at this moment I realised I had been totally wrong about her. Maybe this could be a new friendship? Camp was already going better than I'd anticipated. I looked around a bit and realised that everyone was talking to people. It calmed me and I realised that so many others were in the same boat as me and I really didn't have to worry about anything. Maybe I didn't have much to fear after all.

Soon after I arrived, things became so crazy – everyone finding where they were meant to be sleeping, people unpacking. One child had got lost and the leaders were already freaking out (I bet some of the younger ones now wished they had never volunteered). But all in all it was a good day. Me and Emma talked and got to know each other a bit more. Turns out we were actually able to choose who we stayed with, so me and Emma quickly paired together and went to find one of the tents that were already set up. I hadn't found any fit guys yet, but with all the action going on it wasn't a surprise. I had hardly seen *any* other campers yet. I found out there was a campfire that night (apparently a forty-year-old tradition to have a campfire on the first night for everyone to get to know each other), and I was hoping someone might be there.

The first day was mostly uneventful – just familiarising ourselves with where we would be spending the next four weeks. Me and Emma found our tent and had gotten all settled. We soon met a few other girls in the adjoining part of our tent. It was an odd set-up – a tent for six but split into three sections. There was Tiffany and Molly sharing the part next to us, and Claire and Emily in the next. Six of us all together and they all seemed pretty nice – well, apart from Tiffany. She seemed like a queen bee. But we were soon all settled, and I had Emma, so that was OK.

The day flew by and the time of the campfire arrived. Emma and I got changed into something warmer than the shorts we were both in – I was glad I'd packed those jeans! Soon we were all sitting round this massive bonfire. Some people were roasting marshmallows, some were just chatting, but me and Emma were singing along with another group. The leader of the camp, Dan, called out to get our attention. He seemed nice enough, he was a regular build with a heavy beard. Wearing a checked shirt and a cap that made his eyes hard to see in the darkness he thought it would be a good idea to try and get people singing some camp songs. So far we didn't sound too bad, though there was this one boy, Connor, who couldn't sing to save his life. But, who cares? We were all laughing about it, and Connor was having fun.

They all looked like a nice bunch. I noticed the little groups that had already formed – the boys that seemed pretty sporty, the girls that seemed disgusted by mud but were still here, the group of the youngest campers that surrounded the leaders, then the middle kids that tried to appear too cool for camp. I smiled to myself and kept on looking around.

Then, my eyes landed on him. He was sitting on the other side of the fire, so I couldn't get the best look. But from what I could see over the enormous flames; he had wavy, sandy blond hair and blue eyes. He seemed to be laughing about something, then I noticed that the tone-deaf boy who had been singing had made his way over there. They shared a comfortable handshake and he said something to that Connor guy. I immediately wanted to know what he'd said. He seemed like a surfer guy, he had that kind of vibe around him. As I was studying him he turned his head and our eyes locked. I could feel the blush rising in my cheeks as he raised the side of his mouth in a teasing smirk, but I just couldn't turn away. He had the kind of eyes that I could just dive into; the rich blue pulled me in, and I was washed away from reality. I was far from shore- but I wasn't complaining. It was like I was glued to his gaze. We were both still looking at each other when Emma brought me back to my senses with an elbow in my side. I was kind of thankful; I was not going to get carried away. I mean, this just doesn't happen to me.

"Hey, are you all right? It looked like you zoned out for a while there," Emma asked with concern.

"Oh yea, totally sorry, just staring into space, looking at nothing in particular at all."

"Ah, so you were staring at the beautiful blond that keeps glancing over at you then, were you?"

I snapped my head back and she was right. The beautiful blond *was* looking right at me. But that couldn't be right. I wasn't the type of girl that guys like *that* liked. Maybe he was looking at Emma – that seemed more believable. They were that kind of IT couple, looked like they went together.

"Wait, what do you mean? No way, I was just admiring the fire."

"So is 'fire' his nickname?" Emma teased.

I needed to get out of this situation, like right now. The guy's gaze hadn't left me and now Emma had a mischievous look on her face. I was starting to get nervous; I knew I needed to put an end to this questioning before it properly began.

"Anyway, I'm getting really tired now. It's been a long busy day, you coming?" I questioned, hoping to get off the topic and desperate to get away from the inviting nature of the fiery flames. Emma wasn't falling for it. I could tell by the look on her face that she wouldn't let it drop and I'd be hearing about this later. But she went along with it.

"Yea, sure, let's just tell Dan that we're going to bed and we can head back to the tent." Emma started walking away leaving me completely alone. It was at this moment I noticed that the unnamed blond guy had started making his way over to me. He was much taller than I thought he would be – oh great, so now he looked like a giant.

"I gotta tell you that was a risky move you tried to pull there," he said with a slight chuckle, a smirk creeping up the side of his mouth. Seeing him up close like this I could see that his eyes were a lighter blue than they seemed when I first saw him, and his sandy blond hair was dusted with different shades and a freckle of brown. He looked like he'd just strolled off a Malibu beach.

"What risky move?" I asked innocently.

"The move where you tried to leave without even telling me your name." So, he was a smooth-talking surfer boy then. "You would have kept me up all night trying to guess your name."

"Oh, of course, *that* move," I replied with feigned confidence. "Well, I'm sorry. You looked quite busy over there with that tone-deaf friend of yours."

"Oooo, she's got sass, I like it. Can I walk you back to your tent?"

"Sorry, I was just about to head out with my friend. Oh and here she comes." Perfect timing, thank you Emma. "Emma, I would like you to meet…" I glanced over at him, giving him the hint that I was waiting for his answer.

"Dean. My name's Dean." Nice name for a nice face, I thought.

"Well then, Emma I would like for you to meet Dean," I said as calmly as I could, even though I could sense Dean's eyes on my every move. I could feel my heart racing and I was almost sure that Dean could hear it. "Well, anyway, sorry Dean. As I was saying, me and Emma were just about to leave, you see. It's been a very long day and we're both so tired." I started to turn away, but then I heard Dean call something over my shoulder.

"Wait, I never got your name!"

"Well, I guess you'll have to wait till next time you see me then Dean," I called back. I sneaked one last glance over my shoulder, only to see Dean's wide smile and a glint in his eye. The feeling that I was in trouble was overwhelming.

"He's cute, I told you he was looking at you," Emma whispered to me as she linked my arm on the way back to my tent. I elbowed her in the side, but with a giggle I secretly wished she was right.

I couldn't help but smile to myself. Maybe I'd find a man on this trip after all. Imagine it! Me! The one that no one ever noticed, landing the beach babe on the first night. Me and Emma stumbled back to our tent, our giggles dancing in the air. I got ready for bed, settled down and went to sleep with a smile plastered on my face. It was difficult to sleep, thinking and dreaming of the scene that might await me at breakfast. Soon my eyes grew heavy and I began to rest. Oh, breakfast couldn't come fast enough!

Chapter 3

Wow, I really should've looked at this morning thing more closely! It was seven a.m. and calls outside the tent were waking me. All the leaders were out, yelling at us all to get up and be ready for breakfast in an hour. Now, that might seem like a long time, but for over a hundred campers to all be showered and dressed in that hour was a big ask. The only thing that made me get up was the thought I'd be seeing Dean at breakfast and I realised I needed time to prepare.

Last night wasn't so bad. The campfire light made me look better than usual, and don't forget the tiredness we were all feeling after that hectic day. But now, in the harsh light of the morning, who knows what I'd be dealing with. That thought alone made me jump out of bed and run over to the toilets and showers all the girls shared. It wasn't the nicest thing – there were a few spiders here and there and the floor was already wet. But it was fine – I got in just before most of the campers arrived and wrecked the place. As soon as one shower was free, I ran in and washed my hair as best I could, then came out and dashed straight for the toilet. I had spent ages in the tent deciding what to wear, finally deciding on a pair of light denim ripped shorts and a cropped white top. And with my shorter brown hair, I was pleasantly surprised when I looked in the mirror. Not too sad with what I saw, I added a light touch of blush and mascara. As I was applying my lip gloss in the mirror, I noticed Emma appear behind me with a smirk on her face.

"Oooo, you wouldn't be dressing up for a certain blond hair boy now, would you?" Ah, Emma, of course – there was no way I was going to get out of this with her now. I was really hoping to avoid the conversation; I didn't want to be seen trying too hard before I knew anything would come of it. I wasn't going to be labelled that sad hopeless girl on the second day of camp!

"Oh, ha, ha," I said, blushing at the thought of Dean. "But really, do I look OK?" I asked her now, becoming really nervous.

"You look majorly hot. Wow, I swear, if Dean doesn't dip you and kiss you right in the food hall then I will be so mad."

"OK, OK, that's enough Em please, you're more worked up about this than I am!" I said but couldn't stop from bursting with laughter.

Making my way to the food hall that morning I didn't understand why I was so nervous. I didn't know if Dean was going to be there or what he was thinking. I mean, what if he was just joking around last night or even found someone better than me once I left the bonfire? Oh god! What if it was a dare? Ugh, I needed to get my head straight before seeing him; I only saw him yesterday! As I stepped in the door, I saw that Emma had saved me a seat and I was very thankful. I slid in next to her as quickly as I could and sat there waiting for my turn to go and get breakfast. That's when the Dean came and sat right next to me. Oh no, here we go!

Now, I remind you, I love the idea of cute boys wanting to talk to me, but it never happens. This means I've had no practice in how to actually talk to them. I've watched all those movies where it seems to just work, but that's the movies; things aren't like that in real life. Those moments are planned and scripted meticulously to make them look entirely spontaneous, and no matter how hard I tried, any plan I had to talk to a cute boy would immediately crumble. Maybe there were some girls that could flirt effortlessly, I just wasn't one of them.

"Right then, I need to know your name now, it's been driving me crazy all night," he demanded with a grin on his face. I turned in my seat so I could see his face better.

"Oh-er-right-um...." Great, not even using coherent words right now – this was going well! Dean just laughed.

"You know, it seems like I'm making you nervous," he observed.

"Oh ha, no way, it's just too early in the morning. Don't inflate your ego too much," I mumbled in response.

"Am I going to find out your name now or are you going to tease me even more?" Me? Tease him? Really?

"Her name's Cassandra but most people call her Cassie," Emma interrupted me, leaning over to be included.

"Well Cassandra, it's very nice to meet you properly." Dean didn't break eye contact for me for one minute while Emma was speaking, which was just making my heart beat even more. I shoved out my hand in some sort of awkward greeting. He jokingly shook it very seriously. I didn't get the spark that all the cheesy romantic books always talk about, but that's only ever in the movies anyway.

"I'm Emma, by the way, the best friend and the guard. So be careful," Emma teased with a mock-serious expression.

"Woah, OK," Dean said with his arms up in a feigned sign of defeat. "Consider myself warned," he chuckled.

As we sat and ate breakfast, I had marmite on toast, which spurred a whole debate with Emma and Dean about whether marmite was actually nice. Dean thought so but Emma didn't. It was good that Dean liked it, or that could've been the end of things right there!

While Emma had Weetabix and banana, Dean had chocolate spread on porridge. We laughed and joked, and I had fun, Dean was great and it helped that he got along with Emma. I felt happy. It felt weird.

"All right guys, now that you've all devoured your breakfasts it's time to tell you what we'll be doing today," started Dan as he got everyone's attention. He was a middle-aged man, his black hair peppered with grey, and he seemed like a nice guy. He was the one leading the campfire last night and he appeared to be the main guy in charge.

"So today, folks, we'll first be doing some icebreakers so we can all get to know each other a little better. I mean, it's the first official day and time we started talking to others. I can already see some groups forming, which is nice, but let's get out a little more!" There was a murmur in response and he continued, "Then after the icebreakers we'll be going rock climbing and abseiling to see if you trust each other after you've gotten to know each other. You'll need to get a jacket in case it gets cold and you'll need to make a sandwich for your lunch. Be back here in ten minutes to make your food and then we'll be starting the challenges at nine-thirty."

"Well then Miss Cassandra, I guess I'll see you soon." And with that Dean got up and walked away, jogging over to where his friends were. I'm sure there was a wink, but I wasn't certain of anything and didn't want to get my hopes up. I always did that.

"Oh my gosh, that was so hot! He's amazing Cassie!" I shot a smile Emma's way. This all felt too good to be true though. Why me? It can't be this easy.

Ten minutes later we were all standing on the campsite. Dan had first split us into three groups for some activities that worked in smaller numbers. Dean wasn't in my group this time, but I hoped that for the next one we could be in the same team. First, we did trust falls, which I thought was crazy. We still had to participate though, so here I was. It was actually kind of fun, but I couldn't stop my eyes from drifting over to Dean every once in a while. He glanced over, and when he noticed me watching he shot me a quick wink. I smiled and turned back to focus on not dropping the person about to fall in my arms.

Next, we were mixed again into two smaller groups and played two truths, one lie. It was a pretty good game, but it took me a while to think of my statements. They weren't bad in the end and not many people guessed what the actual lie was. I soon became bored, though, and just wanted to talk to Dean again. Apparently, my luck was about to change, as the next challenge was one all-together, I went to stand with the group and Dean immediately swooped in next to me.

"Finally," he joked, "I thought Dan was trying to keep us apart on purpose."

I was left speechless by this comment, it was such a warm day but I could still feel his warmth so close to me. It was something that I'd be more than happy to get used to.

The challenge commenced and soon people were struggling to fit their bodies through this small hoop. Then it came round to us. Dean wasn't too graceful as he tried to manoeuvre his tall, butch body through the hoop. After some – well, quite a lot – of struggle, he finally managed to get himself through; and then it was my turn.

"Let me show you how it's really done," I said to him, smugly. In less than ten seconds I'd slipped my body through the hoop and it was onto the next person.

"OK, well that's not fair. You're so much smaller than me, it's much easier for you," he protested.

"Ah, the sound of a sore loser," I said, mocking him as I gently nudged him with my shoulder.

"Oh, we'll see who the sore loser is when we get to the rock-climbing," he told me, narrowing his eyes.

"Oh, yeah, yeah, OK. I look forward to it," I replied, squaring up to the challenge.

"Ah, brown eyes, you have no idea what you've gotten yourself into," he said. There was a mischievous glint in his eye, and I took a deep breath with my eyes not breaking away from his. I think I was in trouble. With that we ended the game. There were a few more things that Dan had planned for us, but I just couldn't wait for rock climbing to see Dean would keep his promise.

Luckily, I didn't have to wait for long as forty-five minutes later everyone was standing around the bus waiting to go. I was actually quite excited about it. On the bus, I sat next to Emma and we gossiped the whole way. She asked how I felt about Dean and we laughed at what had happened at breakfast. I asked Emma whether she saw anyone but she shook her head.

"Not yet, but I'm not giving up hope. Maybe I'll meet someone while we're out." We started giggling together about our crazy hopes.

"Maybe Dean has a nice friend," I suggested, but Emma just shrugged.

The bus journey took around half an hour, but the time flew by sitting and chatting with Emma. She had become so close in such a little time, and I was so happy that she was the one that I bumped into first. I wasn't sure where Dean had got to. I assumed he'd just jumped onto the other bus with his friends, but I was sure I would find him once we were there.

We arrived at the rock-climbing centre and there were a range of climbing walls in every direction. There were already a lot of people on the walls, and I was so excited to have some fun.

"Looks amazing, doesn't it?" I heard right next to my ear. I turned my head and Dean was just a breath away from my face. My heart jumped and raced a mile a minute. What was happening to me? The trademark smirk I saw last night returned to the edge of his mouth.

"I, uh, yeah… it looks great." He made me so nervous. I rushed away and went over to Emma, Dean's gaze following me.

"Why did you leave me over there?" I whispered.

"I thought you'd want to be alone with him, try to get to know him, you know," Emma said, wiggling her eyebrows. I understood where Emma was coming from but I just got too nervous being around him – I had no idea what to do, or what to say! I'd never done this before and didn't have a clue how to act around a guy, let alone one as cute as Dean. I just gave her a smile and laughed it off, turning back to Dan as he began instructing us.

"OK folks, so we have a few hours here. We've rented out this whole area just for us, which is pretty cool. So, the only rule we have is to stay in the area – but aside from that just have fun," he announced.

"For the record, never do that again," I said hurriedly to Emma. "It's way too soon for that, promise me you will never do that again." She just rolled her eyes and laughed.

"OK fine, I won't, but you've got to talk to him! How is anything ever going to happen if you don't," she insisted. This time it was my turn to roll my eyes at Emma, and with that we dropped the topic.

We went rock climbing for a few hours. Me and Emma raced each other up the wall. Dean came over and I raced him, too. With Emma there, I was fine. She made it feel relaxed and I worried less. She seemed to get on really well with Dean and it gave me more confidence. We laughed and joked and the time flew by. Even Emma and Dean raced. We all flopped down, exhausted and ate our lunch together, just us three – I liked how easy it was between us all.

After lunch, Dan declared that it was time for abseiling. I was quite nervous as it was something I hadn't really done, but we all stood and put on harnesses. I was very quiet while mine was fitted, with thoughts rushing through my head about the task ahead. But I took a deep breath and made my way over to the wall.

"Hey," Dean said in a comforting tone, "you'll be fine, and I'll be right here if you need anything."

I nodded at him and headed to the wall when it was my turn. I started the steep stairs to the top of the wall and got fitted with the ropes. I gazed over the edge and saw Dean and Emma staring up at me smiling encouragingly. I leant back and let the ropes take my weight. It was incredible!

The afternoon drifted by in a happy haze and in no time we were already back on the bus making our way to the campsite, me sitting with Emma again, Dean at the back with his friends. Every once in a while I glanced back and would catch his eye. He shot me another wink, that blush filling my cheeks again.

As soon as we got back to the campsite, Dean disappeared somewhere, and I couldn't help but think about the moments we had shared together that day. When I tripped up on the wall and Dean came to help, catching me before I fell flat on my face in front of the whole camp, he had saved me from embarrassment and not made me feel bad about it. At first, I thought he was just one of those guys that flirted with everyone – who just seemed nice. But as I got to know him more it seemed as if something could actually happen with him. The thought alone made me smile – the idea of me having my first boyfriend.

I didn't know what was happening, though. It was crazy! I mean, this was the kind of thing I had read about in all my books. It doesn't actually happen – does it?

Chapter 4

A couple days into the camp and I'd shared nearly every moment with Dean and Emma. Of course, Dean spent time with his friends, too, but he seemed to be drawn to me and I to him. I'd received a couple of text messages from my mum just asking how I was doing. I'd responded occasionally but I wasn't saying too much – I needed a break from my family. I hadn't really heard anything from my dad, except an acknowledgement from him when I said that I'd arrived safe and was settled in, although even that was on the group chat. I tried not to dwell on him too much and not let it ruin this holiday.

On the morning of the third day, after we had finished our breakfast, we were told that our next activity was canoeing. That kind of shook me up. I'd never done anything like this and frankly I was scared. What if I fell in the water? What if I couldn't actually do it? I didn't want to look like a wimp to Dean. No way could I embarrass myself this early on in knowing him – that would scare him away for sure. And hey, I needed to broaden my horizons. That was the whole reason I was here, so maybe this would be good – I hoped.

As we stood on the edge of the campsite lake I stared into the murky water and shuddered. The instructor stood in front of us all, explaining how and what we needed to do. The main idea was just to not be an idiot, which seemed simple enough. We all rushed over to grab our life jacket, helmet and oar. As we got onto the water the nerves disappeared. It was so nice! It took me a minute to get the hang of things but soon I was floating around the lake, turning and everything!

But just as I was getting the hang of things, there was one moment that will remain one of the most embarrassing near misses of my life – although it did turn into a rather cute experience that I'd be re-telling for a long time.

We were about an hour into the activity and we'd just finished a series of races – with me even winning a couple, which was awesome! But now we were just kind of floating around the lake having fun. At this point, my luck changed. I dropped my oar into the lake – yet again – but being an expert on retrieving oars, I leant out of my canoe to reach it. I must have miscalculated how far away the oar was, because soon I could feel the boat start to tip further and I knew a face full of water and a soaking were on their way. At that moment, I felt a strong hand yank my arm back and, as I turned, I noticed Dean with his other hand on my boat, steadying it before it capsized. Somehow he stopped me and then grabbed my oar.

"Woah there, Cassie, bit early for a bath isn't it?" he teased, and a blush grew on my cheeks.

"Wow, thanks. I don't think a bath in that water would have been very nice," I winced, flashing him an awkward smile.

We ended up just floating along together and laughing about my near miss. Oh yeah, and he had finally started calling me Cassie, although I had a feeling it was only to wind me up. I liked hearing my nickname coming out of his mouth.

I hadn't thought of a nickname for him yet, but I would get there. He had been so kind and perfect. I hadn't experienced something like this before, so you can't blame me for getting a little excited – honestly, it felt like I was dreaming.

"You really need to be careful. If you had gone in, I'd have had to go in after you and I don't think both of us being soaked from head to toe for the rest of the day is really the best idea… particularly with the state of that water." I mean, seriously, Dean knew exactly what to say to make my insides melt. That may sound ridiculous, but it's the small things that make a difference. He could have easily mocked me for that moment or made a bigger deal out of it, but he didn't.

Once everyone became tired and a little cold in the lake, we all got back to the pier and stepped out of our canoes and dragged them onto the banks. We had some free time now and before I knew what was going on, Emma was dragging me from where we stood and pulling me back to the tent. The next thirty minutes was filled with Emma quizzing me on everything that had gone on with Dean and me trying to be as calm as I could as I explained the story. Dean had also begun walking back and was hovering around the campsite. Of course, I didn't want him hearing the gossip about him, but my attempts to keep things quiet were futile with Emma squealing every minute as I told the tale.

After a while, Emma had finally exhausted herself of questions and we emerged from the tent. Dan told us there would be various activities going on around the campsite, but we didn't have to participate in any we didn't want to. Since me and Emma were so tired from the canoeing, we thought it best to just relax for a little while. But as we were talking about what we wanted to do, Dean snuck up behind us.

"Hey, I was wondering if you wanted to take a walk with me in the woods. Apparently, there's this path that leads to a lake and I wanted you to come find it with me," he said with that cute little half smile of his.

"Oh er, yeah, that sounds really nice. Just let me find Emma and see if she's OK with it. I don't want to leave her alone." I scurried off to go and find Emma. She was with Dan.

"Hi Dan!"

"Hey Cassie, how are you?"

"I'm great. I just needed to talk to Emma quickly." Dan backed away a bit to give us some space.

"OK, so Dean just asked me to go on a walk with him in the woods. I was wondering if you were OK with that…"

"Of course, that's amazing! Go. Go quickly. You can finally have some time alone." I started to turn but Emma grabbed my arm.

"But I want every single little detail when you get back OK?", she said, giving me a wink. I laughed it off and started dreading the amount of questions I would have to answer, seriously debating whether I should just film the whole thing. That way she could just watch and I wouldn't be subject to a major grilling. I gave Emma a quick hug and ran back over to where Dean was waiting for me on the edge of the forest. His hand was outstretched to me and I took it hesitantly.

As we started walking, my nerves began to build. I had never done anything like this before with a guy at all and I was overthinking every… single… thing. I thought my hand was too tight, so I started to loosen it. But what if he thought that I didn't want to hold his hand any more and let go, or what if my hand was sweaty and he thought it was gross and never spoke to me again. Dean must have noticed the silence because, soon enough, he turned to face me.

"Hey, are you OK?" he asked worriedly.

"Oh yeah, I'm fine. I guess I'm just a bit nervous really. I've never done anything like this before." At this Dean started to laugh.

"Do you really expect me to believe that someone as cute as you hasn't done anything like this before?"

"Well, I guess guys just never really looked at me like that before. I never really thought of myself as one of those girls." Dean stopped me and pulled me around so I was facing him properly. His hand grazed my cheek, and my eyes fluttered.

"I mean there have been guys but like nothing ever really happened with them." I could feel a blush threatening my cheeks, but this wasn't the usual nervousness I got from being around Dean, this was embarrassment. Surely he had been with loads of girls, and here I was telling him that I was a sad loser that no one paid attention to.

"Don't you know how truly beautiful you are? You have the cutest smile. I love your hair and the way it has a slight curl at the bottom and how your eyes light up when you talk about something you love."

A smile started to spread over my face. His hand came up and cupped my cheek as he slowly inched closer.

"And your lips – the colour of them is amazing and it drives me mad not kissing them all the time. It gets even worse when you bite your lip like that. I've realised you do it when you're nervous – it's adorable and the little constellation of freckles that decorate your nose, and your eyes. They're such an intricate mix of browns and tiny flecks of gold – I so easily get lost in them when I talk to you," Dean confessed. He started to lean closer to me, but my hands pressed against his chest and pushed him back slightly.

"I've never done this before, just to let you know… in case I'm bad." I was now getting so nervous, I was wondering if this was all a massive mistake.

"You mean you've never tried to find a lake before?" he joked.

I punched him lightly on the chest, "You know what I mean."

He raised his eyes as if in confusion – god, this boy was really going to make me spell it out.

"I've never kissed anyone," I mumbled.

"That's another reason I like you. You don't realise how cute you are sometimes." He leaned in – it was so slow; my heart was beating out of my chest. Our faces came closer and closer, and just as he was a whisper away from my lips he paused, looked into my eyes and said, "Don't worry, sweetheart, I'll show you what to do."

I looked up at him.

"Uh huh, never call me sweetheart, it sounds like an old person's pet name."

I felt more than heard his laugh. "Noted."

After what seemed like years, but was probably no more than seconds, our lips met in a sweet, gentle way. It was amazing. He wrapped his arms around my waist and mine looped around his neck, deepening the kiss. Soon my back was pressed against a tree and Dean was kissing me senseless, almost devouring me. It... was incredible. We broke apart, and he smiled down at me sweetly. This didn't seem real; the fact that a guy this cute would actually want to be with me, spend time with me, kiss me! I didn't think it would be like that the first time. All the horror stories of braces, teeth and tongues I had heard had me worried – but damn, this boy knew what he was doing.

"Wow," Dean laughed, "that was the best kiss I've ever had." He brushed his lips against mine, almost as if he just couldn't get enough, and you know what? I was OK with that – if it meant I got kissed again.

"So not bad?" I asked, suddenly feeling a lot more conscious.

"Not. Bad. At. All." He chuckled.

"Are you saying you're judging from a lot of experience?" I asked him coyly. He just shrugged.

"Oh, so you've kissed a lot of girls, have you?" I questioned, narrowing my eyes.

"Hey, not many, and none of them compare with that kiss. Shall we continue and try to find this lake? Because if we don't stop now, I don't think I'll ever be able to stop kissing those gorgeous lips."

I took a deep breath and tried to do some purposeful flirting.

"OK, just one thing." Swallowing the fear, I just reached up and kissed him again. I could feel his smile against my mouth. His arms soon wrapped around me. And if we never found the lake? Well, I wouldn't mind too much, let's just say that.

Chapter 5

After around fifteen minutes, we eventually stumbled across the lake. It definitely took longer than I thought it would but that's mainly because we were constantly stopping. It seemed we couldn't keep our lips apart for very long. After we'd first stopped and Dean told me how much he really liked me, I didn't worry about how I was holding his hand. I felt like that kiss had made me more comfortable with him and it was good.

When we finally found the lake, Dean flopped onto the dock beside it, laying down his jacket first on the dirty ground. I sat in front of him and together we settled down, me sitting in between his legs, leaning against his chest, him kissing my neck. I could feel the comforting rise and exhale of his breath. I never realised how good it could feel to be with someone. It was all still so new, but it was something I didn't want to lose. It was unbelievable to me how comfortable it could be with someone I had only just met. Maybe it was the sun or glistening water, but I was happy.

"Hey that tickles," I giggled, feeling his breath touch my neck. I twisted my body, trying to turn and face him.

"Oh no," he said with mock sympathy, laughing as he continued. I smiled at this. He made me feel so happy and complete. We sat and talked about nothing and everything –

what music he liked, what books I liked, his family, my family. It was amazing. I got to know him so well.

We stayed around the lake for about thirty more minutes. Then Dean checked his phone and realised we should probably head back before everyone started wondering where we were. As we strolled back through the woods, I couldn't stop the smile that was creeping over my face. Of course, not everything was like I expected. I never got the spark that all the books talked about, but this was reality and the rest only fantasy. Just as we emerged from the woods, Dean grabbed me and kissed me one last time before we got back to the campsite.

"I needed to kiss you one more time before we were crowded by everyone else," he explained. I smiled. No one had ever wanted me the way Dean wanted me right now. I mean, yes, there had been other guys in the past but not properly; it was always a kind of "we almost dated but nothing ever really happened" and then it just got complicated and awkward. It wasn't like I hadn't wanted anything to happen – it just never worked out for me. But here, with Dean, I felt like I belonged.

When we got back to the campsite, Dean dropped my hand as Emma came barrelling over to us.

"Sorry Dean, but I need a serious girl-to-girl talk right now," I giggled as Emma pulled me away, while sending an apologetic look over my shoulder to Dean, who had his trademark smirk tickling the left side of his mouth, lighting up his face. I noticed Dean walk away from the woods, too, and join his friends over by the football field. Connor greeted him, and he joined in with whatever they were doing.

"Soooo, details now. Was it good? Did you kiss? Was it romantic? Was he kind? Come on, details!"

"I'll give you all the details as soon as you stop talking long enough for me to say something," I insisted. That shut her up.

"OK, so we started walking down this stone path. He said there was a lake and he wanted me to go find it with him. He held my hand as soon as we started walking and I've got to be honest with you, I was so freaking nervous. Anyway, I started rambling on to fill the quiet, and soon conversation started up about the most random things. Anything, nothing, everything. It was perfect. When we were about halfway there, he turned to me and kissed me."

"Wait, was this your first kiss?" Emma questioned with a grin on her face. I looked at her and nodded.

"Yeah, and it was a good kiss." I started to blush and Emma's grin grew over her face.

"Hey, shut up, there's just no one decent where I live! Anyway, back to the story. So, he stops me and kisses me. At first I'm like: what the heck to do? I've never kissed anyone before. But then it was like second nature, and it was incredible. Anyways, so we had made it to the lake and we sat there together just taking in the nature around us. After a little while, we started to walk back. He kissed me one more time and then you stole me away to talk about it."

At this point, Emma's face was splitting with a smile. And then the squealing began.

"Cassie is adorable; seriously, he sounds perfect!"

This conversation went on for a while, back and forth between us, with Emma asking so many questions and me having to repeat a lot of it as Emma was too busy squealing. My blush deepened.

That night we went to dinner and Dean came and sat with us, his hand innocently resting on my thigh under the table. I hadn't been able to stop smiling since walking out of the woods. Dinner was carefree and so much fun. I shifted slightly in my seat, readjusting my position, which caused Dean's hand to move slightly up my thigh, making my heart beat erratically. And judging by the grin Dean had on his face, he could tell what his touch was doing to me – so unfair! Later that night I would get my revenge...

Lights out arrived way too quickly. Well, they do say time flies when you're having fun – but I didn't want it to. I was happy to stay there forever, just laughing with Emma and Dean – as long as someone bought us food once in a while. Me and Dean said goodnight around the side of my tent while Emma was in the toilet, and as he bent down to kiss me, I raised slightly on my toes and just gently brushed my lips against his before walking off.

"Hey what was that? What about a proper good night?"

I turned around so I was now walking backwards while facing him.

"That was revenge for dinner time."

Dean looked at me innocently.

"Hey, you knew what you were doing." And with that I heard his laugh in the darkness; and I'm pretty sure he winked at me before turning and walking to his tent across the field.

"I'll see you tomorrow, brown eyes," he called over his shoulder.

That night, lying in my tent I couldn't help smiling as I went to sleep. Maybe my mum had been right, maybe this camp wasn't so bad after all.

Next morning, Dean was waiting for me outside the food hall. I waved at him as I walked over and he walked halfway to meet me. Before I could even blink, he had me pressed up against the wall with his arms trapping my head like a cage. But I was a very willing prisoner.

"Good morning beautiful," he whispered to me. I had never really been called beautiful like that and I could feel the blush on my cheeks. I assume he noticed because his grin just widened.

"Good morning to you, too" was my less-than-skilful response.

Dean ran his fingers through my hair and I closed my eyes in bliss. It was these little moments that I really loved about our relationship. Wait, was this a relationship? Oh my gosh, was he my boyfriend? Is that what I call him now? Are we still just friends? Are we dating or actually going out? I was getting worked into a state here and I could tell that Dean had noticed.

"Hey Cass, what's up?"

"Oh, er, nothing, nothing... I'm fine, really." I could tell my rambling wasn't convincing anyone right now.

"Come on, please talk to me"

"Well, it's just – I mean – well, er, what are we?"

"Huh?"

"Well, like we've kissed and we talk and I mean we've had as near enough as we can to date, so what are we? Like, is this a trial run? Are we dating now? Like, I'm not expecting anything, I was just wondering what we're doing. Obviously, it's been less than a week so there's no rush."

I realised I was rambling on at this point, so I just stopped and looked up at him.

"Well, I mean I want to be your boyfriend. It's only been a little while, but I'm sure already, so that really depends on you."

He was now fidgeting with the hem of my shirt where his hands were resting on my hips.

"I want you to be," I said a bit too quickly and a bit too keenly. But luckily this produced a chuckle low in his throat, which I felt more than heard.

"Then I am," he said with a blinding smile and a light quick kiss on my upturned lips. With that we walked inside for breakfast.

"OK, OK guys, would you please let me talk for a minute."

I was on Skype with my three best friends from home: Lottie, Connie and Lexi. These three girls were the reason I had gotten through a lot of stuff. Without them, I have no idea where I would be. Both Lottie and Connie were pretty quiet, as you already know, and I was pretty surprised they got onto a call in the first place. Lexi was the one that I knew wouldn't be leaving me alone all summer, checking in about how the family was as well as quizzing me on potential guys. Well, there will only ever be one Lexi. Connie had been my best friend since nursery. We had grown up together. She was medium height but was still pretty tall compared to me. Lottie and Lexi we had met in secondary school, but they had become just as close to me. It was the four of us all the time. Lottie was similar to Connie, but whereas Connie had long wavy black hair, Lottie's was a much lighter brown. And Lexi? Well, to put it simply, she was basically blond beauty. She wore glasses that somehow highlighted her washy green eyes, and she was composed of this effortless confidence. Yes, there had been some others in our group but they have been and gone. These three friends were my foundations. Whatever happened in life, they were the people I knew I could always go to; and I knew they were dependable.

I'd already messaged them quickly about Dean on our group chat, due to Lexi's constant badgering, but had never had a chance to go into proper detail. I couldn't tell one and not the others, so I had to wait until we could all call at the same time.

"Come on, you've been holding out on these details for ages!" Lexi moaned.

"OK, I'll spill. So, you know I mentioned that I met this guy recently. Well, we had a date recently and we kissed," I said, not even caring about the smile that was splitting my face.

"AHHHHHHHH!" Connie screeched, "it's about time. I mean, honestly, you deserve to be happy."

"Anyways, it's been going pretty well lately. He's been so sweet and I feel like this could really be something."

The smiles coming from the screen were crazy.

"Why are you all looking at me like that?"

"You deserve this, Cassie." Lottie spoke candidly, "It's about time you put yourself first. You haven't had the best luck in the past."

"Oh Connie, I wanted to ask, how are things going with Ryan?"

That's when it was her turn for her cheeks to turn a crimson red.

"He's doing good. Things are going really well actually. I still get a little shy around him but it's good."

"It took you two long enough. I mean, seriously, you've liked him for like a year now. I'm so glad you finally did something about it," Lexi commented.

"I know, me too," Lottie confirmed.

Connie and Ryan had been crushing on each other for ages now. They were both the artistic type but both too shy to do anything about it; they barely ever even talked. But after the three of us had annoyed and pestered her about it enough, Connie finally grew up and decided to do something about it. They had been dating for about two months now and I had never seen Connie as happy as when she was with Ryan.

"I really missed you guys, you know. I've made a few friends here but it's still not the same without you." I smiled at the three faces on the screen thinking it would still be a whole month until I saw them face to face.

"Gasp! Wait, did you say you'd made another friend? Have you replaced us already?" Lexi exclaimed. "Guys, we've been replaced!" she said with pretend sadness. This was when the fake crying Lexi was famous for started. She's used this so many times we just know that it's not true. But it has got us out of trouble in school many times.

"Of course not, you guys," I chuckled and assured them, "but her name is Emma and she's actually so nice. She's really helped me not be a complete loner here."

We continued catching up, talking about Lexi and her boyfriend, too, Lottie quietly listening, as always, chiming in with her limited input. That's when there was a knock on the door.

"Hey! It's just me," Emma called from outside, "didn't want to interrupt with your friends"

"Oh hey, yeah, come on in, you're not interrupting. There are actually some people I want you to meet," I assured her.

"Wait, you're not keeping someone hostage in there are you?"

"Ha, nope. I assure you they're all safe in their own homes. Keeping them in here would be too much of a giveaway."

Emma opened the door with a laugh. "Oh, that's what you meant when you said meet people," she said as she noticed the three smiling faces on my phone screen. "HI, I'm Emma "

"Hey, this is Connie, Lexi and Lottie." They all simultaneously waved through the screen. "These are my friends back home, I was just catching up with them."

"Oh, has she filled you in on the new hottie she's bagged?" Emma said to the three of them.

"Yeah, she's told us some, but been a bit stingy on the details. Care to enlighten us?" Lexi asked.

They started chatting together as if they were lifelong friends – laughing, joking. I just sat back smiling at the four of them. My three best friends for years and the girl that I'd only known for like a week but who had become as close to me as the other guys. It was at that point that things began to feel right, a feeling that had been foreign to me for so long. After they had spilled their secrets and Emma had filled them in on everything between me and Dean, they all hung up.

Emma and I had fallen into a good rhythm this week. We would meet up with Dean just before breakfast, then the three of us would spend the day together doing whatever was planned. Dan seemed to have different activities each day, and already we had gone go-karting and biking. Emma gave me and Dean space when we needed it and she didn't seem to mind. We also hung out with Dean's friends, and Emma seemed to get on well with them, so it made me feel a little better when me and Dean did sneak off for a little while.

I was having a fantastic time. I had met a great guy, and all my friends, new and old, were either with me physically or on a screen. I was scared it wasn't going to last. I knew it would all be different when we left, but I still had three weeks until that happened so I would just enjoy it as long as I could.

I loved the fact that Emma and Dean got on so well; it just made things so much easier. It was less of a challenge to split my time between them, now that I could spend time with them together. For the first time in a long time, I had a feeling that things would be OK. Instead of my monotonous life, I had excitement. Things were good.

Chapter 6

Before breakfast we were told what the activity would be for today, and a mix of emotions bubbled up when I heard. Ready for it? Cliff jumping. I was going to be jumping off a cliff today. Obviously not as dangerous as it seemed – in all honesty the cliff wasn't very high and we were diving into water – but this was crazy for me! I was looking forward to it, but I suddenly felt massively under pressure. I wanted to look nice for Dean, and now that we were officially dating – an actual boyfriend, for the first time ever – I felt like I needed to impress him somehow. I only had half an hour before breakfast and before I saw Dean again. I mean, we had already hung out and flirted and stuff, but it was different now and I didn't know how I was meant to act with him. Have things changed? Should we act differently? You can tell I haven't done this before!

My mind was racing and I was going crazy over what to wear. I finally settled on my favourite denim shorts, a cute black and white striped crop top and my trusted Converses. I thought it looked pretty nice and I felt good in what I was wearing, so I grabbed a hoodie and left the tent. As me and Emma made it to the cafeteria, I noticed Dean standing outside, just like every other day.

"Well, good morning, Dean, how are you doing on this splendid morning?" Emma said, beaming like a Cheshire cat.

"Hey Emma, how are you?" he responded with a chuckle.

"Oh well, I am absolutely fine Dean, feeling great today."

I elbowed her, trying to get her to shut up.

"What was that for?! I was merely asking Dean a simple question about how he was doing this fine morning."

I noticed a slight laugh coming from Dean.

"You shush," I pointed at him, "and you," I turned to Emma, "can shush too". But this was pointless as it only made Emma laugh a little harder.

"OK, well I'll meet you love birds inside," she said to us.

Emma sauntered inside, but not before glancing back at me and raising her eyebrows. I just laughed and shook my head. But before I knew what was happening, Dean's arms were looping around my waist from behind.

"Good morning, you're looking beautiful today," he whispered in my ear, "not that it surprises me".

My heart glowed. All the nerves from this morning disappeared knowing that I was comfortable with him. I turned in his arms, looking into those beautiful eyes that were growing so familiar to me. He leaned down to kiss me and his warm lips touched mine as light as a butterfly. I melted into him and his arms tightened around my waist.

"We should probably go inside now," I said between kisses.

Dean started a trail of kisses down my neck, and my heart raced at a ridiculous speed.

"Just a little bit longer out here, it's been like a full ten hours since I saw you. I don't know how I managed to survive". I laughed at this and continued to kiss him.

We walked inside the food hall and went to join Emma. I grabbed a nice cup of coffee with some buttered toast and sat at our table. Breakfast was much like any other day and soon we were getting ready to go cliff diving. I ran back to the tent and quickly put my white bikini underneath my clothes. Once I was done, I raced out of the tent and over to the coaches, where the campers were beginning to gather. I noticed Emma standing with Dean, so I walked over to them and was greeted with a warm hug from Dean and a sweet smile from Emma. We walked to the bus and soon we were off. After a ten-minute drive, we jumped off the bus and raced over to where the instructor was waiting for us with a pile of life jackets near the edge of the cliff. We each grabbed a life jacket, zipping it up and securing it.

"OK everyone," the instructor called, "now that you all have your life jackets on, I want you all to make a line. You can either pick another person to jump with or go on your own."

I looked over at Emma.

"You sure you don't want to jump with Dean?" she whispered to me.

"No way," I assured her, "you're my best friend here. If I'm jumping off a cliff with anyone, it will be you," I joked. "Plus, Dean can jump with Connor or something."

After five minutes of chaos, everyone was sorted into the queue. Some people were jumping on their own, but most had found a pair. Dean and Connor were a few people in front of me and Emma. The queue was steadily getting smaller as each person jumped off the cliff. I saw Dean and Connor jump off the cliff together with a whoop. Soon it was mine and Emma's turn. I stepped up to the edge of the cliff and looked over. It wasn't as big a jump as I'd anticipated but it was still quite a leap. I could see other instructors at the bottom waiting for us in case we needed anything.

"You ready?" Emma asked me.

I looked at her and then glanced back down – it was time.

"Ready as you are," I replied.

With a quick smile flashed at Emma, I grabbed her hand.

"One…" she said.

"Two…" she continued.

"Three…" we said together.

And with that, I jumped!

"That was so amazing!" I screamed as I burst through the water. I looked up from where I had just jumped and I was in awe. I could see Dean standing on the dock, looking down at me with such a warm gaze. I swam over to him and climbed up the ladder onto the dock. Once I was up, I ran over to Dean. He stumbled back against my weight, his arm tightening against my waist to keep us from falling.

"I'm glad you enjoyed it," he chuckled.

"That was the best thing ever! Do you think we can do it again? That was so cool. Honestly, did you see me up there? I was flying, like actually flying!" I rambled while Dean just looked at me, laughing slightly at my enthusiasm.

"If you want another turn then please make your way up the stairs and join the queue once again," the second instructor told us with a gesture towards the stairs.

"You up for it?" I turned to Emma and asked.

"Oh no, you have got to be kidding me. I'm not doing that again," she insisted.

I laughed at her apparent rage, but I was slightly deflated. I didn't want to do it on my own. I spun towards Dean.

"Well come on boyfriend, what about you?" I asked him. He seemed hesitant at first, but the enthusiasm on my face must have convinced him as with a sigh he relented and agreed. I squealed with excitement and turned to Emma.

"Will you be OK if I leave you with Connor for a bit?" I asked her.

"I'll survive," she teased, with a wink in Connors direction. But I couldn't help but notice that she seemed slightly deflated.

With that, I turned towards the stairs, grabbed Dean's arm and dragged him away. I raced up and joined the end of the queue. I was bouncing on my feet, waiting with great anticipation for my turn to come.

"Easy girl, it'll be our turn soon," Dean teased.

I rolled my eyes at him and continued bouncing, barely able to contain my excitement! Finally, after what seemed like years, our turn arrived – and this time I wasn't afraid.

"Let's do this!" I cheered, grabbing Dean's hand. I ran towards the edge of the cliff, I took a deep breath and launched off the edge.

It was incredible. It would be a long time before I got to do something so invigorating again, so I was not going to waste the time I had now. I managed to convince Dean to do some more jumps with me, and it seemed that after seeing Dean and I do it so often, Emma couldn't resist at least one more go. Dean went a few more times with his friends. They tried backflips and all sorts of tricks, and it went well until Connor miscalculated the angles and hit the water with a painful yet somehow satisfying splat. When he emerged from the water, the redness of his back was undeniable. We could all see the agony on his face, and I actually had to stop Dean slapping Connor on the back.

Seeing Connor's discomfort, we all decided to call it a day and settled down on the bank by the dock waiting for the final people to finish their turn. A few towels and blankets had been sorted for us so we tried to get dry before going back to the coach. About an hour later, everyone had finished jumping and left the water. I grabbed my bag and checked my phone – just past four. We'd be leaving soon, so I picked up my top from where I had left it to dry and put it back on.

"All right everyone, it's time to get back to the coach now, please," Dan told us. There was a collective groan. Clearly a lot of us didn't want to leave this breath taking place, but with a sigh Dean helped me up, and hand in hand we strolled back to the bus.

In no time we were back to the campsite. I changed into something warmer, and Emma and I went into the food hall where they had set up various activities they had for us that evening. I spied some playing cards and grabbed Emma's wrist, pulling her over to where they were.

"Fancy a game of twenty-one?" I asked her.

"You're on," she said with a nudge on my arm.

We played a few rounds, and I was mostly winning. We were just about to deal out for a new round when Dean, Connor and a few other friends walked in.

"So, what's the game?" Dean asked.

"Twenty-one," Emma said. "Want to join in?"

"I have a better game," Connor chimed in. "How about we play cheat!"

There was a collective agreement about it, and they all joined the table. Emma dealt out the cards and the games commenced. Within a few minutes, the game was in full swing with plenty of excitement all around the table. Dean seemed to be doing very well – he had nearly lost all his cards. Emma wasn't so bad but had been tripped up a few times. Connor was the worst liar, by far, at the table.

"Wow Dean, should I be worried that my boyfriend seems to be such a good liar?" I teased, scrunching my nose in his direction.

"No idea what you're talking about," he replied and proceeded to stick his tongue out at me.

After a few rounds – with Dean winning every single game – we decided to call it a night. Connor had become too heated and started complaining that Dean was cheating, and let's just say that Dean was not pleased about the accusations. With that, we all decided to head to our tents. The day's running, jumping and swimming had made me so tired that I was happy to head to bed. I kissed Dean goodbye quickly, and Emma and I started back. After I got ready for bed, I settled down and said goodnight to Emma. I was feeling good right now and I couldn't fight the laughter bubbling up in my throat.

I woke up the next morning going about my regular routine now- shower, dress and food hall- and I felt my phone vibrate in my back pocket as I was walking towards Dean where he was waiting outside the food hall. I grabbed it and saw the name that flashed on the screen – "Dad".

Oh. My heart started to beat. I hadn't heard from him all week and now he decided just to call me? This couldn't be good. I told Dean that I had to answer the call, said goodbye and quickly walked away to somewhere private.

"Hi dad," I said, short of breath.

"Hey Cass, how are you doing?" he asked.

I flinched slightly at the nickname. I went by Cassie most of the time, but my family usually called me Cass. I hadn't heard it in a while. My mum usually chose more affectionate names, like "sweetie" or "honey", and my big brother insisted on using my full name. As for my other siblings, well, they usually chose Cassie. My dad was the one that said Cass mostly, but I hadn't spoken to him for so long that the name didn't really register.

"Yeah, I'm doing good dad, it's nice to hear from you," I told him.

"Well," he cleared his throat, "I thought I would just give you a call and check up on your first week away."

"I've been having a really good time," I replied, keeping my tone as even as I could manage. "How are things at home?"

"They've been… OK. Hailey is doing really well. She's been seeing her friends a lot. Bradley has just been spending his days playing football. He's really enjoying his summer football programme. And Jake has been spending time at university with his friends," he told me.

"Well, that sounds great," I replied – and I noticed very quickly that he didn't say anything about mum.

"And Mum?" I asked.

"She's fine" was all he said, nothing more. The line was quiet.

"Well, my friends are waiting for me, so I guess I should go."

"Oh, um, yes," he cleared his throat again. "Well I should leave you to it," he said. The line went quiet again.

"Are you OK, Dad?" I asked, an edge of worry in my voice. It was then that I realised that he didn't seem like himself. Even with everything going on between my parents, he managed to remain himself with me and my siblings – but this wasn't him.

"Yeah, yeah, I'm fine," he told me, but his voice sounded distant.

"Well, I should go then," I said. "Love you, I'll talk to you later."

"I love you too Cass," he said.

This time when he said my name, I smiled, remembering the fun and wonderful memories that would always accompany it. I just hoped I could return to that place at some point. But for now, I simply wanted to enjoy my summer.

Chapter 7

I woke up the next morning thinking about how happy I was with Dean. He made me so happy. He got on well with Emma and made me smile. He was kind, considerate and *very* good looking. There was a part of me that still felt unsure and confused, although I think I just wasn't used to it yet.

I headed down to breakfast with Emma and saw Dean, I settled into my usual space and it passed in a happy blur. After breakfast we found out that today we were going swimming. My stomach began to fill with nerves at the thought of wearing a swimsuit in front of Dean. I was worried, to say the least.

I hardly ate anything during breakfast. I felt so nauseous I wasn't sure whether I could keep any food down – so I didn't try. Me and Emma were in the tent, getting ready to go. She was rambling on about her excitement and choice of costume. Hearing her stream of anticipation made me more enthusiastic, but there was a part of me that was dreading it. Not so much the swimming – I loved swimming – but rather the required attire. I would be in a bikini, in front of everyone. I didn't feel the most confident and I had my doubts about why he was with me. I mean he was hot and funny and like the perfect guy, and I was just me. I didn't know what to do or think. The idea of being there, totally exposed, was so nerve-wracking.

The day started like any other, with us all piling into the bus and setting off. When we arrived, we split into guys and girls and went to our changing rooms to get ready. At this point, I was almost certain I didn't want to swim, and I knew Emma could sense it.

"Hey girl, what's up? I can feel your nerves from here," she said, a concerned look etched onto her face.

"Oh no, it's nothing. I'm just really self-conscious about my body, and the whole

swimming costume thing is a sticky one. I know I'm not supermodel skinny and I know Dean likes me and… I'm just being ridiculous. Wait, you know what? It's fine, I'm just being stupid" I started to walk away but Emma grabbed my arm before I could move.

"Oh Cassie, I get that." A look of shock crossed my face and it clearly didn't go unnoticed by Emma, who wanted to reassure me.

"Not expecting that, I see. Cassie, look at you, you're amazing and, you know what? You have amazing curves – and look at your boobs! You're hot and that's what Dean sees. You're beautiful, inside and out, never doubt it, and I'll be with you each step of the way. And if you do feel really nervous, then I'll be there and you can just come and change. You're not the only one that feels like this. I'm the same and it's annoying every time. But the best thing to do is just own it! Come on, jump in quickly and you'll be fine."

I knew with Emma by my side that I'd be OK, so I put on my costume and went out to the pool. Dean was already there with his friends, playing some weird kind of volleyball game. Me and Emma jumped right in and went to join them. I tried to play but kept getting distracted by the view of Dean's tanned and toned bare chest. I watched him leap out of the water each time to hit the ball, his muscles flexing with the movements. With Dean looking like some bronzed god, there was no way I could focus properly on the game. Clearly fate was laughing at me, when, as I was completely distracted by Dean's chiselled chest, the ball hit me square in the face with a big thud. The game stopped and Dean rushed over to me, examining my face to see that I was OK.

"I can't believe you just got hit in the face because you were so busy checking me out," he chuckled. "I really am flattered!"

"Oh, don't admire yourself too much – I wasn't checking you out, please," I replied as evenly as I could with Dean standing so close.

"Well, what a shame," he said but then proceeded to lean in closer to me, "because I've been checking you out this whole time. Have I told you yet how extremely sexy you look in that swimming costume?"

My body warmed at his words. I mean, my costume wasn't anything special – just a normal white bikini, the same one I wore yesterday – but the way Dean was looking at me made it look like the most exotic swimwear ever. He grinned, slowly lowered his head and bent down to kiss me, his lips tasting of chlorine. His arms snaked around me, pulling me impossibly close to his body. Just then, a massive splash exploded beside us. I'd been so lost in my world with Dean that I hadn't noticed Emma and all of Dean's friends crowding round and splashing us. We both looked at each other and burst out laughing. There was colour in his cheeks and I couldn't tell whether he was blushing or just worn out. We both went back to the game and tried to avoid checking each other out every two minutes.

When we returned to the campsite, Dean and I were both desperate to have some time together. So we snuck off to our spot, the gloriously glistening lake, to do what we wanted without the watchful eye of Emma or Connor. This had become the tradition every time we could get a free moment. I didn't feel guilty because Emma had become very close to one of Dean's other friends, Mason, who was really sweet. It was a shame that it wasn't Connor because I was pretty sure he liked her, although he didn't seem like the kind of person who would be mortally wounded by rejection

from Emma. The fact that she did have someone of slight interest meant that when me and Dean went off Emma usually went to Mason and they hung out. I was happy that she had someone to stick around with, otherwise I'd feel so bad about going off with Dean and ditching her.

We stayed at the lake for about an hour before Emma texted to say that Dan wanted us all to go to the food hall. It was quiz night!!! Yea (totally fake enthusiasm). I was terrible, and I mean terrible, at quizzes. We used to play them at my old school – and I knew nothing. Like it was the most random thing, and each time I'd try and inevitably fail. Why would now be any different? It turned out the quiz was going to be tent against tent, with a prize at the end of it. I found the rest of the girls from our tent – not really my kind of people but we were all desperate to win. Dean's tent was next to where we were sitting, and me and Dean made it our own little competition. If Dean won, I had to give him a kiss – not a problem, even if he lost! But if *I* won, Dean had agreed to take my washing duties for a day, so I was so pumped for victory. I really hated washing up!

The competition lasted about an hour, and soon it was result time. Dean was trying to intimidate me, but I wasn't budging.

"Well then everyone, I have the results," Dan announced. I sat up higher and waited in anticipation. "So, from first to last......" he started and began listing a lot of the other tents. He was in fifth place and neither of our teams had come up yet. Then it was the top three.

"OK, so third place is tent four, which means that second and first place is between tent twelve and tent seven.." I held my breath, waiting for Dan to continue. "So, in second place is… tent twelve." A cheer erupted from our table. We had won! Tent seven had won! I looked over at Dean to rub his face in it. My smugness was undeniable.

"Looks like you'll be having extra washing now," I teased.

"Yeah, yeah," he rolled his eyes, and laughed. On that note, we all stood up and started back to our tents, it was already dark and time to go to bed. I started walking out of the food hall and Dean grabbed my hand to stop me. I spun to face him.

"So, I hope you enjoy washing u–" My words were silenced by Dean's lips pressed against mine.

"Well, it looks like I won too," he mumbled.

"Hey, that wasn't part of the deal!" I replied.

"I don't see you complaining," he chuckled.

"Uh huh – well with that I think I'll go to bed now," I told him and turned towards my tent. "Goodnight Dean."

"Sleep tight brown eyes," he called.

That night I went to sleep, but there was something keeping me up. I could sense trouble coming, an uneasiness in my stomach warning me that soon my contentment might hit a wall. At that point, I didn't know what was going to come of it. Oh, but how I wish I had been prepared….

Chapter 8

The next morning, I woke and thought back over the past week. One of the best weeks in my life. It had been such a glorious seven days, shared with Emma and Dean. She had spent more time with Mason, and I could see something happening

between them. The thought made me smile. As I sat up, my heart began to race. There was something about today. I brushed it aside, got up and dressed, just as I usually would. I emerged from my tent and started over to the food hall, which was when something caught my eye.

Maybe I was magic, the way I could feel it, but this was that day that disaster drove into camp – in a silver Volvo and in the shape of a very cute boy with delicious wavy brown hair, begging to be messed up. Even at that moment, I wondered what it would be like to run my hands through those sweet curls- even if he happened to be a total stranger at this point. I was frozen to the spot, staring at this guy, captivated by his person. I could only see the back of him, but his strong muscles tensed through his shirt as he shook a camp leader's hand. He was dressed in a crisp white T-shirt with blue jeans that hugged his legs, admiring his long strides as he strolled over to Dan. Thoughts ran through my head. Who was he? Why was he here late? What was he like? Emma bumped into my shoulder, and it shocked me out of my daze.

"Hey, you OK?" she questioned,

"Yeah, yeah, I'm fine. Who *is* that?" I asked as calmly as I could, even though I felt my heart jumping out of my chest as I spoke. I was surprised that Emma couldn't see it!

"Oh, that's a new kid. His name is Noah. I'm not too sure what his deal is, but I'll do some digging. He's kind of cute though."

I couldn't lie. I really liked Dean, but there was something about this Noah, something intriguing. I didn't know what it was. I was definitely *not* attracted, no way. It was more like a weird feeling, which I couldn't explain. He made me uneasy. I hoped that Emma could find some good gossip to help me straighten out what it was that got to me.

Noah's first day at the campsite passed in a blur. It felt like everywhere I went he was there. And it was starting to annoy me. I couldn't get him out of my head, and now I couldn't get him out of my eyesight. Multiple times that day I caught him looking at me – nothing weird, just staring. But he didn't come and speak to me at all. I tried to steer clear of him and stay around Dean and Emma, but the more I attempted to stay away, the more he was around! It was as if Noah was making it his mission to be everywhere I was. By lunchtime, even Emma started to notice he was always there and she could tell I was getting annoyed about it.

"What is your problem?" she asked me with a scowl on her face. I could tell she was getting annoyed with me, with some justification as I had been pulling her every which way today.

"It's nothing – just that Noah kid is really annoying me," I replied, trying to keep my tone light to show that he wasn't affecting me nearly as much as he actually was.

"Well snap out of it! You're really annoying me today, and it's such a nice day I want to enjoy myself." And with a final brush of her blonde hair she stormed off.

I think Dean too could tell I wasn't up for talking as he'd been keeping his distance from me for the past hour. I was starting to feel really guilty and alone now, not having my boyfriend or my best friend around. Emma was annoyed at me and Dean was afraid to come over. He'd been his kind, charming self all morning, and all I could do was give short, stupid responses.

I didn't even know the guy, why was he annoying me so much? What was it about him?

That afternoon I cautiously approached Emma. I had only known her a little while but already knew how her temper could get, and it was something you did not want to mess with.

"Hey Em, I'm really sorry about how I've been acting today. I don't even really know why I'm being this way, but I don't want you to be mad at me so I'm really gonna try to not wind you up any more," I said, showing her how remorseful I really was.

"It's OK, don't worry about it. I'm just really confused about Noah. Did you two like to hook up before and he never called you or something?"

Taken aback, I replied in a hurry, "No way – nothing like that! I've never met him before in my life."

"Really? Because he's been checking you out all day – like seriously, he's been doing it constantly. I don't understand his problem, but he literally looks like he wants to lick you!"

"Oh god, Emma, please! He's not looking at me in any way. Honestly, I don't even know the guy."

The rest of the day passed in a similar fashion. Emma continued to insist that something had happened with me and Noah, and her guesses were getting even more insane. I told her constantly that nothing had happened or was happening, but there was no changing the idea that she now had in her head. It was hard to admit it, but I could see why Emma would think that. Seriously, every time I looked over at Noah he was already looking at me, and then, when he realised he was caught, his eyes would immediately dart away as if nothing had happened. There was one part of me that was desperate to go over there and yell at him, and another part that

wanted to walk straight up and kiss him – wait, no, not kiss, I was with Dean and I was happy and he was a great guy. I definitely did not want to kiss Noah! There was no way I could! I didn't even know him. It was like I had this pathetic hope that if I kept denying the impulse then I would start to believe it myself. And so far? Not exactly working.

With me trying to ignore Noah and the effect he had on me all day, I was exhausted by the end of the night and so ready to just go to sleep. Clearly, though, that wasn't on Emma's agenda. The evening finished the way it always had – shower, teeth, pyjamas. But rather than bed, there was a never-ending quiz from Emma. I'd already said goodnight to

Dean the way I always did, with a goodnight kiss – my new favourite way of saying goodnight (at least with Dean) – and we were now sitting in the tent. Emma invaded my bed and bombarded me with question after question.

"Are you sure you don't know him?"

"Would you ever do anything with him?"

"Do you think he's hot?"

The list goes on, but I won't bore you with the onslaught of questions, particularly the ones that were way too insane. I'm sure you can tell where it was going, and with Emma the questions were getting crazier and crazier.

There was part of me that dreaded tomorrow. I knew I would be facing the magnifying glass of Emma, the concerned looks of Dean and the hidden glances of Noah. This was really *not* something I'd anticipated for the summer.

I woke up the next morning thinking over yesterday and dreading what was coming. It felt like Dean was trying to tiptoe around me – he hadn't been his usual witty self, full of energy and jokes. He had hardly spoken to me last night and I can only think of one reason – my ridiculous mood swings. I felt incredibly guilty. Here was this incredibly nice guy, so cute and kind and smart, and all I could do was think about another guy, who for all I knew could be an escaped criminal – or a creep! Not likely, I know, but not impossible.

There was just something about Noah and I couldn't get him out of my head. But why? I mean, yes, he was obviously really hot, but it was more than his looks – something… deeper. And why now? I'd gone my whole life, up to now, not having a properly serious relationship or even a date with a guy! Then, when I get to this camp, there are suddenly two guys that seem to be fighting for my attention and one of them I haven't even spoken to yet. Noah might not even like me, but I can't stop thinking about him. Why did this have to happen? I wish things could have just been easy – find the guy and get together with him. How hard is that? But I was always told that the best things in life are never easy, so here I was, accepting this challenge and fighting for the great things waiting for me.

With a deep breath I got dressed and ready for breakfast. But at the food hall things were far from normal. Our regular breakfast chatter was missing today and it seemed extremely hard to say anything to Dean or Emma. I managed to get through the whole of the meal without looking at Noah once, but I could feel his eyes on me the whole time. Just the knowledge of his presence made my heart beat faster. I didn't understand his problem. We didn't even know each other. I knew I had to ignore Noah and sort things out with Dean, He was my boyfriend after all and I really liked him. I was *not* going to throw that away for some stranger – nope. I glanced over and noticed that Emma was suspiciously quiet but I'm pretty sure that's just because she

was annoyed, thinking I was keeping this massive secret from her, which obviously wasn't the case. There was no convincing her of that, however.

"Hey, Dean," I whispered to him. "Er, I'm sorry if I've been really moody lately. I don't know what's gotten into me. I've just been feeling a little off for a couple days, but I'm getting better now. I really am sorry. I've taken it out on you, which really isn't fair. You've been an amazing boyfriend. It's only been a week but you're very special to me – yesterday was just a little weird."

"Look, I'm not going to lie to you and say it hasn't annoyed me, but I can see you're going through something so it's OK. But what *is* going on. I want to help, so please don't shut me out."

"I won't, but this is just something I need to work out. It's OK, it's really nothing."

"Does it have anything to do with the new guy that arrived a couple days ago?"

"Why does everyone keep asking me that? First Emma, now you!" I said, quite explosively, which probably didn't help my case.

"Woah, woah," Dean said, with his hands up in the universal sign of surrender, "I didn't mean anything by it. I was just asking my *girlfriend* a question."

It was the emphasis that he put on "girlfriend" that really got to me. It made me feel terrible. He was right, I *was* his girlfriend and I was getting really defensive about another guy.

"You're right, I'm sorry. I *am* your girlfriend and I'm acting really mean to you. But it really means nothing. I don't even know who he is – I've never met him before."

"I believe you. It just seems that he knows you, like the way he keeps looking at you just seems weird."

"Yeah, see Emma said the same thing, it's a bit crazy really."

"You know if it gets too weird for you just say something to me and I'll have a word with him. No one treats my girl like that," Dean said with his signature wink, my heart warming at being called his "girl".

"Say it again."

"What? You're my girl Cassie and that's a fact. I'm not gonna let anyone treat you badly."

"You really are too good for me, you know that," I replied with a massive smile on my face.

"No Cassie, *you're* the one that's too good for me, don't forget that." He kissed my lips sweetly and I could feel his smile. "Come on," he said, "we need to get ready to leave – new activity today."

We had another goodbye kiss and parted ways to go and get ready for the activities. I waved goodbye as Dean walked out of the food hall and then turned to join Emma walking back to our tent. But, as I spun around, I ran straight into a very firm and solid chest, my hand splaying out over tight muscles. A hand landed on my waist to steady me. I lifted my eyes and turned my head. Looking up through my lashes I saw the chocolate curls that had been taunting me all day yesterday, those delicious curls I so desperately wanted to run my hands through.

"Hi, I don't think we've been properly introduced. I'm Noah."

Oh god…

Chapter 9

The sensation of my heart flipping in my chest was overwhelming; feeling like it was

going to explode. I became dizzy and lost for words. How could one person create such a storm of emotion and do it when I don't even know them! I was oddly drawn to Noah and I couldn't explain why. This was the first time I was seeing him close-up and there was an undeniable beauty to his face. He had these misty grey eyes – a colour I had never seen before. His nose had a dusting of light freckles, and a small, pale scar sat just above his eyebrow. He had these rosy plump lips just begging to be kissed, and as I examined his face he raised a single eyebrow. There was something about that gorgeous hair mixed with those grey eyes- that had somehow gotten darker and now resembled a frenzied storm- that I could easily lose myself in, and I wouldn't be complaining if I did get lost. I mean, they were... beautiful. An essence of beauty and peace surrounded him and I was drawn towards it.

"Hey, are you OK?" he questioned. I realised I had been staring at him for quite a while now and had remained silent the whole time. Come on brain, think of something to say – come on, literally anything!

"Hi" was my masterful line.

"I've been wanting to come and talk to you for a while now. Er, I realise you've probably caught me looking at you quite a bit. I'm not a weirdo or a stalker or anything. I was just, um… fascinated, I guess? I hope that doesn't sound too freaky." He paused and gave a little laugh. "I guess I was a bit frightened by that boyfriend of yours. He seems quite intimidating, and I didn't want him to think I was battling him for anything, and I certainly didn't want to be beaten up or whatever, but… yeah." He ran his fingers through his hair absentmindedly, causing the curls to stand up slightly, creating an adorable mess. It seemed like a little nervous habit of his that he did without even realising and I had to stifle a giggle. He had seemed so cool and above

everyone else, but here, with me, he appeared young and harmless. I liked it.

I found Noah's little rambled speech quite endearing. He made a very strange and awkward situation much calmer and funny. I desperately wanted to get closer to him and just feel his body warmth against mine, although I was already feeling hot and flustered just by standing near him.

"Oh, ha, ha, no it's fine, don't worry about it," I said. "I mean, Dean is a nice guy anyway. I'm sure he'd be fine with it, and yeah, I *had* noticed you looking at me so I'm glad you kinda explained it because I was getting a bit nervous and confused. Actually, you saying you're not a creep could indicate that you *are* a creep, you know. My friend Emma has been quizzing me about it constantly, claiming that we like hooked up or something and that this imaginative tension is insane between us. I'm pretty sure at one point she thought we had committed a major crime together and were both hiding and worried about getting caught!"

Oh god, I *was* the one rambling now. I'd told him way too much, and if Emma found out she would probably kill me. She'd be mad that I'm even talking to Noah right now. She thinks that Dean is such a nice guy and, apart from his preference on marmite, basically perfect. If she had any idea about the thoughts running through my head about Noah right now she'd go insane and – no joke – probably slap me.

Noah just kind of looked at me as if trying to work out whether I was serious or not and then laughed.

"Ha, well I can assure her that it definitely wasn't anything like that. I mean, come on! If we'd committed a crime, we wouldn't be stupid enough to go to the same camp. That would be an extremely good way to get caught. Big red flags – come on!"

"Thank you, that was exactly my point. It's like she thinks we're amateurs," I laughed along with him. He had a good sense of humour and I felt immediately calm when I was around him.

"Anyway, we can't talk about it too much or people will start getting suspicious," he responded. "Oh! Are you looking forward to the next activity?"

"Yeah, I think the water activities in the lake are going to be fun. I heard boat races are a possibility," I told him. "Apparently we're meant to build our own boat and then see which one will last the best."

"Oh no! I fear for anyone on my team. I'm terrible at that kind of thing," he confessed. I got the sense that Noah was downplaying his skill though as his nervous neck rub made another appearance.

"Only time will tell," I smiled at him. "Anyways I need to go and get ready, put on some better clothes," I pointed down at my white shirt. "This will not be good for the lake."

"Well, I don't know, it could be interesting," he laughed. I smacked his arm for that comment, which only made him laugh harder.

"I'll see you there, weirdo," I said, giving him a little grin as I walked away. I looked back to see Noah run his hand through his hair but quickly turned away. Just that one small motion did something to me, and I wasn't going to let *that* happen.

Dean was waiting for me by the lake, smiling. I'd changed my clothes and put on an older black vest over my white bikini. His smile just made my insides melt. He was genuinely happy to see me even after I'd been so horrible to him. Honestly, I couldn't ask for better. Any thoughts of Noah were immediately forced from my head. I had a great guy here, so screw the new random guy. I couldn't explain what I felt around

him, but I knew it wasn't something I wanted to risk losing Dean over.

"Hey babe, how are you doing? Ready for the challenge?" Dean asked, dropping a swift kiss on my lips.

I smiled back up at him. "Oh, I am so ready for this," I replied with a grin. The weirdness of this morning with Noah was completely gone from my mind. This is what I wanted; this was good and it made me happy.

"You remember what happened the last time we were at this lake?" He grinned down at me with a little wink.

"Hey, shush, you know we weren't meant to be down here at that point." But I couldn't contain my giggle as I remembered the nights we'd shared down by this lake, some of the best nights of my life.

"Hey girl, you over being crazy?" Yep, there was Emma's candid tone. I was shaken out of my reverie as I turned and smiled at her, glad that I hadn't lost her. I gave her a massive hug and felt happy again.

"Ha, ha, don't worry, loony Cassie has gone for good. I'm back," I told them and did the jazz hands, which got a laugh out of Emma. With that, they both cheered, and I let out a sigh of relief.

"All right everyone, are we ready?" Dan bellowed from the front of the group, grabbing our attention. "Right, so there's no point in me dragging out this speech and I know we all want to go on and start the adventure, so let's do that. We're going to split into partners for the first round and see how we go."

I immediately turned to Emma. "No, you idiot," she said. It's been weird with you guys – go and be with him. I'll drag some other poor sucker to be my partner for this round.''

"Aw, thank you Em, we'll pair up for the next round," I told her. "And hey, maybe you can see if Mason is around for this activity."

"Wait, what?" she asked, confused.

"Oh, come on! I think it's good. You and Mason would be really cute!"

"Oh no, wrong idea, Mason is just the guy I get on best with when you and Dean decide to scurry off," Emma told me. I glanced at her and noticed the disappointment on her face. I was disheartened by the loss of her potential man.

"Enough of this," she said light-heartedly, but I could still see the sadness in her eyes. "Go find your man."

"And maybe I'll help yours at some point," I told Emma with a wink. She rolled her eyes at me and shooed me away. With a laugh, I turned away and strolled over to Dean.

"Looks like you're stuck with me," Dean grinned and looked at me with such warmth.

"I think I'm OK with that," he chuckled.

The time passed in a haze. I was so happy with Dean and we had such a great time – *and* we even won the challenge. The goal was to make a boat out of wood and hollow plastic barrels that would stay afloat and that both members of the team could stay on. Most of the craft fell apart, and the one that stayed together didn't float. Our boat was the only one that managed to survive the challenge and get back to shore. Emma wasn't so lucky. She trudged over to me with water dripping from her clothes, drenched almost head to toe. Dean and I had to stifle a laugh.

"This," she said with a gesture towards her soaked clothes, "is not funny! I'm freezing and soaked. Mason, that stupid guy who I thought would be a good partner, was a

total moron. He clearly can't tie a rope to save his life! And he's drier than me – not fair! There's no way I would've been with him after that! I'm pretty sure he did it on purpose because I said I didn't like him."

"Well, do you want to pair up with me next?" I asked, barely concealing my laughter. "I'm sure Dean won't mind." I turned to him, but I could see he was in no state to talk with his face turning red, clearly trying to hide his amusement, too.

"No way! I'm not trying that or anything else involving that lake again! I will opt to relax in the sun and hope that I can dry off, maybe even catch a tan."

As Emma trudged away, me and Dean finally released our laughter.

"Don't get me wrong. I feel really bad for Em – but look at her! I'm sorry, it's just too funny."

"All right everyone! Time for the next challenge. Now, it seems we've all become too comfortable with who we are, so I think it's time we switched things up," said Dan, as a collective groan sounded from all camp-mates. "Yeah, yeah, I know, I'm evil. Now let's get on with it, before even more of us end up taking a bath in the lake."

And on that final note, I stole a glance at Emma who seemed to be soaking up the sun and looking a bit happier.

"Well, I guess that's my cue to find a new partner," Dean winked and strolled away. I watched him go slightly panicking. Dean and Emma were the only real people I had spoken to so far. Sure, there were the other people in my tent, but I hadn't really spoken to any of them. Plus, they didn't seem like the kind of girls who would have fun building a boat. I glanced over at Emma to see whether I could make a break for it and join her in the sun.

That was when I felt the hair on my skin stand up. I knew it was him. My body reacted in a way I didn't understand. I hardly knew Noah but he created this whirlwind of emotions that I couldn't control or understand.

"Fancy taking pity on me and being my pair?" he said. "This girl has her eye on me, and I don't trust her. I guess being the new boy doesn't work so well in my favour. It seems everyone has already made their friends, and I'm kinda stuck."

There it was again, that adorable little rant he went into when clearly nervous, and as if I'd willed it to happen, the fingers through the hair followed. I had a faint dream of running my own hands through his hair and making it stand up on its ends like that, as he moved closer to me.... No! Come on Cass, you're with Dean and you really like him. Don't do this! It was at that point I realised he'd stopped talking and I was staring at him awkwardly.

"Ha, ha, sure. As long as you promise not to drown me in the lake, I guess I'll take pity – but you owe me."

That earned a real laugh from Noah, which got Dean's attention. He was paired up a little way down the shore with Connor, his eyes fixed on the two of us- his jealousy radiating towards me. Dean entirely ignored what Connor was saying to him. He didn't seem happy with the scene. At all!

"Well, we better get started," I said and stepped away from Noah a little in a weak attempt to put some distance between us and reduce the tension held so tight inside me. I turned to Dan as he was instructing us on our next challenge, which seemed simple enough, but I was worried. The idea seemed to be that one person was blindfolded and would have to steer the boat, while the other had to instruct them on where to go, all while trying not to tip the boat. Easy, right?

So, between me and Noah, we'd established I'd be the one blindfolded. I wasn't so pleased about that, but somehow Noah has convinced me.

"OK, OK, you're doing good. A little to the left, that's it, yep. OK, now tilt a little to the right. We need to avoid the branch. No, right Cass,'' Noah instructed me and steered my arm slightly to help.

That surprised me. No one called me Cass, apart from my dad, and obviously that was a little tense right now. But Noah's touch – just that simple graze on my elbow, my god, my body caught fire. What was happening to me? I hardly knew the guy and he was doing this to me. I didn't like it. I was uneasy. And it was at this moment that things turned upside down. Noah was trying to guide me, but I was so caught in my own thoughts that I ended up missing what he said and clearly went in the wrong direction. *Bam*! Right into the branch we were trying to avoid. And then… *Splash*! Both of us went right into the lake. I then understood why Emma had been so moody – this was cold, murky and horrible. Also, my foot was caught – that damn branch again! I mean, hadn't it done enough damage already? I was soaked, and then my leg was stuck too!

"Cass!" I heard, knowing it was Noah. I just had no idea where he was. I could hear him above me, which made me sure that he had surfaced and noticed I wasn't with him. I was still stuck under the water but soon felt him snake his arm around me, hold me and help me free my leg. He pulled me close to him so we could get to shore and I felt my heart kicking in my chest. My breath had become short, but I knew it had nothing to do with the mess I was in. It was him. I could feel his tight muscles as his top clung to his chest and I clung to him. Wow, clothing really could hide things!

Who'd have thought that such a body was under that top!

I crashed through the surface of the water and noticed the true beauty of Noah's white top, hugging his chest and showing me what had been hiding underneath. I silently compared him to Dean. Sure, Dean had a good body and was tanned and delicious, but Noah? Oh man, he was making it hard to breathe. His chest was so defined, and I was savouring the moments I could be so close to him. We got safely back to shore, and Dan came out to check up on us.

"Don't worry, we're all OK here – nothing we couldn't handle, right Cass?" Noah looked at me expectantly. OK… words. That's what I needed right now.

"Oh yeah, yeah. We're all OK. My foot just got caught, but I'm OK."

I tried to stand on my own, now realising that Noah's arm was still holding my waist, but as I did, I felt a searing pain shoot up my leg.

"OK, maybe not." I tumbled back into Noah's chest – damn that chest – and luckily he caught me with no problem.

"I got you," I heard him whisper, pretty sure I was the only one that heard it.

"Well, I guess you should take her to the first aid ward," Dan said.

"Right, I'm on it," answered Noah, tightening his grip on my waist. I let out a little gasp, which I hoped he hadn't heard. From a quick glance at his face, there was no sign of acknowledgement.

"I think I'd better take her." I jumped at hearing Dean's voice. I turned to see him and could tell he was far from happy.

"It's really no problem, mate. I mean, it's kind of my fault in the first place," Noah chuckled, which made me suddenly fear that he knew how much his touch affected

me. But he can't have – no, I was just being paranoid.

"Well, *I* am her boyfriend, and maybe you've done enough – right, *mate*? Like you said, it was *your* fault," Dean said through gritted teeth.

"Yeah, it's fine Noah," I said, breaking into the conversation before anything went too far. "Dean can take me. Plus, you're soaked – it might be good if you get dried up. Wouldn't want you getting a cold. T- thank you for saving me."

"No problem, it was the least I could do," he said with a smile.

"Come on Dean, my ankle is really sore" – and my waist suddenly felt cold with the absence of Noah's gentle touch. Dean took me in his arms and helped me away from the lake.

A feeling of emptiness swept over me. I wished it was because I was soaked head to toe, but I knew the cause was the absence of something else. Something that was soaked in water, too, standing by the lake, watching me walk away. I could feel his eyes bore into my back and I desperately wanted to look back, but I knew Dean would know what was up and I couldn't do that to him. I liked him far too much.

So, I limped up to the first aid ward and sat while my ankle was checked out. I felt like I had messed up more than just my ankle that day.

Chapter 10

"So, my little cripple, that was quite a scene," Emma stated as she plopped down next to me on a chair in the first aid ward. Trust her to just blurt out the truth.

"What are you talking about?" I questioned, choosing to play the oblivious card, hoping it would get me out of this situation.

"Oh, come on, don't give me that innocent act." She rolled her eyes. "We all saw that little display with you and Noah at the lake, and don't get me started on Dean! He practically had steam coming out of his ears seeing you two joke around. What *is* going on?"

I knew I couldn't escape this one, Emma was too persistent. With a sigh, I gave in and the flood gates opened. The words poured from my mouth and there was no way to stop it.

"OK, so... he is a total stranger but there's just something about him. I have known him the same amount of time you have. I promise. I can't explain it. Probably doesn't make sense right? But then there's Dean, and he's so amazing and cute and nice and I don't want to mess anything up with him." I let out a sigh. "I just don't know what to do.''

I looked at Emma expectantly, hoping she would know what to do to help me. But she just looked shocked. I don't think she was expecting my confession.

"Well, um, OK. That was… a lot. OK, let's think about this. So you and Noah seem to have this strange connection, or whatever, and he seems to like staring at you and making things weird with your boyfriend, who, for some reason, is mad jealous over this guy that showed up a couple days ago. Well, that isn't a lot at all."

I rolled my eyes . This was not helping.

"Right, that's the situation right now. Any ideas? Because I don't think I can do much about the Dean thing on my own," I confessed.

"OK, we can deal with this. Now, Dean seems to be pretty jealous of Noah." I nodded. "But Noah doesn't seem to be leaving you alone." I shook my head. "And do you want him to?" I hesitated and looked at Emma. "Right, OK, we can deal with this. We just

need to keep the two of them away from each other. That way we can try and resolve all the issues and there won't be any more… situations, like today."

"OK, that works, thank you Emma," I said with a sigh of relief.

"But Cassie, best plan for now. It might be hard – and he might always be around – but if you mean this about Dean, just stay away from Noah."

I knew she was right and I smiled and nodded. At the moment, this was the best I could have hoped for. I didn't know what to do. It was all new, so I needed to find all the hope I could. I grabbed my phone and messaged the girls at home. I knew they would be desperate to help and maybe they could give me an outside view.

Me: *Update – Dean asked me to be his girlfriend. I said yes.*

Me: *Fast forward a few days and there's a new boy.*
Me:*Super cute and seems to like me too.*   Me: *Awkward situation in the lake today.*

Me:*I'm a mess, more information to come.*

Lexi: *Oh damn.*

Connie: *Wow.*

Lottie: *That's a lot.*

Me: *Yep, it is a lot, I'm trying to sort it out and any advice would be amazing.*

Lexi: *You better, I need this excitement in my life*

Connie: oh yeah me too, this holiday is fun but this is juicy.

Me: *I'm glad my situation brings you happiness and excitement.*

Connie: *We love you!*

With that I pocketed my phone once again and left the first aid ward. The nurse had checked me over and the ankle had just been sprained when it got caught on the branch. I'd sat there for a while with some ice on it and the swelling had gone down. I could walk on it, so the nurse thought I was OK to leave. As I left, I noticed Dean standing outside. I mentally prepared myself and went up to him.

"Hey babe," I said with a smile and leaned in for a kiss, which he returned – but not as keen as usual.

"Hi," he returned with a tight smile, "how are you feeling?"

"Much better, my ankle is feeling OK," I said with a smile. "Are we OK?" I asked, worried that I had messed up too much.

"Yeah, we're OK. I'm sorry, I guess. I was just a little threatened by that Noah guy," he chuckled, but I could tell that was just to cover the fact that he was serious.

"Please, there's no need to apologise. About what happened at the lake – it was just the challenge. We had to partner up with someone and he's still the new guy, so he was on his own and awkward. He just helped me out when my foot was stuck."

"Better being alone and awkward than flirting with my girlfriend," Dean muttered under his breath, I pretended I didn't hear and continued.

"Anyways, look, there was really nothing to worry about or be upset about. I really like you and want to be with you. He asked me and I just felt too bad to say 'no'."

"OK, it's fine, I trust you, it's OK. I guess I was just worried about losing someone as great as you."

Wait, what was he saying? As great as me? No way! An achingly large smile covered my face as I leaned up to kiss him.

"Wow, I got really lucky with you," I said.

"No, I'm the lucky one," he responded, returning the smile.

Me and Dean parted ways and I went to see Emma. Sadly, my route wasn't clear. There was Noah, leaning against one of the trees, just watching, with that look on his face. A flame burnt inside my stomach again seeing that face.

What was he doing? Why was he just standing there? Oh god, was he waiting for me? I took a deep breath and approached what I only knew was going to be trouble. But, for some reason, the prospect of trouble excited me rather than scared me. I was walking straight towards him – my feet just couldn't stop. I was drawn to him. And- to tell the truth- I don't think I wanted it to stop.

"Hi Cass,'' he murmured, running a careless hand through those luscious waves, consequently messing up his hair as he looked at the floor. And there it was – that feeling in my stomach. Oh no, this was getting worse.

"Look, I'm sorry if I created any problems for you. I guess I just don't have any friends here, and you were nice and there's something about you I seem to really like, and well, I guess… I didn't want to stay away," he paused, raising his eyes to meet mine, "maybe I couldn't stay away."

I was taken aback by the frankness of his words and the intensity of his gaze. I averted my eyes and looked down to the floor, breaking the spell. Yes, that was safer.

"Um anyways, look I'm sorry," Noah pleaded. "I thought it was just a bit of fun. I didn't mean anything by it, but I sense I may have made things a little awkward so I'll just leave you to go and join Dean." With that, he started to step away.

"Wait no!" I interrupted, blocking his path. "Hey, it's fine. Look, Dean knows it was only a game and we were just doing the activity. I explained it to him and he's cool now. I mean, come on, you're still the new weirdo. It's gonna take some time to adjust to the groups, but you'll be fine." I paused, he just looked away. "Anyways, look, Dean is cool. And I really don't want you to be on your own, so from now on you at least have one friend here," I smiled trying to ease some of the awkwardness.

"So, how is the ankle healing up Cass?" he said, changing the subject rather smoothly after a slightly awkward pause.

"Eh, it's all right. I mean, it's still attached to my leg, which is a good sign," I joked, "it's fine – still a little sore but I can walk on it."

"That's good to hear. I still feel really bad about it all," Noah mumbled.

"Look, you have no reason to. It could've happened to anyone. It was just my luck that it happened to me," I laughed. This was nice. We talked a little more, but Emma's words flashed into my head. I quickly ended the conversation and darted away to the tent. I could feel Noah's eyes follow me as I fled across the campsite, but I refused to look back. I knew that could only lead to bad news.

"So, I see everything seems to be cleared up?" I heard Emma say when I got back to our tent.

"Yeah, I smoothed things over with Dean. Plus I cleared things up with Noah and I feel much better!" I responded cheerily.

"Wait, wait, wait!" Trust Emma to be dramatic. "You spoke to Noah again? Today?"

"Well, yeah." I realised maybe I shouldn't have said this. "He was waiting by the trees as I was walking over to come see you and I guess he wanted to apologise again. But I think it's good – we cleared the air and he seems cool now."

Emma just looked at me. "Oh dear, dear little Cassie. Can't you see this boy likes you?!"

My head shot up in disbelief.

"Come on, Cassie, can't you tell? He chooses you to be his partner, when I know for a fact, there were a number of girls who would've had no problem pairing up with him. He offers to take you to the first aid ward *even* though your boyfriend was sitting right there watching the whole thing. Then he waits for you, for god knows how long, to 'clear the air' after seeing you with your boyfriend. I mean, that was so clearly just a ploy to come and talk to you!"

I was still just staring at her, caught completely off guard by this sudden claim. I had no idea how to react. How could Emma think Noah liked me? First of all, I could hardly deal with one cute guy, let alone two! And second, I hardly knew him and hadn't even really spoken to him apart from a couple of awkward situations that didn't end well. Obviously, I'd seen the way he always looked at me, but I never really thought anything of it.

"Emma, how can you say that? I've hardly spoken to the boy, and the two times I did speak to him have been a disaster."

"Exactly! You're that cute clumsy girl who doesn't seem to be affected by his looks or

air of mystery." Ha, if only she knew. "And you've got an amazing body, face and personality, with all the curves in the right places. I mean, damn, don't you see that?!"

I was now shocked for the second time. What the hell was happening? Apparently, two great guys like me and I had a 'rockin bod' (Emma's words not mine).

"OK, come on Emma, let's just pause for a moment. This is crazy and I need a distraction. Talk to me."

"Um OK. So things didn't work with Mason, but Connor seems pretty cute. He came and joined me as I was drying off after the lake challenge and we chatted a bit. He seems really nice, doesn't live too far away and is kind-of funny"

"Wait Em, Connor?" I was a little confused. I thought she didn't like him.

"Oh, don't be like that Cassie. I know I said I didn't like him, but things can change, and he actually seems pretty great!" I couldn't help but smile to hear her talking about someone like that.

"Aw, Em, that's so good. I'm really glad you found someone," I said sincerely.

"Yeah, he seems really good."

"Just be careful Em. He seems a little bit of a player."

OK, maybe I shouldn't have said that.

Emma looked at me and her face dropped.

"I'm sorry Cassie but we can't all land the two hottest guys at camp at the same time and use that oblivious cute little act," she retorted.

"Oh woah, Em, I didn't mean it like that – I'm sorry. I just worry about you that's all," I explained, a bit taken back by the sudden change in her manner.

"Well, how about you focus on the fact that you have a great boyfriend but seem to be off flirting with this other guy that you don't even know! Dean is great and it's only

been a week and you're already keeping things from him." With that, Emma walked out the tent and away to the rec hall.

I couldn't believe it. How could I say something like that? I kept creating problems for myself, burning the people I'd grown so close to so quickly. I had to put this right. I just needed to work out how.

Chapter 11

I stayed in the tent for a little while and then, with a deep breath, emerged and went to find Dean. I hadn't spoken to Emma all afternoon. She'd disappeared and I had no idea where she was – obviously avoiding me. I decided to spend some time with Dean instead to clear my mind.

We had a great afternoon together, visited our favourite spot down by the lake again, walked around and enjoyed the sun. It was really nice just to spend time with him, but I was still aware of Noah's presence around the campsite and couldn't help myself glancing over at him. Each time I looked, he was looking at me – damn it! Maybe Emma was right – I needed to make things right with her. I felt terrible – she'd shared something she was so excited about, and I shut it down immediately. I decided I would try and make things right at dinnertime, and now that fateful time had come. OK, it sounds dramatic, but really it isn't. Here we go…

I walked into the food hall, holding hands with Dean. I spotted Emma as soon as I walked in, hunched over the table pushing her food around the plate. Dean nudged me from behind, encouraging me to go over. He knew how much Emma had come to mean to me even in a short time and I needed to make this right.

"Hey Em," I called, approaching timidly and fully preparing myself for water being chucked over my head. "Can we talk?"

She grumbled in response, but I took that as a yes and decided to sit down. I searched the room for the Dean and saw him encouraging me and watching, just in case this didn't go as planned, from a safe distance.

"Look, I'm sorry about what I said. I didn't mean it. I guess I was just being stupid and didn't think."

"You got that right," Emma muttered

"Look, I'm really happy for you and it's so great that you found someone, and I can't wait to get to know him a little better. I guess I just reflected my own worries and the stuff I was used to with guys, and shouldn't have done that. I don't even know him properly, but I would like to, if you like him," I smiled at her, hoping she would accept the apology. Emma turned to me.

"I know you were only looking out for me, and I guess it was good that you were. I went to talk to him this afternoon and it turns out he has a girlfriend back home. Guess he was just looking for a bit of summer fun," she responded glumly and went back to her food.

"Oh Em, I'm so sorry."

"Hey, I guess it's good. I mean at least good I found out now instead of a few weeks down the line and realise he was a cheating pig the whole time. At least I didn't waste my summer on him.'' She was being optimistic, but I knew she was really upset about it.

"Look, you'll find someone, I know it. Maybe Dean has a friend?" I mentioned in a futile attempt to cheer her up. "Then we could go on double dates." This made her a little more excited about the idea.

"That would be nice," she said, smiling at me. I knew she was really trying right now, and I was so thankful for it.

"So, am I forgiven for being a total moron?" I joked.

"I guess so," she replied. "I mean who else will put up with my insane amount of sarcasm?"

We laughed. Dean, still watching from the sidelines, then deemed it a safe zone and made his way over to join us, placing a small kiss on my forehead.

"Well, isn't that cute,"' he chuckled. "I'm glad you two are OK. In all honesty Emma I don't know what I would've done if I had to deal with a stroppy Cassie for the whole time. One afternoon was bad enough!''

I gasped and elbowed him in the chest, but by now we were all laughing. See, this was what I wanted, back to the easy feeling I had when we were all together. Dinner passed with relative ease. We laughed and joked and had a good time, despite a tingling on my neck as if someone was watching me. I knew better than to look, already aware of who it was. The sensation that flowed through my body when he was near wasn't going away. This was not good.

As me and Emma made our way to the tent, I spotted Noah coming out of the food hall. My body itched to go over to him. I don't even know why, but I wanted to be near him.

"Hey, you all right?" Emma nudged me and I snapped back into real life.

"Oh, what? Yeah, I'm fine," I said as I turned back to her, "just enjoying the evening sky, I guess."

I could tell by Emma's look she didn't believe that at all, and I couldn't blame her. But she let it go. We got back to our tent and quietly got ready for bed. I lay there for a while with all these thoughts racing through my head.

"Night Em," I called over. But all I got was a mumble in return – clearly, she was already asleep.

An hour passed and I was still tossing about and couldn't sleep. My phone lit up, and as I went to check it, it vibrated.

Noah: *Hi Cass.*

Wow, OK, there's one person not saved in my phone that called me that, and now I was confused how he got my number.

Me: *Hey, who is this?*

Noah: *It's Noah. Sorry about the random message, I got your number off Emma.*

I looked over at her. What was she thinking? I mean, I wasn't mad but I was still confused.

Me: *Oh, hi there, yeah, that's cool. I'm surprised you're up.*

Noah: *I could say the same about you. I couldn't sleep.*

Me: *Yeah, me too.*

Noah: *Were you OK? I noticed you and Emma seemed a little tense earlier.*

Me: *Oh yeah, we're OK. It was just a silly little thing, we're good.*

Noah: *Well, that's great. I'm glad you're OK.*

We chatted a little longer, but it soon got so late.

Me: *Look, I better get to sleep, I'm sure we have a busy day tomorrow.*

Noah: *Yes, you're right. Well, I'll see you tomorrow.*

I put the phone down. This was meant to be getting easier, but with him making contact and being such a great guy, I couldn't get him out of my head. I shut my eyes and forced myself to get some sleep.

The next morning came all too quickly. I was exhausted but managed to heave myself out of bed.

"Rise and shine sleepyhead," Emma called from the tent entrance. With a groan, I flopped back down into bed.

"Can I just stay here forever, please?" I moaned.

"Ha! No way weirdo. Dean is meeting us for breakfast, remember? Can't leave the old lover boy waiting can we."

She had a point. With very little enthusiasm, I crawled out of bed and got ready.

"Why are you so tired anyway?" Emma asked, eyeing me suspiciously, a mischievous glint in her eye. "We didn't go to bed late last night."

"Oh, I just couldn't sleep, I guess. I was tossing and turning for hours."

"Wow, that's funny. I swear I saw a phone screen light up. Almost certain it woke me up for a minute," Emma asked probingly. OK, I needed to get out of this situation. Quick.

"Huh? Well, that's odd. Oh, I remember now! I checked my phone briefly hoping some distraction would help me sleep. I just went online for a little bit, scrolling mindlessly, that was what you must have seen.'' I shrugged flippantly, hoping to appear nonchalant. Emma still didn't seem entirely convinced but she let it slide.

"Come on, like you said, Dean is waiting and we don't want to miss all the good food for breakfast," I joked and made my way out of the tent.

As I started towards the food hall with Emma, I saw Noah yawning, looking almost as tired as I was. By the look on Emma's face it didn't pass her notice either.

"Just checking your phone, huh?" Emma nudged me.

I just rolled my eyes, pretended not to hear and went to get my breakfast.

So, the activity today was a ten-kilometre walk. I can't lie, I was looking forward to it. I mean, I don't do loads of walks but I do love hiking and the great outdoors.

"OK everyone," Dan said after breakfast, "we're doing our walk today, so we're going to split into different groups. We'll all do a different circular walk and meet back here this afternoon for what I imagine will be a very deep sleep!"

"Something you seem to need," Emma whispered to me.

"There will be four groups, so listen closely for your names," Dan said. He ran through everyone's names. I heard groups one and two and none of us were in them. Then group three came, and Emma's name was called out, then Dean's. I hoped and prayed for my name to be called but it never came.

"And group four will be Jess, Mike..." I paused waiting for my name.

"Noah," my head shot up. "And Cassie," my heart began kicking inside my chest from nerves or excitement I couldn't tell. I immediately looked over at Dean, and to put it kindly his face was not the happiest. I looked over at Emma and she was clearly amused and intrigued at the situation. Lastly, my eyes landed on Noah, whose gaze was already fixed at where I stood. We would be spending all day together (with no Dean or Emma), and there was no way to avoid him. I tried, but failed, to hide from the heat of his stare.

"Hey baby, this should be fun," I said to the Dean, forcing a pained smile.

"Yeah, apart from the fact that we won't be spending the day together and you're stuck with *that* guy," he grunted, jerking his head in Noah's direction.

"Look, I know, but you have nothing to worry about, I really like you and you're the one I'm with," I reassured him. Dean nodded at that and seemed a little more at ease.

"I'll be right back," I said as I walked over to find Emma. "Hey, look, can I ask you something?"

Emma raised an eyebrow. "OK, I'm interested. Of course, what do you need?"

"Can you just distract Dean while on the walk. He seemed better but I know he's still stressed about Noah. So, just talk to him and steer clear from any… sensitive topics."

"Is there a reason for that?" Emma questioned.

"No, no, no, of course not, no" I paused, "no, no, no."

"Oh yes, that seems very convincing!" Emma rolled her eyes. "Look, all I want to say is don't mess Dean around. He's a really nice guy and it wouldn't be fair."

"Oh, of course Em, I *do* like Dean so much and there's nothing with Noah. I'm happy with Dean and he's so nice and good to me. I don't want to do anything to upset him or to mess up what we have."

"OK, that's good then," Emma smiled, "I just want you to be happy." I smiled back at her and gave her a tight hug. She was so amazing.

"Look, I'll see you later. I've got to go and catch up with my group," I said as I turned and started to walk away.

"Be careful, don't fall over!" I heard Emma call. To anyone else that would be a harmless message, but to me, I knew she meant more than avoiding falling on the walk...

As I made my way over, I saw Noah waiting for me.

"So, it looks like we're stuck together." He looked at me and ran his hands through his hair – oh dear. Clearly, he was nervous from that b.

"Yep, seems as if you're stuck with me for now," I smiled back at him.

A comfortable ease spread over us. Today was going to be difficult, and it hadn't even begun.

We set off on the walk, and me and Noah fell into a comfortable silence. I had this odd itching to reach over to him and... I don't know, just to be nearer. I shook myself out of it – I shouldn't have these thoughts, I don't like him like that. But no matter how hard I tried to hide it, my hand kept reaching out towards him.

"So... how have you been?" Noah asked me. I just looked at him. There was something about him. It was so nice that he was still trying, and the idea just made me smile.

"I've been OK. My ankle finally healed after some crazy guy pushed me into a lake," I joked.

"Oh wow, he sounds like a great guy. You know maybe he just had to make the activity a little more fun," he teased and bumped my shoulder with his. "So come on, tell me about yourself."

"Um, what do you want to know? I'm not that interested really."

"Oh, come on, I'm sure you're far more interesting than you're telling me." I knew he wasn't going to let it go and I waited expectantly for him to go further.

"OK, what's your family like?"

"Hmm OK. Well, I'm a middle child, older brother and two younger siblings, one brother, one sister. Parents still together, got a dog. That's kind of it really."

He looked almost victorious.

"OK," I said, "what about you?"

"I'm kind of similar. Got a dog too, parents are together, but I've only got one sibling, a little sister. She's pretty adorable and we get on pretty well."

It was nice with him with no interruptions – his mystery was lessening. Maybe his enticement would reduce too.

"OK, well that's good to know. Learning more about you makes me less convinced you're a crazy weirdo," I responded. "What about your hobbies, what do you like to do?"

He paused for a moment, then said, "OK, I like football – playing more than watching. I play games quite often, music is pretty good and reading is how I spend a lot of my time." I was really impressed by that.

"Go on then, your turn," he said.

"Well, OK. I'm a massive book nerd. I love music too. Working out is pretty fun and a certified TV watcher."

"Ohhh , that's opened up two very important questions… favourite book and best TV show?"

"Hmm, let's think about this. Can I choose a top five?" I asked him. He thought about it for a moment then flashed me a grin.

"I'll give you three."

"So, favourite books – I don't even think I could pick one" I admitted, which gained an exasperated look from Noah. "I read *Little Women* recently, which was incredible; and not to be clichéd, but *Pride and Prejudice* was awesome too.''

I looked at him and he was just watching me and listening.

"Now, to choose a TV show. It would be an equal tie between a lot of them. So", I said and began to list them, "*Brooklyn Nine-Nine*, *New Girl*, *The Office* and *Gilmore Girls*. And that is only a few"

"Wow so not many then," he teased.

"Oh, and *Miranda*!" I interrupted. He paused and looked at me, seeing if it was safe to speak.

"Well, I have to say I agree with you on those TV choices, but I would add *Game of Thrones*," he said, which I just met with a blank expression.

"Have you ever watched it?"

"Can't say I have," I said with a grimace.

His face turned to clear shock. "I can't believe you haven't watched it – that's insane!"

I laughed and once I'd told him I hadn't seen the show I was subjected to a complete summary of the show. I was so confused by what he was talking about, but it was quite funny, he was obviously so excited.

I became a little too amused by him and my attention was so fixed on his gorgeous

face that I wasn't concentrating on the less-than-smooth path.

"Oh damn!" I exclaimed. I could feel my feet slipping in the mud and wasn't certain I would stay standing for much longer. My legs started to go and that was when I felt an arm slide round my waist and warmed flooded through me, keeping me up. Noah had grabbed me, and suddenly I was pressed against his body, his arm holding me tight. It was like the lake adventure all over again. I could feel his chest under my hands and my breath became short. As I looked up at him he was already gazing down at me. It felt as if his eyes were staring straight through me, deep into my soul. It scared me but I couldn't tear my gaze away – something in me was drawn to him. I didn't want him to let go. I knew that I'd feel the loss as soon as his arm went, which would be all too quick for me.

"Don't worry, I'll always catch you," he murmured his mouth a whisper away from my ear and I couldn't do anything other than stand and watch him.

Then I remembered Dean. Kind, sweet, funny Dean, who I cared about so much. Who made me feel calm, safe and happy. As I looked up at Noah, I knew that this wasn't OK. Emma's words ran through my head – and she was right. I scrambled out of Noah's arms, straightened myself and looked down at the floor.

"Uh, um, thanks. That could have been bad," I coughed and joked, trying to forget what just happened. I cleared my throat and tapped him on the arm as a thank you while taking a few steps back, just trying to put some distance between us. But I knew this was futile. The rest of the walk passed with no further accidents, and I tried to keep up a safe light conversation with Noah. I just had to get back to the camp and then I would be with Emma and Dean and all would be OK.

Noah and I talked more about our favourite things, and he asked a little more about my family. I immediately stiffened and I'm sure my discomfort didn't go unnoticed as Noah quickly changed the topic of conversation to our dogs, asking what breed and how old. I was surprised by his keen attention and how quickly he noticed my uneasiness. It was only a small thing, but it made a difference. I wasn't ready to talk about things yet and he didn't push. It made the whole situation that little bit easier. We kept on walking and soon stopped for lunch. I sat next to Noah as we enjoyed our food and relaxed in the sun. It was so easy with him and, while I felt guilty over Dean, there was a side of me that didn't want this day to end. It seemed so uncomplicated here, with him.

After an hour, we'd all finished our lunches. We had time to relax and then set off again to complete the walk – five-kilometres to go. Noah jumped up and reached a hand down to me. I looked at it for a moment.

"Oh, come on Cass, I promise you I won't bite," he joked. I rolled my eyes at him but soon reached for his hand. He yanked me up and I stumbled slightly, righting myself before he could reach out and grab me. I didn't want to know what I would do if I felt his touch again.

The afternoon passed quickly – all too quickly. The long walk had seemed effortless with Noah – he seemed to boost me. Soon, we were walking back towards the campsite, and I would have to say goodbye to Noah. I wasn't sure what was going on when I was around him, but I liked who I was when I was with him.

Chapter 12

As we walked back into the campsite, me and Noah parted ways with a smile and a little awkward wave. When he was out of sight I went straight back to the tent and tried to calm myself down and get my thoughts straight before I faced Dean and Emma. OK, so maybe Noah and I had shared a moment, but it didn't mean anything. I'd lost my footing and started to slip! I would've fallen over if he hadn't grabbed me and he saved me from major embarrassment. It was fine – that was all it was. It didn't mean anything. If it had been anyone else there, they would have done the same thing! OK, I needed to talk to someone. I grabbed my phone and called Lexi.

"Hey stranger, what's up?" she said as soon as she picked up the phone. "I haven't heard from you for ages. I was worried you were dead or something!"

"OK, ha, ha, I need your help!" I said in a rush. "Or I mean maybe someone to talk to and rant to at least."

"OK, this sounds juicy. Come on then, dish it out. Is this anything to do with your man?"

"Well... kind of..."

"No way! Don't tell me it's about that other one too?" she said. I paused, and there was a gasp on the other end of the line.

"Tell. Me. NOW!" she practically screamed.

"OK I will. I need some advice." I heard some odd noises. "OK, come on Lexi, you need to stay quiet until I've finished."

"I promise."

"OK, so things are really good with Dean, right, but there's this new guy in camp who

arrived a couple days late and we had this crazy thing by the lake and Dean got really jealous and, I don't know, me and him kinda had a moment again today but I don't know if it was a moment or if it actually meant anything. But there was this moment in the lake and then we went on the walk and he caught me from falling and, ugh, I don't know! What do you think?" Silence. "Lexi! Come on, you're always talking. This isn't the time to suddenly go quiet on me!"

"OK, woah, I'm sorry – that was a lot to take in," she said, "so give a little more detail on what actually happened."

I took a deep breath and told her the whole story with Noah – about the lake and my leg getting caught and him saving me, then the walk and him catching me from slipping and the talks over lunch, the messages.

"Is he hot?"

"Oh, trust you to ask such a question! His name is Noah, by the way," I took a breath, "and he isn't the worst looking boy I guess. He has this hair… and his eyes."

I moved the phone away from my face as an unbearable squeal came down the line.

"Look at you, girl! Go away for the summer and have boys falling over you left, right and centre," she joked. I just rolled my eyes.

"So, what do you think?" I asked.

"Do you like this other guy? Or was it just in the moment – like that hero idea. He did save you both times. Maybe only from a fall and a little bit of embarrassment but it was still him saving you."

See, this was why I called Lexi. Maybe she was crazy sometimes, but she still got it and was great with the advice. Plus, she was an outside view. Emma seemed way too close to all this, and I couldn't exactly share the problem with Dean or Noah.

"Yeah maybe you're right," I said. "He was just being nice, and each time he was just saving me. It's not like it was this major thing, plus I hardly know him so there was no way I could like him, right?" I breathed a sigh of relief. "Thank you, I needed this."

"Hey, it's fine. I'll always be here if you need me, plus I love good gossip," Lexi laughed.

"How are your parents Cassie? Have you heard from them?"

"Well, yeah, kind of. My mum has sent me a few messages – just checking up – and my dad called me."

"Wait, what? Your *dad* called you?"

"Yeah, that was exactly my reaction. He just called to check up on me. He didn't mention my mum."

"Do you think they're OK?"

"I'm really not sure Lex, I don't know what kind of scene I'm going to return to in a few weeks," I confessed.

"Well, whatever it is Cassie, you have me and Lottie and Connie to love you and support you no matter what happens," she assured me.

"Thank you, Lexi, that means so much!" I smiled at the phone. Knowing I had them by my side, supporting me, made me confident that I could survive all this. I wasn't sure how, but I would be fine.

"OK, I should go," I said. "Dean should be getting back from his walk soon too so I'm going to go find him. Thank you for this and I'll talk to you later."

"OK hun, I'll talk to you another time. Keep me updated on the camp situation and your family OK? I want to know you're OK," she said to me. I agreed and hung up the phone.

After my talk with Lexi, I felt reassured. The reaction my body had to Noah was merely just the proximity to him and the fact that he'd saved me. I've had the feeling with Dean too, well maybe not the exact feeling. So clearly it was just the situation, it meant nothing. I took a deep breath and left the tent. I felt calmer, and it was fine.

I looked around and noticed Emma and Dean walking back towards me, deep in conversation. They hadn't noticed me – I just watched a little. It was great to see them getting along, Emma nudging Dean's arm and laughing at something he'd said as they leant towards each other. Emma looked up and saw me. Her face dropped a fraction, but immediately a bigger smile took over as she walked over and gave me a big hug. Dean followed close behind and gave me a kiss.

"Hey guys," I said, "how was your walk?" They both looked at me then grinned at each other.

"It was really good." Emma said, looking at Dean as he nodded. "There was one point Dean tripped over a rock and it was so funny, he almost face-planted the path."

"I still blame you for that one," he told her.

"Hey, how was it my fault, I wasn't even that close to you!"

"Oh yeah, come on, you definitely did it," he retorted.

"Oh, you would think that Dean," she teased. They both broke out in laughter, and I just smiled at them.

"Oh wow, that sounds… fun?" I said hesitantly.

"Oh yeah, it definitely was, it was really funny," Emma confirmed with another round of laughter. "Anyways, how was your walk? Stuck with Noah for the whole day."

"Oh yeah, it was fine," I said, not trying to give away anything about Noah, "a little

boring really but it was a nice walk I guess."

Dean seemed quite relieved but Emma wasn't convinced. I'm positive she thought that if it was just the two of us then surely something would've happened. I guess there was some truth to that, but I wouldn't let on.

"Well, it seems like we have some free time," Dean said after a little moment of quiet. "Maybe if Emma doesn't mind, I could steal Cassie away, spend some time with her after not seeing her all day."

I waited for Emma's response.

"No, of course not, it's fine. My feet are aching and I'm so exhausted. I'm going to go and chill in the tent for a while, probably have a nap. Wake me up for food, otherwise do *not* disturb me." Emma gave me a hug and whispered "have fun" with a wink as she walked away. I turned to Dean with a smile.

"So, our place?" I asked. He smiled back.

"You just read my mind." And with that we set off for the lake.

On the way down we chatted about the walk. Dean told me about him and Emma and how they were chatting and laughing and getting on so well. I smiled at him, and it was really nice to hear. We chatted more about just little things, and it was these small moments that made me realise how important Dean was to me and how much I liked him. He slipped his hand into mine as we walked, and we felt so calm. Surrounded by this serenity, I never wanted to return. I was at peace with Dean and I didn't want to leave this bubble. The sun was shining on our faces, but I could see it

begin to set as the night begins to take over. By the lake, Dean sat behind me and I leant into his chest.

"Hey Cassie, I'm glad I met you, you know."

"I'm glad I met you too, Dean. I don't know what I'd do without you"

He kissed me gently. I was torn between what kisses I preferred – we had shared so many – and I couldn't wait for the next kisses we'd share. Dean was amazing and I was so lucky to have known him.

We stayed there for a while, just sitting, chatting and taking in the sun. I loved our little spot, but soon real life was calling us and we had to head back to the campsite as the sun set even lower. We walked to the campsite hand in hand with silly grins on our faces. As we got back, we parted ways and

I went to find Emma. With one more look over my shoulder, I saw Dean smiling at me and my heart filled with warmth.

"All right sleepyhead," I announced as I burst into the tent. Judging from Emma's sleepy demeanour and the snores I could hear from outside the tent, I had to try harder than that. With a sigh, I plumped down onto her bed, which stirred her out of sleep.

"Oh, you're back – I was enjoying the peace and quiet," she grinned at me. "Did you have a good time with your lover boy?"

"It was so nice, being together, having time with just the two of us," I smiled, remembering the sweet kisses we'd stolen down by the lake.

"Awwww, look at you all smiley and loved up," Emma said. I blushed at her choice of words.

"All right, come on, we gotta go. Apparently, Dan has something planned for this evening."

We made our way to the main area, where people had already gathered. As I was walking over, I felt my phone vibrate in my pocket. I gestured for Emma to keep walking, telling her I'd catch up with her. As I glanced at the screen, I noticed another message from my dad.

Dad: *Hey Cass, just wanted to check up on you.*

OK, it is getting weird now. I had officially spoken to my dad more since being away than my mum and that never happened! My dad wasn't the kind of person who messaged often. When I first got here, he was so cold to me, but now after a week he is messaging more. It didn't feel right. Fortunately, I didn't have time to dwell on it as Emma was calling my name as they got ready to start the evening's races. I quickly shoved the phone in my pocket, ignoring the message from dad, and ran over to the group.

I noticed Noah standing at the edge of the group. I looked over to him and he'd already seen me walking over, his face lighting up. I felt a stir of emotion fill my chest and quickly averted my gaze. Dean was standing nearer the middle with some of his camp mates, so me and Emma walked over to their group. When he noticed me, he bent down and gave me a light kiss on the lips, which made my tummy flutter. He threw his arm round my shoulder and pulled me closer to him. Emma had walked over too, and I could see Connor's eyes follow her. She kept her gaze straight ahead and unwavering – oh, how I envied her that talent! If only I could manage that with Noah.

"All right everyone!" shouted Dan. "I hope you're ready for tonight because there will be consequences for those that don't win." This earned a groan from most people. "I've arranged a few challenges and activities for tonight. There will be both rewards and penalties for those who win and lose. So, let's get started!"

We all cheered and got going. First up was a series of races. I was with Emma for a few of them and we did pretty well – not winning, but at least not losing. Then Noah and his partner tripped up in one of the races.

"Ha, tough luck," I heard Dean mumble bitterly under his breath, clearly pleased by the turn of events. I just let it slide, as if I hadn't heard.

Me and Emma were up again next. I'd been a bit too distracted by Dean to hear what Dan had said about the race, but I got the main idea of it. Emma seemed confident, so I just trusted her.

"OK, so are we all clear? Good. In Three... Two... One... *Go!*"

Emma was off. Oh, all right, so it was a relay obstacle – I could do that. I kept my eye on the course as Emma weaved around each part and was in the lead. When Emma was getting closer to me, I prepared myself. She hit my hand and I was off. I was doing pretty well to begin with, it was easy. I loved this kind of thing. I looked up at Emma and she was cheering me on. Then I made the mistake of looking to the left, where I saw Noah staring at me and instantly felt the intensity of his look. For just a second it threw me off and I landed on my face. Dean started forwards to help me, but I was up immediately and racing back to Emma. Much to my dismay, the fall had cost us the race. Oh god, I had cost us the race. Emma looked at me and just laughed.

"What happened there?" she asked.

"I don't know, I just looked up and lost my concentration. I tripped over. I'm sorry clearly I just got distracted"

"Hmmm, you sure it didn't have anything to do with the person standing a little bit down from me?" Emma raised her eyebrow at me suspiciously.

"What? No way! I don't even know what you're talking about." I hoped that being oblivious might help me.

"Oh, are you sure? Because I swear, I could have seen you looking over that way," Emma stated.

"But it looks like I'll be roped into the challenges for the losers now. I wonder what Dan has planned for us to do." This was an obvious change of topic, but Emma clearly understood and let it go.

"I bet it's gonna be really gross or something. I'll enjoy watching you suffer," Emma joked. I pushed her and laughed.

"Come on Cassie, you're my best friend but it's going to be so funny!"

"Wow thanks, real friend right there aren't you!" I exclaimed, rolling my eyes.

We watched the rest of the races take place. After that little incident with Noah and the obstacle race, I didn't feel like doing any other challenges. I cheered on Dean, who won a few of his races and came over to me for a victory kiss when he won. I giggled as he triumphantly pressed his lips against mine. I leant into him, hesitant to let him go. As I pulled away, I smiled at him. I made sure I didn't pay any attention to Noah in the rest of his races – not only for my own sanity, but also to show Dean that there wasn't anything between us.

Soon the races were over, and Dean walked over to me once again.

"Well done baby, at least there's one winner in this relationship," I joked.

"Yeah, you really took a tumble there. I'm not sure if I can be seen with you for a while – that could dent my camp cred," he teased.

"Your 'camp cred'?" I just looked at him. "I'm sorry, I don't think I can now be seen with *you* after you've used that phrase – major turn off," I teased back.

"Hmm, well I guess we can just be a couple of losers. I'd be happy to be a loser if it meant I could be with you," he said as he leant down to kiss me – if you could call it a kiss – gently brushing my lips with his. The touch was as light as a butterfly, but it still warmed my heart.

"Well, I guess I better go and find out what my consequence is for losing my race," I told him and slowly walked away.

"I'll see you later," Dean called to me. "Hopefully it's not too bad a punishment."

"And hopefully my punishment is *not* with Noah," I muttered to myself as soon as I was at a safe distance.

Chapter 13

I walked over to where the other unfortunate campers that had also lost their races were standing, waiting to hear what Dan had in store for us. I noticed Noah standing to the side and with a small smile in his direction I went and stood next to him.

"So, I wonder what Dan has planned for us," he whispered to me. I nodded in agreement, hoping that it wouldn't be too bad. Dan approached us and began to explain.

"Right," Dan started, "looks like I've got you all gathered. Now, I'm sad to see you all here but rules are rules, so let's see what consequences I can dish out." He had a look at the board he was holding. "OK, so we have setting up and clearing up dinner, activity coordinator, the toilets need cleaning, and the younger campers need supervision for their tent tidying. When you hear the one you want to do, raise your hand and the first hand raised will do that one."

I decided I would pick the dinner clear down as it seemed like the least amount of effort. I could just stand there and wash up or something. Dan called out the ones before it and arms went up. As he got to the dinner clear up, I got ready to raise my arm – there was no way I'd be stuck cleaning out the toilets.

"And dinner clear up." Up shot my hand. I noticed a few other hands being raised but I didn't pay any attention – I just wanted to make sure that I was part of the clear down group. Dan continued with and filled the rest of the duties. I waited to hear my name called for dinner clear down duty, hoping I had been quick enough to not get stuck with toilet duty.

"Great, that's everyone," Dan announced. "So, just for confirmation, listen for your name and your designated duty." Dan went down the list of names saying their jobs.

"Cassie, you'll be clearing up." I sighed, relieved that I had got there in time. Then I heard the name I was dreading.

"Noah," I held my breath praying fate would be kind, "you're on dinner clean up too, along with Jake, James, Lily and Helen."

Well... apparently fate hated me. I must have done something wrong in a past life to be subject to these never-ending situations.

I kept my head to the ground, but I could feel Noah's eyes on me, his body next to mine, almost daring me to look up at him, to meet his gaze. I was too stubborn, though, for that to happen!

"All right, well you all have your duties, and you all know when you're expected to do them, so I'll see you for your consequences. Until then, enjoy your evening." And with a wave of Dan's hand we were dismissed. I escaped the group quickly but not before I heard Noah say my name. I knew I should've responded, but I wouldn't give him the satisfaction of a reaction, so I kept walking until I found Emma.

Part of me knew this evening would end in bad news. I should've been nice to Noah and did try when I could. I was nice to him when I saw him and I spoke to him often, but there was something inside me that I knew I couldn't let anyone see, a part of me that reacted to him in a way that I wasn't prepared to accept. It was best for all involved for me to keep my distance. But even while I told myself those words, there was a part of my body that didn't want to stay away and that couldn't wait for dinner to finish. Dan might've thought it was a punishment, but if it meant that I could spend time with Noah away from watchful eyes then I was thankful for it.

As I dashed out of the food hall to escape Noah, I spotted Emma and Dean sitting at one of the benches. Their demeanour was similar to when they came back from the walk, sitting with heads bent close together and laughing energetically. I made my way over and they both looked up as I neared.

"So, what was your 'punishment', as Dan so gracefully put it?" Emma asked as I stood behind the bench and wrapped my arms around Dean's neck affectionately.

"Well, he was generous enough to give me a choice," I answered

"Wow, how lovely, what did you end up with then?" Dean commented.

"So, I managed to get clear up after dinner. Me and a few others are stuck with that one," I sighed. "I mean, at least it's much better than toilet duty, which some poor unfortunate camper has been landed with."

They both laughed.

"Well, that's true, at least you landed the lesser of two evils," said Emma.

"Anyways, please distract me, I don't want to think about all the cleaning I have to do later."

"OK, well what do you want to do?" asked Dean.

"Um, let's just chill. I shall enjoy my freedom before I'm forced into my manual labour," I joked.

"I love how you never get dramatic about these things Cassie," said Emma facetiously.

For the next couple of hours, we just relaxed on the grass. I rested my head on Dean's shoulder and took in the scene – the gentle breeze rustling the trees, the sweet chorus of the birds high above me, the final glorious rays of sunshine. I was happy.

Unfortunately, that happiness was short lived, however, as it was soon dinner time. I sat with Emma and Dean, relaxing and laughing along with them. But in my mind, I couldn't avoid drifting to what was waiting for me, thinking of the time I'd be spending with Noah in no more than an hour. I could just see him across the food hall. He had his head down, eating his dinner and pushing his food around his plate, ignoring whatever the girl next to him was saying. But as I looked over, it was as if he sensed me watching him, because his head shot up and immediately his eyes connected with mine. I could feel a wave of emotion and was unable to tear my eyes away, my breath quickening at the intensity of his attention. There was a pull between us, and it was getting harder to ignore.

The rest of dinner passed in a blur. Emma and Dean were talking, but I was just sitting there, unable to concentrate, playing with my food and inwardly freaking out.

"Right," said Dan, as dinner came to an end, "those of you that have already paid your punishment are free to go. Those of you that were lucky enough to not lose then you're also free to go, and those of you who lost, you know what time it is. So, let's go!"

"Well, I guess I'll see you guys later," I said to Dean and Emma as I dragged myself out of my seat.

"Have fun, babe," Dean said, giving me a light kiss on my forehead.

"Yeah, have fun with your manual labour, as you so graciously put it," Emma added, and her and Dean left the food hall.

I turned around and saw Noah rise from his seat, looking at me. I smiled at him and walked over to Dan for our instructions. As I neared Noah, I was desperate to make this encounter as comfortable as possible.

"Looks like we got a fun job," I joked. God, please let this not be awkward!

"Ha, ha, yeah, really got lucky today," Noah responded. "At least the company isn't the worst," he grinned. Oh god, he really wasn't making this easy for me!

"We better get started," I said, "unless we want to be stuck here all night."

"Wouldn't be the worst thing, considering," he murmured. I stumbled for a moment, shocked at what he said.

Dan told us the jobs that needed to be done and everyone began to split up, choosing what they wanted. There were already people cleaning the tables and sweeping.

I turned to Noah, "So, I guess we should start on washing up – it seems to be the only job left."

"Yeah, that makes the most sense – you wash, I'll dry?" he asked. I nodded. As we made our way to the sinks, I thought of all the things we could talk about. It stayed quiet for a while, as we got to the sinks and started up. Having Noah this close was doing something to my senses. His smell was intoxicating, surrounding me like a warm blanket. As I passed a plate to him, our hands brushed. It was the smallest of touches, but I could feel my whole body light up, like a shock had shot straight through me. I imagined those hands wrapped round my waist again, holding me close as his smell enveloped me, his lips leaning closer and closer until....

"So," I said, as I cleared my throat, needing some conversation to stop my thoughts, "how are you?" A pathetic attempt, but at least it was something. Noah cleared his throat.

"Yeah, I've been good, enjoying the summer and camp I guess. Dan has done well with the activities I've seen so far, and I've finally made a couple of friends, so I can't be classed as the new weird guy any more," he chuckled, "so I won't have to run to you to save me from awkward situations any more." I nodded with slight disappointment at the prospect of not seeing him as much. I handed over another plate, just for something to do, making sure to avoid any kind of contact this time.

"Well at least there's that," I laughed along.

"How is the ankle feeling?" he asked. I looked at him, a little surprised by his care. Dean hadn't checked again since that day.

"It's good, fully healed now. It was swollen for a few days but all recovered now. Dean and Emma were really great, helping me out."

"Wow, prince charming right there," Noah muttered. I looked at him, shocked by his sudden change of tone. He noticed my gaze and turned to smile at me, unaware that I'd heard him.

"What was that?" I dared him to respond louder, looking at him expectantly.

He looked stunned – mission accomplished.

"Oh, er nothing."

I felt smug, but victory was short as he then had to go and run his fingers through that glorious hair.

"I was just saying that you missed a spot on this plate," Noah said as he leant over to show me. His scent was even stronger and it was doing things to me.

"Hmm," I said, slightly disorientated by the proximity and unable to concentrate on his words, "oh, where?"

"Right… there!" he said as he wiped his wet towel over my face.

I gasped with shock. "Oh, you're evil!" I laughed and splashed him.

"But, I can do worse," I said, attacking him with the bubbles in the sink.

He immediately leaned over, grabbed bubbles and began to throw them right back at me. I giggled and grabbed even more bubbles. Soon a whole bubble fight had broken out and bubbles were flying, littering the floor. As Noah stepped towards me to get more bubbles, he slipped, hitting his knee on the wet floor.

"Oh Noah, you don't have to take a knee to admit defeat," I mocked, hurling more bubbles at him.

The bubbles started to run out, so I swapped bubbles for water.

"OK, OK, you have the upper hand with a superior weapon, so I shall admit defeat and concede," he joked, which made me laugh even harder.

Sobering up, I asked, "So, not-so-new and mysterious Noah. What do you want to do in the future?" It seemed like a safe question.

"Hmm, let's see. In the grand scheme of things... I have no idea!" he claimed triumphantly. "Now, if we're thinking of the nearer future, one of my biggest dreams would be to travel."

I stopped cleaning for a moment and just looked at him. Sharing the same goal was not making this whole avoidance thing any easier.

"Oh, um, wow, that's really cool," I responded.

"I've always loved the idea of seeing everywhere. I'd hate not to see the world, thinking how small we as individuals are and how much of the world there is to see. I'd hate it if I went my whole life not going anywhere." He smiled at me and I froze. He couldn't really have said anything more perfect to me at that moment.

"Wow, that's... wow!" I was at a loss. "OK, where's your top place to travel to?"

"I'd love to go to Japan – its culture and landscape seem incredible. But another one of my goals is to visit every single state in America." I just gazed at him.

"OK," he continued, "I know what you're thinking, and I have no idea how I'd do it. Maybe rent a car, or maybe a van and live out of the van. It just seems like a great idea."

Now he was off, and I was mesmerised by his passion.

"I just think, most Americans don't leave their country in their lifetime, so clearly there must be something good that's keeping them there and that's what I want to know."

I was still just looking at him and I realised that he was probably expecting some kind of response.

"No, that doesn't sound crazy," I told him. "It's actually something I really want to do too. I desperately want to travel and going to all the states is high on my list too. Now, Japan would be really cool to visit, don't get me wrong, but Italy has always intrigued me."

He was the one smiling at me now, and I took this as encouragement.

"I mean, just think about it – all the pasta and the pizza and the ice-cream and the culture and the nature and the ice cream." He laughed.

"The ice cream must really matter," he laughed. I turned to watch him and his eyes were already on me, my breath caught in my throat and the noise around us fell away. I couldn't tear my eyes away from him -even with the dirty plates piled up around us. The others around us were still cleaning and finishing their duties but there was this connection between us.

"Well, the ice cream is important," I murmured. Noah shuffled his hand along the sink, where it was resting, and lightly grazed mine. I felt it again, that jolt, like sparks lighting up my body and burning inside me. I cleared my throat and turned back to the sink.

"Well," I said, clearing my throat, "we better keep going. These dishes aren't going to clean themselves." I chuckled and got back to work. Noah followed suit and turned back to the clean plates to start drying them once again. We fell into an easy rhythm after that, creating a good and light conversation and working through all the places we wanted to see. But I still couldn't deny the aching need I had to be around him, the pull he had. His presence both set me at ease and stirred up a whole storm inside me. I didn't know I could feel this way – so calm and yet so restless around him. God, what was this boy doing to me?

After the brief, intimate moment we shared, me and Noah quickly finished the washing – with no further incidents. While we cleaned the plates, the rest of the people finished their jobs and slowly filtered out of the food hall. It was just me and Noah left. I looked up at him.

"Well, it looks like we're done – good job, partner." I held out my hand for him to shake, which he took with a laugh. At his gentle touch, I took in a great breath.

"We do make a good team, you and I," he said, turning up the side of his mouth with a cocky look. Our hands were still connected, and I wished I could stay this close to him for much longer. Wow! I had to get away from him… and soon. I released Noah's hand and stepped back.

"It's getting late, I better head back to my tent," I said. "I'm sure Emma is wondering where I am."

"And I bet you want to get away before Dean sees us together," he said with a slight edge to his words.

"Uh um, no no," I stuttered.

"I'll see you around Cass," he called to me as I walked away, smiling at the nickname.

"Bye," I called back. "Oh, and for the record, you'll always be the new mysterious weirdo to me."

"Hmm, mysterious?" That has its possibilities." He smiled as I rolled my eyes and turned away.

Dan may have said that this was a punishment for losing, but it felt far from that.

I started to run over to where Dean and Emma were, but I felt my phone vibrate once again. I remembered I hadn't responded to the message from my dad, so I pulled out the phone to see who it was. My brother Jake was calling me. Now let me tell you, I loved my brother, but he wasn't the kind of person who called, unless there was no way of avoiding it. I immediately answered the call.

"Hey Jake, how are you? Is everything OK?" I asked him, walking round to the side of the food hall so no one could see me.

"Hey Cassandra." I rolled my eyes and smiled at the use of my full name. "Yeah, I'm all good. I just wanted to call and see how you were, being away from home."

"Yeah, I'm fine Jake, it's been great so far. Dad mentioned you've been with your uni friends a lot this summer, how are they?"

"They're great, it's been a good distraction if I'm honest," he confessed.

"Distraction from what?" I asked.

"Well… mum and dad, you know," he answered.

"Oh well, that's true, their arguing is getting ridiculous," I agreed.

"No Cassie." Not my full name I realised, he never used my nickname. "Not just arguing," he told me.

"What are you talking about Jake?" I asked him, an edge of worry in my voice.

"They're separating, Cassie," he said softly. My phone nearly dropped from my hand as I sank to the floor.

"No Jake, this must be a joke, you're wrong. Their arguing was bad, but it wasn't *that* bad." The words came out in a stream. He must have been kidding with me – no way would they separate and not tell me.

"Cassie, it's true, they told me a couple of days ago. They haven't been happy for so long. It isn't permanent, they just need some time away."

"No Jake, no. Please say you're joking, say this is some kind of sick joke!" The tears began to flow down my face and I was helpless to stop them.

"I'm so sorry you didn't know, I thought they were going to tell you themselves," Jake said.

Soon things started making sense – the radio silence from mum, the extra messages from dad, the way he was so weird about mum on the phone.

"I… I need to go, Jake, I need to talk to mum."

"OK, Cassandra, but call me later please," he demanded, clearly worried about leaving me. I said I would and hung up.

With shaking hands, I dialled my mum's number and lifted the phone to my ear.

"Hi sweetie," she said as I answered. I could hear the tiredness in her voice.

"Mummy?" I whimpered through a flood of tears.

"Oh baby," she said.

"I just spoke to Jake – tell me he's wrong," I begged, "please tell me he was lying!" The other end of the line was silent and I knew it was true. I began to sob even harder.

"What happened?" I asked, trying to rein in my emotions.

"Sweetheart, we haven't been happy for a while now and we've spent so long trying to do what was right that we lost ourselves – we just need some time apart. We aren't saying this is permanent, but your dad is going to go and live with one of his friends for a while." I heard my mum take a deep breath and continue, "This doesn't mean you'll never see him or that we'll never go back to how we were but we need this time to see what we both really want. This will be good, honey."

"When did you decide this?" I asked her.

"Last week," she confessed.

"Why didn't you tell me!" I yelled.

"We didn't want to ruin your summer, sweetie," she said softly.

"But keeping this from me mum? I had hardly heard from you, and dad was being more attentive and I don't like being out of this all!" I paused. "Mum, I am eighteen, I could handle this. You should've told me instead of leaving me to find out from Jake, who thought I already knew!"

"I didn't realise he was going to call you," she mumbled.

"That's not the point mum, you or dad should've told me," I insisted.

"I know, I know," she said in a resigned tone.

"Look mum, I understand why you kept it from me, and I love you, but right now I can't talk." I could feel my chest getting tight and I didn't need this right now.

"OK sweetie, but please don't shut me out, I'm here and I love you," she told me.

"OK mum, love you too," I replied, and before she could say anything I hung up.

My chest had become unbearably tight and I was struggling to breath. I turned to my phone and looked for Lexi's contact. She knew what to do when this happened. I tried to call her but I only got her voicemail.

"Um Lexi, I... I think it's happening again and I can't control it – I really need you, please call me back." I hung up, chucked my phone in the grass and placed my head between my knees trying to steady my breathing.

"Cass, are you... ? Oh god," I heard Noah say. I lifted my head and saw him looking around the corner. He rushed to sit in front of me and grabbed my hands in his, drawing soothing patterns on my palms.

"Hey, hey, it's going to be OK. Take a deep breath," he told me. "Hey, just listen to me, listen to my voice. What can you hear?" he asked. I closed my eyes and took a deep breath, listening to what was around me.

"Uh, I can hear the birds? And... uh... the people in the campsite," I stuttered.

"Yeah, yeah, that's right, they're playing football, being obnoxiously loud," he chuckled. "Right, what can you smell?" he asked.

"Um," I took another deep breath, "the... the fumes from the cleaning things, uh bleach, and a little bit of the chocolate cake we had for... for dessert," I told him, my words becoming more even.

"That's right, that's it. That cake was amazing, wasn't it? I had mine with cream. Did *you*?" he asked me.

"Er uh, yeah, cream." I could feel my chest begin to loosen and my breath became more even as Noah continued to rub my hands.

"That's it, Cass, you're doing amazing, keep breathing," he said and let me work through my breaths. I looked into his eyes and saw the panic and concern that he had for me. I shot him a thankful smile. As my breathing returned to normal, he moved and sat next to me, leaning against the wall of the food hall.

"You wanna talk about it?" he asked me after a moment's silence. I looked to the sky for a second.

"My parents are separating," I confessed, "I just found out."

"Oh god, Cass, that's horrible, I'm so sorry," he said, still holding my hand, rubbing comforting circles on the back of my hand. I shrugged in defeat.

"I knew it was coming, they've been arguing for so long now. I just wasn't expecting it now, if that makes sense." He looked at me and nodded. "I just don't know what to do, my dad is moving out and it's all going to be so different when I get home. I don't know what I'm supposed to do!"

"Hey, hey," he said, putting his other hand on mine. "It's OK, you're only eighteen, no one expects you to know what to do."

"But I need to be there for Bradley and Hailey," I insisted.

"No, you don't," he said, "they have your parents, who will still love them even if they're not together, and you have your older brother, who will be there. This isn't all on you Cass, it will be fine," he assured me. I rested my head on his shoulder and let the final tears fall from my eyes. We sat there for a while in a comfortable quiet, listening to the other campers and looking at the stars above us. It was an incredible sight. I closed my eyes and smiled at the ease of being next to him. With so many others, it took me a while to share anything and show vulnerability, but with Noah it was easy. I was comfortable and happy.

"Thank you," I whispered to him. I lifted my head and looked at him, "Thank you for not judging me."

"Cass, I would never judge you," he told me as he brought his hand to my face and wiped away a stray tear.

"I just hate looking weak and I hate these attacks I have," I confessed.

"Cass, you are many things, but weak is not one of them," he said as his hand stayed on my face, lightly stroking my cheek. I was glued to his eyes, unable to tear myself away. After a moment, he leant towards me. I lifted my head towards him but he pulled away.

"I want to kiss you Cass, you have no idea how much I want to, but not like this. You've just had bad news and you're not thinking straight. When I kiss you, and I do mean *when*, I want you to be focused on us, not distracted by the sadness you feel. Come on, I'm sure Emma is worried about you."

With that he stood up and pulled me up with him.

"Thank you again, Noah," I said to him, trying to undercut some of the awkwardness I was feeling over what had just happened.

"Are you going to be OK?" he asked with a concerned expression on his face. I nodded silently, not trusting my words. "Well in that case, I'll see you later, Cass." He kissed me lightly on the cheek, his lips hovering there for a moment, and then he stepped back and walked away. I watched as he turned the corner and as he went over to his friends. I leant against the wall again and this time my breath was quick – but for a whole different reason.

Chapter 14

Once I'd steadied myself, I pushed away from the wall and started back to my tent, the events that had just occurred running through my mind. I had almost kissed Noah! While I was with Dean, this was bad. I reached the tent and pushed back the front flap. Emma was chilling inside, waiting for me to get back, I assumed.

"Soooo, how was your 'manual labour' as you put it so eloquently?" she questioned.

I knew I should handle this delicately to avoid her suspicion. I tried to keep my tone as even as I could while I explained what had gone on – not everything, of course.

"Hmm, it was all right I guess, pretty boring, I was stuck on washing up. Anyways, how was your evening?" I asked, changing the topic very quickly to avoid any interrogations.

"Yeah, it was really nice. Me and Dean just walked around, hung out with some of his friends. Connor tried it on with me again, which earned him an elbow in the stomach I wish I could've given him more but I wouldn't want to get in trouble – he isn't worth that. Dean thought it was quite funny too."

"Ooo that sounds like a great time, any of the other ones catch your eye?" I gave her a little wink.

"Okay, a bit of overkill with the wink," she laughed, "but no, I mean they're really nice, but there wasn't really that kind of feeling with any of them."

"Oh, that's annoying, but at least it was a good time."

"Yeah, it was a good time – would have been better if you weren't stuck on clear up duty all night," she joked. "Anyways, I'm exhausted so I'm going to try and get some sleep."

We said goodnight to each other and then both settled down. As my eyes started to droop, I felt my phone vibrate. With a groan, I turned to check it.

Noah: *I know it was supposed to be a punishment but I had a great time with you.*

Me: *Yeah, I can't lie, it wasn't the worst.*

Noah: *I'll take that as a compliment.*

Me: *If that will help you sleep, go ahead.*

Noah: *Ha, ha, you know you had fun too.*

Me: *Hmm, well I guess I'll give you that one.*

Noah: *Yes!! Ha, ha I take that as a victory.*

We talked for a little bit longer. I asked him more about his idea to travel to America – it was nice.

Noah: *Anyways, I will let you sleep.*

Me: *Wow finally, here you are keeping me up.*

Noah: *Hey, you could have ignored me.*

Me: *Ah but I'm too nice. Anyways, night.*

Noah: *Goodnight.*

Noah: *Wait Cass, are you sure you're OK?*

Me: *Yeah, I'm much better, thanks. Sorry about earlier.*

Noah: *It's OK, it was just the moment. As long as you're OK, that's what matters.*

Me: *I am. But I should sleep now.*

Noah: *Right yes of course.*

Me: *Good night.*

Noah: *But you can always come to me if you need to Cass.*

Me: *Thank you.*

With that I put my phone under my pillow and closed my eyes. My thoughts drifted to Noah and the moments we'd shared. That was a side of me that no one saw. Only Lexi, Connie and Lottie ever saw the true depth of it and had witnessed one of my panic attacks. I didn't like showing that weaker side of me, but with Noah it hadn't mattered. He hadn't made me feel little or ashamed to cry. Soon my eyes began to feel heavy and sleep took over.

As soon as I woke up, I knew I needed to call Lexi again. I had a missed call from her and she would be disturbed by the message I left her. I'd had some bad attacks in school before and she was always worrying – and the stuff going on with my family, and the fact I was hours away, wouldn't make her worry any less. Plus, she'd love this update with Noah and would give me good advice. But I needed to get ready for breakfast and didn't have much time left. The call would have to wait until after, so I got up and began getting sorted.

My thoughts were running wild at the thought of seeing Noah, a stir of panic and excitement bubbled up in my stomach. How would he be with me? Would he even talk to me if I was with Dean? What did he think of yesterday? I tried to focus and took a few deep breaths to calm myself down, concentrating on getting ready for breakfast instead. There was a little bit of a chill in the air, so I decided to wear my ripped blue jeans with a white, cropped tank and a shirt over the top. As I left the tent with Emma, I shoved my Converses on – of course.

Breakfast went smoothly. We met Dean outside the food hall and he greeted me with a sweet kiss and a nervous smile towards Emma. I watched, rather confused. We walked inside and went to sit at our table. As I sat down I saw Noah in his usual spot, surrounded by his friends – he was quite popular now. He glanced up as if sensing my presence and waved in acknowledgement with a kind smile. I smiled in return and sat down. The time flew by in a whirl or chatting, laughing and eating. I was just enjoying being in the company of Emma and Dean, but one look at Noah, laughing with his friends, brought it all back to me – our glances, our light touches, our moment last night. A blush rose on my cheeks… I *really* needed to call Lexi.

As soon as breakfast was over I headed off to call Lexi. I went into the tent and sank onto my bed. She picked up on the second ring – I could always trust her to be around for the gossip.

"Oh god, Cassie, finally! I've been worried sick, what happened? Are you OK? Can I do anything?" she said as soon as she answered the phone.

"Hey Lex, I'm OK, Noah helped me and calmed me down."

"Ah OK, that's good, but what happened Cassie? Was it caused by something or was it one of your random ones?"

I took a deep breath. "My parents are separating," I replied. "Jake called me yesterday and told me. Mum had been keeping it from me – I only just found out."

"Oh no, Cassie, I'm so sorry, how do you feel?"

"I'm still a little numb," I admitted, "I don't think I've fully come to terms with it yet but at least that explains the calls and messages from dad recently."

"I can't believe he didn't tell you. He must have had some idea even when he called you. Is there anything I can do?" she asked.

"At the moment, no. Noah helped me out last night and he calmed me down. He saw I was having a panic attack and he was really good. But I don't feel like talking about the separation right now, I'm still coming to terms with it, in all honesty."

"That's fine, but what did Noah do?" she asked me.

"Well, I was around the side of one of the buildings and he must have heard me because he walked over to check, and when he saw it was me, he came and sat with me, talked me through it and just stayed with me until I was ready to get up."

"Oh Cassie, that's great, I'm glad you had someone."

"That's not all Lexi," I said to her, "we almost kissed."

"No way!" she screamed.

"Yes way, I was next to him, and it was getting late and he was so nice, I just turned to him and leant in."

"But why didn't you?" she questioned.

"He said he didn't want to kiss me while I was preoccupied and sad with my family problems. When he kissed me, he wanted my focus to be on him."

"Oh wow, Cassie, that *is* crazy, what did you do?"

"I mean, what could I do Lex? I just went silent, I felt so awkward. After that he just helped me and went to join his friends."

"He did then message me too, asking if I was OK."

"Oh Cassie, that's so sweet!"

"Yeah, it is, but that's not it."

"Oh god, really?"

"Um well no, there's a little more of an update with the whole Noah situation."

"EEEEKKKK, oh my gosh! I'm loving this and very jealous of you living this summer instead of me. Go on, fill me in on *everything*!"

"Wow, I'm loving the enthusiasm in my chaotic love life! OK, before my whole breakdown and stuff we had these races, right, and I lost one."

"Hey, how did you lose? You're normally so competitive."

"Uh, actually that's part of the thing. I was looking up and then I saw Noah and I tripped over."

"Wow, talk about head over heels", she joked.

"OK, OK, calm down. That's not all of it."

"OK, keep going."

"Well, the losers of the races then had punishments. They had to carry out some sort of consequence."

"Seems odd, but OK," Lexi commented.

"Well yeah, kinda. But we then got to choose which punishment we got to do, and me and Noah picked the same one." I started to hear her squeal. "And before you go crazy, it wasn't done on purpose, it just happened."

Still a squeal rang out on the other end of the phone.

"OK, what was that for? I told you I didn't do it on purpose. I didn't want to be with him."

"Ah but," Lexi paused, "that leads me to two conclusions… either he noticed you picked your consequence and wanted to do the same one to be with you, or it's like fate and you two just keep getting pushed together, and you don't even realise it!"

"OK Lexi, that's just crazy," I rolled my eyes, "fate doesn't exist, things just happen."

"Yeah, yeah, OK, you deny it, it's only a matter of time." I could feel her smugness through the phone.

"No, that's why I need your advice! Look I've started to realise that maybe I can't completely ignore what happens between me and Noah – on my side, anyways."

I then worried if this was all in my head. What If Noah didn't even think of me that way? Maybe I was just making it more than it was.

"OK, OK, Cassie, stop freaking out! I can hear you overthinking all the way down the phone." She knew me so well.

"Well, what do I do? I don't know if I properly like Noah or if he likes me! Then there's Dean… I mean, I really like him too! But it isn't really fair for me to mess him around like that."

"Wow! Well, this is kind of a situation for you, isn't it?" she pointed out.

"You don't say! That's why I need your help."

"OK, well, look, at the end of the day it's unfair to string along either of them – you're right there. So, I think you just need to look at who you really want and care about. Who do you feel is right in your heart? Who makes you shiver when they're around? Who do you get excited to see? Who do you want to spend all your time talking about?"

I took a deep sigh. I realised Lexi was right. I couldn't do that to either of them and I had to realise who was really more important to me.

"Yeah, you're right. OK, I need to do this. Thank you for the help. I needed a chat."

"Hey, you never need to thank me, I'm always here for you," she said, "I mean I'm loving the gossip so it's really no problem, you better keep me involved!"

"Thank you, Lex," I said to her, relieved to have gotten it all out.

"Oh, and Cassie," she added.

"Yeah."

"Please talk to me. I'm worried about you being there with everything going on. Please don't shut people out."

"I'll try not to Lex. I have people here too, and I won't shut them out," I assured her.

"OK good – enjoy your summer babe, go soak up the sun."

I laughed at the sudden change from serious to joking and I hung up. I knew I could count on Lexi and she never made me feel bad about anything.

I emerged from the tent and made my way back to Dean and Emma, who were sitting in the sun together. I didn't want to tell them about what had happened last night with Noah or about my parents – I just couldn't bring myself to see their sympathetic faces or hear their sorrowful tones. As I approached them from behind, I heard their laughter. their heads were bent together in a conspirator sort of way. Dean then noticed my arrival and they sprung apart, as if scared that they had been caught. I was a little confused, but I'm sure I had just surprised him. Dean leapt up and planted a light kiss on my cheek.

"Hey babe, how was Lexi?"

"Yeah, she was great, thanks. It was good to catch up with her. Felt a little homesick, I guess."

By this point we'd both settled back onto the grass and Dean had his arm around me as I leant against him. I attempted a glance at Emma, but she was looking into the woods. It puzzled me. She almost looked disappointed or saddened and I couldn't understand why. I decided that I would check in with her later, but at this point I let it slide, not knowing if she would want to talk about it in front of Dean.

"All right everyone!" Dan called out, announcing that there was a new activity.

"Well, we better get going," Dean said as he stood up, "let's see what Dan has in store for us." He pulled me up and then Emma. I couldn't tell if it was just me or whether he held her hand a little longer than necessary. I brushed it off and realised I was being stupid. He was just helping her.

We walked over to where Dan was gathering us. "So," he started, "today is pretty exciting. We'll be heading to a water park, which means we're actually allowed to swim there." Dan looked pointedly at me, which caused me to laugh and glance over at Noah. I noticed this time he wasn't looking at me, though, but was busy with his group and… this girl. I quickly looked away, ignoring how I felt when I saw him with another girl – a burning envy.

"So, I want you all to get your swimming stuff ready and we'll meet back here in fifteen minutes ready to leave."

Everyone slowly dispersed and went to get their stuff sorted. Me and Emma walked back to our tent together. It seemed odd, she seemed odd.

"Hey Em, are you all right?" I asked her worriedly. She just nodded.

"Are you sure? You seem a little quiet," I insisted.

"Do you still like Dean?" She turned to me and asked rather abruptly.

"What?" I was taken back by her question.

"Well, do you?" she insisted.

"Of course I do! Why are you even asking?"

She deflated a little.

"Look, I'm sorry if I've seemed rude, just I haven't heard any more about the Noah stuff and I don't want to see Dean strung along and hurt," she confessed.

"Well, that makes sense, but I promise you, I do really like him and the reason you haven't heard more is because there hasn't been anything else." The lie stung as it left my mouth but I knew it was necessary because it wouldn't matter.

Emma sighed and nodded.

"OK, good," she said as she hugged me, "and I'm sorry again, I feel bad now."

"Please don't!" I hugged her tight. "It means a lot that you care."

"Well, of course." Emma swallowed and nodded, accepting what I said.

"Come on, let's get our stuff sorted."

I linked my arm through hers and we carried on to the tent. I put on my white bikini and grabbed my shorts and a top. Emma changed into her black bikini and we headed out of the tent and towards the bus. As we got there, Dean was waiting, and his smile grew once he saw us. He greeted me with a tight hug and Emma with a tight smile.

We got on the bus together and sat down at the back. Noah got on after us and sat a little further up the bus. *That girl* who had been next to Noah at breakfast sat down with him, and I felt a sharp pain surge through my body. Luckily, the journey went quickly, and as soon we were at the water park, I turned away to relieve myself from the nauseating scene in front of me.

"Before we get off the bus," Dan called from the front. "Just to remind you, you'll have the day to walk around and do what you like. But we'll be meeting back here at five to return to the campsite. So have fun, be merry and don't walk around on your own."

Me and Emma looked at each other and smiled.

"Let's go!" I whispered to her. We started ahead with Dean trailing behind us, while

The whole crowd dispersed in different directions.

I scanned the group before they disappeared and saw Noah with that girl again. I had to turn away quickly before I felt that burning in my stomach again. I kept trying to convince myself there were no feelings there but seeing him with another girl fuelled something in me and I didn't like it. I couldn't deny the jealousy but I was just desperate to believe it wasn't there, I was with Dean and I liked him so much! Anyway, I didn't want to focus on that today – I just wanted to have a great time. Emma grabbed my arm and dragged me away from the group and we set off for the rides. Soon my thoughts of Noah were no more than just a slight nagging at the back of my mind.

This day was just the distraction I needed, running around the water park and not focusing on my troubles. It was good to get away from the campsite and not worry about Noah and my family issues. I'd had a few messages from my mum when I woke up, but I wasn't in the mood to talk to her right now – there was no way I would've been able to deal with her lies or excuses. I'd had nothing from my dad, but Jake had messaged last night to check up on me. He told me Hailey and Bradley were doing OK and they were dealing with it. Wow, my little siblings were doing better than I was!

In no time at all we were racing for the queue at the largest water slide. It was one of those where you could sit in groups, which was great for the three of us. I looked up and saw a group slide down. We waited in anticipation, slowly shuffling to the top of the slide. We chatted together and joked about some of the past activities. Some of Dean's friends had joined the queue, so we scooted back to join them so that we all had a partner for the rides. Connor continued to show a clear interest in Emma, trying to talk to her and leaning closer to her as we lined up. I looked over at Em and gave her an encouraging smile, but she just rolled her eyes and gave a brief shake of her head. She deserved better than him.

I decided to let it go… for now. I knew I could find Emma a great guy if she'd just be open to it, but I pushed it to the back of my mind and decided to talk to Dean about it later. He knew Emma and he knew his friends – maybe he'd know if any of them were a good match for her. We both knew Connor and Mason were a no, but maybe there was someone else.

Lost in these thoughts, I hadn't realised how close we were to the top. I turned around and looked out at the park. It made me realise how truly high the slide was. It was incredible, I could see so much from here, maybe too much… because it was at that moment that I saw him… again. A little down the queue, Noah was leaning against the rail chatting to *that girl* again. I rolled my eyes at her constant desperation. I noticed he was with a couple other people, but his main attention was on her. I felt my stomach drop and the warmth drain from my face. It was at that point I realised that I couldn't deny I had some sort of feelings for him.

I turned back to the slide and saw Dean looking at me. I held his face and kissed him right there. Not one of those light gentle kisses we'd shared recently but a true kiss, to show him how I felt about him and cared for him. He slid his arm around me and ran his hand through my hair. As I pulled away, he looked at me and smiled.

"I wish we were back in our spot," he murmured, his lips just a breath away. I reached up and pressed a light kiss to his lips again.

"Looks like we'll have to wait until we get back to the campsite, then we can escape," I murmured in agreement.

As I turned around, I noticed Noah further down the queue again and saw him turn away, his face distorted in an expression of fury and true disgust, almost as if he'd been stung.

The rest of the day passed without incident. We passed Noah and his group a few times – there were a few girls with them, but I kept on forward. We stopped in one of the fast-food places for lunch. It was great to hang out with some of Dean's friends too. I realised I hadn't hung out with them much – Connor and Mason mostly. Emma got on well with them too, which was really nice to see. I loved being with Emma and Dean, but I couldn't deny how great it was to be with a group too. Dean kept a loose grasp on my hand all day. I was content right now and I didn't want that to change. But as my mind floated towards Noah, I could feel change in the air.

Chapter 15

The rest of the day flew by in a wet and sunny haze. We went on as many rides as we could manage – and we managed a lot. Exhausted from running round the park in the sun, I was relieved when it was time for us to head back and meet everyone at the coach. As soon as I sat in my seat, my eyelids felt ten times heavier and I craved a long sleep, envious of Sleeping Beauty and her chance to sleep for a hundred years – I was that tired. So tired, I hardly noticed Noah get on the coach and sit down next to *that* girl who'd been hanging off him all day.

I was nearly too tired to notice, but not quite.

I felt my eyelids grow even heavier. I tried to fight it, not wanting to miss a moment of this amazing day, but with a touch of Dean's lips on my forehead I soon drifted off, a wave of contentment washing over me.

Apparently, I slept the whole way home because in no time Emma was nudging me awake, trying to get me off the coach. With a groan I whacked her hand away. Soon, I felt a yank on my arm, which jolted me awake.

"Jeez Em, you trying to pull off my whole arm," I moaned.

"Well, I wouldn't have had to if you weren't such a heavy sleeper. Damn, how do you get up in the mornings?" she responded – so sweetly.

"Ugh, well I'm awake now." I stood up and stretched my arms above my head, glancing around the bus. It had started to empty, but there were still a few onboard, one, of course, being Noah. As I raised my arms, my top came up too, revealing my stomach, and I noticed Noah's eyes scan over me. My face burned. I quickly yanked my arms to my side, pulled my top down and looked back at him. I was nearly blown away by the heat of his stare. His gaze shone right through me and for a moment I was unaware of anything around me – I didn't understand how he did this to me. Immediately, I turned away, before it got too heated, and I rushed to gather my things. Out of the corner of my eye I noticed Noah doing the same thing, clearly as flustered as I was.

"You ready?" I turned to Dean and Emma. They were just staring at me.

"Hey, what just happened? It's like you were a million miles away," Emma commented. "I was trying to talk to you, and you just didn't seem to register anything."

"Oh, I must just be so tired, I can't seem to focus. I just need a massive cup of coffee," I joked.

I could see Emma calculating it in her head and soon enough she seemed to believe me. I snuck a glance at Dean, but he just seemed concerned by my tiredness rather than suspicious of anything. We all stepped off the bus.

"I'm just going to freshen up before dinner." I excused myself and headed to the washroom. I just needed to cool down, and hopefully a splash of cold water would also wake me up a little. I walked in and stood facing the mirror for a while, a blush still creeping up my face as I remembered the desire that Noah showed. I bent down and splashed some water over my face and took a deep breath. I looked at myself. *I was fine, it didn't mean anything, Noah had been with that girl all day, clearly he didn't like me, but it didn't matter, I didn't like him and I was with Dean, come on!* With one last breath, I focused, splashed some more water on my face and walked out the bathroom. I collided with something – something strong that wrapped its arms around me to steady me. Then I recognised *that* smell, and the scent danced around me, enveloping me, and I immediately knew who it was. I quickly steadied myself and stepped back, away from him, worried about what I would do if I was near him for too long.

"Uh," he cleared his throat, "hey Cass."

"Oh, hi," I choked out.

"You've got to look where you're going," he joked.

"It seems you're always around to save me when I make a fool of myself," I responded with a weak smile.

"Yes, but usually I seem to be the person who causes it." He seemed shy, raising his arm and running his hand through those soft curls in his absent-minded habit. The action had caused his shirt to ride up, revealing the slightest hint of stomach while his biceps tensed. My mind wandered, wondering what it would be like for those arms to hold me tightly.

"We can call it even then. I think that balances the scales, I'll make sure I'm around to save you…" he laughed.

"Well, I…"

"I should…"

We both started at the same time and laughed, some of the tension now diffused.

"You first," he said with a smile.

"I was just saying how I should go and see where Emma and Dean had gotten to. I was only freshening up quickly."

The smile fell from his face.

"Right, yeah. Well, I better go find my friends anyways." He started to walk away but then paused "I'll see you later, I guess," he grumbled and continued on.

I found Emma and Dean in the food hall. They were playing a game of cards and leaning close together. I couldn't see Dean's face, but I could see Emma, she looked a lot happier than she seemed earlier, smiling and unaware that I was standing only a few metres away, watching the whole exchange. It was nice to see, but I was confused. She seemed so odd when she was around me, but with Dean she seemed happier. I guess it was good that Dean could make this happen. I approached them and gave Dean a hug from behind. He lifted his hand stroking my arm.

"Hey babe, feeling refreshed?" he asked.

"Yeah, I feel much better thanks – a bit of cold water did the job. So, what are you doing?"

"We're playing cards," Emma responded, "and currently Dean is losing epically!" She teased.

"Ha, ha, that's my best friend! Hard luck, Dean," I said, high-fiving her. I sat down and they dealt me into the next round.

We played for around half an hour and then it was time for dinner, so we headed over to our table and sat down.

"I hope everyone had a great day today and you're ready for dinner," said Dan. "I can imagine you don't want to hear me talk any more today." A low laugh spread across all of the campers. "I'll take that as a yes, so without further ado, enjoy!"

"I am *starving*!" Dean exclaimed.

"Well, you always are," Emma joked. It was good to see her in a better mood.

Dinner passed as usual, with us talking and me avoiding Noah's glances, and soon dessert came.

As we went to get it, Dean slid his arms around my waist and whispered in my ear.

"So how do you feel about sneaking away a little later to our spot and having a look at the stars?" I looked back at him and nodded my head, and with a wicked grin he bent down to kiss me. Now, dessert couldn't come quick enough.

I told Emma that me and Dean were going to go for a walk. She seemed slightly deflated and disappointed but soon recovered and smiled.

"Have a good time," she said, but there was something sad behind the smile. I gave her a hug and went to join Dean. He held out his hand and I took it happily.

"I've missed this," he said lovingly as we walked down towards the lake.

"It has, we've hardly had time to ourselves recently," I replied, "this is nice."

We continued walking and soon reached the lake. Dean sat down and I nestled in between his legs and leaned against his chest. I was content – I could stay here forever. But then Emma came to mind.

"Do you think Emma has been OK recently?" I asked.

"Well, that was random," Dean commented.

"Well maybe," I said, "but she seems a little off lately and I was worried."

"I mean, I don't think so." He paused. "She said she's been feeling homesick for the past few days so maybe it's that,"

I turned to look at him, and he continued.

"Yeah, I mean she was feeling a little upset because her brother is leaving home in September and she's here for the summer and she's not spending much time with him. She's feeling a little sad and a little guilty, so maybe that's just hitting her a little more." He glanced at me. "I'm sure she'll be fine, though she seems OK to me."

I turned back to look at the lake. She'd told Dean all that but hadn't mentioned a single thing to me – I didn't even know her brother was leaving home! Had I done something? Maybe I'd been too involved in myself to see what was going on with her. I feel horrible now. How could she have told Dean all about this and not me?

"Did you enjoy today?" Dean asked me after a moment of silence, tactfully changing the topic.

"Yeah, it was really good today. It was so much fun," I replied. "It was exhausting but so worth it."

"It was an exceptionally great day, particularly," he lowered his voice, "while we were waiting for the first slide." I giggled at the memory.

"That was a *very* good time, wasn't it?"

"Mnhmm." I felt, more than heard, his response this time with a rumbling in his chest.

I turned around and he brought his face to my lips. It was glorious, as his hands came round and held me tight against him. I couldn't tell whether he had pulled me or I had moved, but soon enough I was in his lap straddling his legs as he devoured me. His hands held my face, and I threw my arms around his neck. He pressed me to him and I shuffled around trying to move even closer, but, as I did so, my leg hit a branch.

"Ouch!" I pulled away and checked my knee. "Wow, maybe the forest floor isn't the best place to make out!"

Dean let out a low laugh and nodded in agreement. I straightened up, looked at him and laughed.

"Come on, we better get back," he said as I climbed off his lap. He stood up and pulled me with him.

We slowly made our way back to the campsite, pausing every once in a while for a kiss. We both knew there wouldn't be much alone time once we were back with Emma and Dean's friends, so we took advantage of each moment. We reached the edge of the woods and I saw Emma heading towards the tent. I said goodbye to Dean with a kiss, and he went to his group of friends as I joined Emma on the way back to the tent.

"Hey!" I called after her. She paused, turned to see me and, with a smile, replied,

"Hey girl, how was your alone time with Dean?" I could tell she was trying to appear enthusiastic, but she was clearly exhausted.

"Yeah, it was nice." I hesitated. "Hey look, I just wanted to remind you that I'm here. I'm sorry if I seem distant but I *am* here, and if you ever need to talk about anything –and I mean *anything* – then I'm here for you." I stepped closer and hugged her tight. She seemed puzzled by my outburst.

"Of course, I know that. What's brought this sudden outburst on," she laughed as she wrapped her arms around me too.

"Well, Dean mentioned to me about your brother and that you seemed homesick, and I just wanted to say that I'm here if you need me."

Emma stiffened as she hugged me and stepped back. I assumed it was then mentioned by her brother.

"Oh Cassie," she said with a sympathetic smile, "I'm sorry I didn't mention it to you. I could tell you were a little homesick with your calls to Lexi and I didn't want to pile on. Dean asked one day and I just kind of burst, I guess. But I'm OK, I promise."

She still seemed exhausted, but I thought I'd let it slide just because I didn't want to push her too much. Emma knew I was here and that was what mattered.

I hung out with Emma that night, just the two of us. I realised I hadn't spent much time with her. We went into the food hall and played a few rounds of card games, and sat and talked. Sure, getting to know Dean over these past couple of weeks had been great, but spending time with Emma, just us girls, was something I'd desperately missed.

She asked if anything more had happened with Noah, to which, of course, I replied with a no. I needed to get straight in my head what was going on between me and Noah before I burst out to Emma. I wasn't ready for the onslaught I'd receive in return from her if I told her everything that had happened, plus I wasn't even sure myself what was going on. I turned it around to get the focus away from me and asked if any of Dean's friends had caught her eye after the water park. She blushed and said no, but I could tell there was some hesitation.

"Are you sure? You're not entirely convincing," I smirked at her.

"Ha, ha, nice try but no. I mean they're nice, don't get me wrong, but I don't have that kind of connection with any of them. Plus I'm not sure which one of them I'd trust."

As soon as she spoke of that *connection*, my thoughts drifted to Noah. *We* seemed to have that *connection*, the idea that we'd been pushed together and were unable to ignore each other. Or at least I couldn't ignore him. After seeing Noah flounce around with the bimbo that was always hanging off his arm, maybe he didn't feel the same. But even so, I was reminded about fate and that we couldn't fight it. But I still didn't believe it. I just didn't want to think of what that would mean for Dean and I.

"Well, that's boring," I joked, "but don't worry Em, we'll find someone."

"Aw, you're going to become my little Cupid aren't you?" Emma teased.

"You bet I am," I responded with total seriousness. "This is *our* summer Em and we're going to make it great!"

"OK, Cassie!" She laughed at my enthusiasm. "You just tell me when you've found me my soulmate," she suggested, rolling her eyes.

I decided not to pester her and dropped the subject, while Emma quickly jumped in with another topic to keep the conversation safe. The rest of the evening passed in a comfortable way. Spending time with Emma was so good – and long overdue. I just hope we didn't lose this amazing friendship we'd found. Even if it hadn't been long, she was already so important to me.

Chapter 16

I woke up. It was getting into the last week of the summer. I couldn't believe that my time at camp was almost over. This has been some of the best times of my life.

I sat up in bed and stretched. I felt happy today and I jumped out of my bed and onto Emma's. She gave a grunt.

"Ugh, Jeez Cassie, come on, it's too early. Why do you have to be in such a good mood?" she groaned and slowly sat up.

"Oh, come on Em, the sun is shining and we're on the last week of camp. We've gotta enjoy each minute!" I said leaping off her bed and sorting out my stuff to get dressed.

"Let's goooooo!" I yanked her arm and pulled her out of bed.

"Ugh. OK, OK, I'm getting up," Emma moaned, but I could see a smile dancing over her face. She loved my craziness and it had been too long since we'd joked about it like this. I reflected on this. I'd only known Emma a few short weeks, but over that time she'd become so close to me and so important. I hoped that our friendship would last beyond our summer bubble.

Ten minutes later, Emma and I were up, ready and heading to the food hall for breakfast. But my timing was clearly wrong, because as we got to the entrance... so did Noah. And *that* girl. I rolled my eyes, seeing her hanging off him. I mean, come on, she just seemed a bit desperate, constantly around him – a bit excessive, if you ask me.

"Hi," I smiled at him.

"Hey," he said but kept his head glued to the ground. I glanced at Emma, and she was staring intently at us.

"It's good to see you," I said.

"Yeah, er you too." Well, this wasn't awkward at all! "We should get inside, don't want to be late for breakfast," he laughed.

"Er yeah, well see yo…" He walked away before I could finish.

"Well, *that* was weird," Emma commented. "Really nothing else going on between you two, huh?"

"Honestly, there's nothing," I replied. "I have no idea what that was. But it was weird right?"

"Very – dude, he was looking at you like you'd broken his heart and slept with his best friend!" Emma agreed.

"Well, I can assure you that none of that has gone on while we've been here," I told her with a laugh.

And with that we walked into the food hall for breakfast.

Dean was at our usual table with a few of his friends. As soon as we had got our food, me and Emma made our way over. While walking, I couldn't resist a look at Noah. Of course, there he was, at his usual table – the only difference was *that* girl was sitting next to him. Ugh! I rolled my eyes and went to our table. I sat next to Dean and he leant over, giving me a sweet kiss on the cheek. I grinned up at him and leant my head on his shoulder.

This was how I wanted my summer to be, with a good set of friends and a great guy, relaxing and enjoying the sun, no drama. This was great. As I sat back and enjoyed the moment, my eyes drifted around the room, taking in everyone in their groups, laughing and joking. My eyes inevitably landed on Noah once again. But this time was different. This time, he was staring right back at me, his gaze boring deep into my mind, seeing all of me. I lifted my head from Dean's shoulder and Noah's gaze grew more intense, as he knew he'd captured my attention. I could feel my heart buzzing in my chest. My breath quickened and yet still the intensity grew. I could feel a fire in my stomach lighting me up inside.

Then I felt a nudge – Emma was elbowing me and it shook me out of my daze. My eyes flickered towards Emma as she gave me a puzzled look. As I dropped eye contact, the spell was broken. I looked over to Noah but he was back to his food, no indication that anything had just happened.

"Hey you spaced out for a minute there. All OK?" Emma questioned me.

"Yeah, yeah, of course – I just zoned out for a while, I guess, thinking about what Dan has in store for us."

I gave her a weak smile and focused back on my food. I looked up one more time, but he was gone. The feeling of disappointment was devastating.

I continued eating, chiming in the conversation where it seemed acceptable so that no one was concerned about my silence. Emma still seemed slightly apprehensive, but she let it slide. After that awkwardness with Noah as we walked in, I don't think Emma was going to be mocking me about it as much anymore. She realised it was still a bit of a sensitive topic. I hadn't even dared bring Noah up in front of Dean again – guys could be so territorial, and I couldn't deal with him going mad again like he did at the lake. A blush rose on my face at the thought of us there. That place had come to mean a lot to me in such a short time. The moments with Dean, our adventures and secrets, even the awkwardness with Noah during our water challenges. My head was filled with memories of the lake, its water glistening like magic.

I shook my head and brought my attention back to breakfast. Dean was laughing at his friends while he held my hand under the table. It felt a little uncomfortable – my arm pushed against the table and my hand at an odd angle – but the action was so sweet I didn't mind. The idea that he wanted to touch me and be close was adorable. I glanced over at Emma, but she seemed so distant. One of Dean's friends was speaking to her, and while she responded, she just didn't seem in the same room as us. Her eyes were staring into the distance, and while her mouth was moving, I'm not sure she even knew what she was saying. It was quite worrying. I had spoken to her and she knew I was here, so I didn't want to push anything or seem like I was hounding her. But she was constantly absent-minded and I didn't know what to do about it. I looked at her quizzically and she noticed my gaze, forcing a weak smile. I was still confused as to why she was acting so spacey but I knew that this wasn't the time to talk, so I dropped it… for now.

Dan had planned a water fight for the whole camp later that day. There were going to be four different teams and each team had a cardboard castle that they had to protect and keep dry. It sounded cool – not just a regular boring water fight. After breakfast, we all dispersed to change into something we didn't mind getting wet.

Once we'd all prepared ourselves we split into our groups – thankfully, me, Dean and Emma were all together. Noah was on one of the other teams – with *that* girl.

"All right, you have until all the water balloons and water run out, and then we shall see who will," Dan proclaimed. "Let's begin in Three… Two… One… *Go!*"

Madness ensued – water flew everywhere, and within the first five minutes, everyone was soaked. *That* girl with Noah had decided to wear a white top, which I know was no accident, and immediately it became see-through. When I saw it, I rolled my eyes, which Noah didn't miss. He fixed his gaze on me. I quickly turned away and hurled a water balloon at one of the other teams. I glanced over at Noah again and he was standing there with *that* girl as she stood there leaning on his arm. I stared in disgust at her obvious flirtations. She clearly just didn't care and it was ridiculous. My eye roll was impossible to stop. I turned to Dean and Emma and saw him grab her around the waist. He swung her around as she let out a warm laugh. My eyebrows drew together as I looked at the exchange, but she seemed happier and I was just glad she wasn't being quite so distant.

The water fight soon finished, and everyone was thoroughly soaked. Noah's team won and *that* girl jumped in his arms while he wrapped his arms around her and lifted her off the ground. Could anyone be more forward? I huffed and turned away from the two of them.

"Well, I hope you all enjoyed that and have become nice and cool in this hot weather," Dan called out. "Now, have some time to chill or do whatever you'd like and there will be some activities later for those who you want to join in." Dan turned away, leaving us all to decide what we wanted to do.

"Hey, the boys want to go and play a game of football to dry off," Dean told me as he walked over.

"Ah, that sounds really good – have fun. I'll come and cheer you on later," I said with a kiss on his cheek. He strolled away and Emma walked over to me and threw an arm over my shoulder.

"Hey girl, how are you doing?" she asked.

"I'm doing good – glad to see you in better spirits too," I responded.

Emma turned to me with a quizzical look on her face.

"You know today at breakfast you seemed a little sad and distracted." I said.

"Oh," she blushed slightly, "well, no I'm OK, guess that was just tiredness. I'm feeling much better now."

I wondered if it had anything to do with her hanging on to my boyfriend all through the water fight, but I kept that to myself.

"Look, I'm going to go and change quickly just to dry off a little," Emma said. "Give me like five minutes then we can chill together. Are you changing?"

"Na, I'm OK," I replied, "it's pretty hot – I'm sure I'll dry soon."

Emma nodded and smiled and jogged off in the direction of our tent. I sat down on the grass, leant my head back and closed my eyes, enjoying the summer sun. Suddenly, I could feel a shadow pass over my eyelids and the warmth of my sun disappeared. Wow, Emma was quicker that I thought. But when I cracked my eyelids open it wasn't Emma staring down at me. It was Noah, and he wasn't looking pleased.

"Hey," I said, trying to put on an innocent front as I stood up. He just glared.

"What is your problem?" He snapped in a direct tone I hadn't heard before.

"What do you mean?" I spoke sweetly.

"That whole mess during the water fight – don't think I didn't see the eye rolls and the disgusted looks you shot my way. So, come on, *what* is your problem?"

He spat out the last four words and they felt like bullets hitting my chest.

"Woah, OK, look I'm sorry if you think there were any disgusted looks. There weren't really," I said defensively.

"Oh, come on, you couldn't hide those looks even if you tried, and *you* clearly didn't."

I just looked at him silently, stunned and unsure what to say.

"OK fine, give me silence. Just next time back off. I'm not doing anything against you or hurting you in any way, so just stop it. You made things clear the way you hang over Dean, so don't get mad at me if another girl who shows me interest is actually doing something about it." With that he stormed off.

I was frozen. His words had dropped like poison – I had never heard him speak like that. But I couldn't fault him – he hadn't done anything to me. It was simply my fault for thinking everything would be fine. Seeing Noah constantly with that girl had fuelled something inside me. When he smiled at her with that lopsided grin and ran his hand through his hair, it felt like I was being stabbed. I knew I had to do something – but what?

Chapter 17

The activities in the afternoon were optional, which I was relieved by. I'd sat silently through lunch, occasionally smiling up at Dean or Emma, but mainly focused on my food. Neither of them seemed to mind as they were in their own little world. I was too tired for it to even really register or for me to care. I replayed the moment where Noah laid into me and I stood there with my mouth agape. After seeing Noah with that girl I knew there was no denying how I felt about him, and these feelings were growing by the day. He affected me in a way that I couldn't explain.

I looked over at his table and saw him smiling and laughing with the rest of his friends and longed to be the one he was laughing with. The desire for him to be flashing that smile at me was overwhelming. I felt a pain in my stomach that I couldn't explain. The sight of him – even the thought of him – joking with others while he hated me was something I couldn't stand. I was still staring at him when he glanced up and for a fleeting moment our eyes locked. I felt my heart do a somersault, but the moment was short lived. Soon, his face was filled with disdain and his eyes had broken the connection with mine. It was as if I hadn't been seen, as if he felt nothing. Suddenly, I felt too nauseous to finish my lunch and I abruptly excused myself from the table and rushed outside, craving some fresh air and a view that didn't include that striking face I couldn't resist.

I stumbled outside and sought support against a tree. I tried to take deep breaths and stop my hands from shaking. I could hear voices calling my name, Dean and Emma had come looking for me. I slunk behind the food hall hoping they wouldn't find me. I started to focus my thoughts and my breath started to come more regularly. When I pushed myself off the building I turned back to where I had come from. But there he was. Noah. He had a face of anger laced with worry.

"What do you want?" I mumbled, not bringing myself to look at him.

"Don't start again Cassie, I saw you run out so thought I would check," he replied irritably, "but whatever, if you're acting like this I'll leave you alone."

"Fine," I croaked. My voice began to waver again. He clearly heard it too as he stopped walking and turned to face me again. His anger had melted away, now he just seemed worried.

"Are you OK?" Noah's deep voice said from behind me as I leant against the food hall once again, my legs feeling too weak to hold me up.

"So, you want to talk nice now," I commented, happy he hadn't left but still hurt by his earlier words.

"Look Cass, let's not do this. I just wanted to check up on you. With everything going on with your family I just wanted to check. You haven't told me anything since the moment by the food hall," he said warmly, taking a step closer to me. My cheeks warmed at that memory.

"Oh right, I really am sorry for how I acted Noah. I didn't mean it. I've just been so tired lately."

"Look, don't worry about it. Have you heard anything more from your family?" he asked.

"Well, my brother messages and my mum has called but I haven't answered them. I just can't bring myself to do it," I confessed.

"Hey, it's OK Cass," he said as he brought his hand up and placed it lightly on my arm, rubbing comforting circles.

"But it isn't," I admitted for the first time.

"Maybe not, but it will be soon," he assured me, "don't shut them out Cass. Whatever is going on is only temporary, they love you and they want to support you, they just want to know you're OK."

"You're right," I sighed, and he was. They didn't deserve silence just because I was feeling sad. "I'll talk to them."

He began to smile.

"And Cass, if there's ever anything I can do, well, just tell me. Don't worry about what happened… I just don't want to see you like this." I just looked up at him and smiled – it was a sweet moment.

We walked back out to the front of the food hall- making sure there was a safe distance between us.

"Thank you. You really helped, I appreciate it," I told him with a warm smile.

"You don't need to thank me Cass, I'm here whenever you need me." he replied, returning the smile.

But the moment didn't last long. A wave of surprise hit me as a warm hand snaked around my waist and Noah stepped back, giving us more distance.

"You OK?" Dean asked me, "you ran out so quickly, we were looking for you for ages."

"I'm sorry for worrying you, I just got overwhelmed and needed some air." I told him, I saw Noah's quizzical look at me not telling Dean the truth, but Dean didn't notice, just nodded before turning to Noah.

"What are *you* doing?" He pointed at Noah, poison now lacing his voice.

"Just checking up on Cass, making sure she was all right," he said neutrally.

"Well, her *boyfriend* is here now, so thanks, but I can deal with it," Dean said venomously.

"Right, yeah," Noah replied. He cleared his throat. "Well, bye Cass," he said briefly, placing his hand on my arm before leaving and walking away.

"What was he doing?" Dean demanded as he removed his arms from around me.

"He just came to check up on me, that's all," I assured him.

"How chivalrous of him," he snarled but added in a softer, more concerned voice, "Are you doing OK, Cassie? You've been pretty distant lately." I pulled his arms back around me and leant back into his chest, savouring this moment, not knowing how many more I would have with him like this. I knew it wasn't fair to Dean for me to hide the feelings I had for Noah – I just couldn't bring myself to confess them yet.

"Yeah, I'm OK. Just felt a little nauseous, I guess. Didn't sleep well or something."

"You sure it doesn't have anything to do with that Noah guy?" Dean asked accusingly, whipping his head back in Noah's direction. I looked him in the eyes and saw confusion, concern and anger.

"Wait, what?"

"Come on, Cassie, don't treat me like a fool. I'm a guy and I know what it looks like when another guy likes a girl, I see the way he looks at you," he confessed.

My eyebrows knitted together. "What made you think that?"

"Well," Dean sighed, "beside that moment in the lake, I saw that weird thing outside the food hall a couple days ago and I got confused, so I asked Emma and she didn't really say anything. But I could tell just by the way his eyes followed you."

"Honestly, I'm not sure what Emma said but he was acting weird with me just before breakfast and I have no idea why."

"Look, I do really like you," he said.

"I really like you too Dean, honestly… ." He held up a hand to stop me.

"But, if you don't want to be with me Cassie, then you need to tell me, I can't be the only one in this relationship, it needs to be both ways," he pleaded and I could see the sadness in his eyes.

"Please, Dean," I said as I turned to face him and slid my arms around his neck, "I want to be with you, honestly. I'm with *you* aren't I? Not Noah"

He hesitated but must have seen something in my face that confirmed what I'd said because he bent his head and kissed me sweetly. I snaked my arms tighter around his neck and pulled him closer and deepened the kiss. I could feel him laugh against my lips, and he didn't pull away. When I thought I had thoroughly proved my point, I pulled back, not wanting to give the whole camp a little show. I smiled up at him.

"Come on then," he smiled, "we better get back in and finish our food, otherwise Dan will get worried." I looked up at him and knew I couldn't face going back in there right now.

"Hey, I'm still feeling a little unwell, I think I'll sit out here for a little longer. I'm enjoying the quietness and the summer sun." I shot him a weak smile and he conceded. As he walked back into the food hall, I found a nice spot in the field looking out into the woods. The peace was rejuvenating.

My solitude was short-lived as people began to filter out of the food hall, and I took that as my signal to leave. I couldn't face Emma's questions or Dean's worries, and there was certainly no way I was going to deal with any sight of Noah.

"Err, you better head to the first aid bay and lay down for a while – don't want you having any more accidents now do we?" Dan joked when I told him I wasn't feeling well.. I managed a timid laugh and made my way to first aid. They set me up with a bucket, in case I was sick, and some cold water.

I peered out the window at the events unfolding. Dan had started the activities and I noticed Emma strolling over to join the group with Dean and the rest of his friends. I began thinking about everything that had happened. Thinking hard about what I could do. I pulled out my phone and tapped on Noah's contact.

Me: *Hey, look I'm sorry for any animosity towards you. I don't know what came over me and I just must not have been feeling well. But thank you for coming to check on me.*

I sent the text and waited anxiously for Noah to respond. I glanced out the window again to see if I could spot him. Aha! There he was. I sat gazing at him, safe in the knowledge that he didn't know I was here and couldn't catch me staring at him. He was talking to his friends, when I noticed him looking startled. He glanced down and grabbed his phone from his pocket. After a moment he placed it back – without typing anything. I was confused. Maybe my message hadn't gone through yet. I checked but could see that the message had been read. He just chose not to respond. I flopped down onto the seat, feeling deflated and with a sense of lost hope. I didn't know how to make this better. There was a knot in my stomach – I knew that if I spoke to Noah face to face I would either yell at him or break down in tears and I didn't feel like doing either in front of Noah *again*. Not to mention that if Dean saw us that would just add to the mess. It was hopeless. For the time being I would just accept that things might not be OK.

I stayed in the first aid ward for as long as I could, but after a few hours the nurse who was helping me could tell I wasn't sick. She didn't kick me out, but I also knew she wasn't hoping that I'd stay. I left, knowing I couldn't hide away from my problems forever. There weren't many more days. I would just avoid Noah until then. I no longer cared how I felt – he'd attacked me and it was all too hectic. He stirred a storm inside me and I couldn't take it any more. Things with Dean were comfortable and good, and I didn't want to throw that away. At least that was possible. As soon as I left the sick bay, I glanced around the campsite and Emma spotted me. She ran over, giving me a tight hug.

"Oh Cassie, I missed you this afternoon. How are you feeling? Dean mentioned you felt ill, and you left so quickly that I couldn't check. And then you disappeared for the whole afternoon."

"Yeah, I'm sorry Em, I just wasn't feeling good," I confessed, hoping she wouldn't see through the lie.

"Well, as long as you're better now," she said, smiling.

"I mean, I'm a little better but I'm not feeling in the mood for dinner right now. I think I'm going to head to the tent and lie down."

"I'll come with you," she said.

"No, please don't," I sighed, "I just need some time alone. You go and enjoy the evening – I'll see you later or something. Let Dean know where I got to will you?"

"Of course," she said with a hug, "let me know if I can do anything. I'll see you in the tent later, we should catch up properly."

I nodded at her and slowly made my way to our tent. I looked around and noticed Noah glance at me. This time it was me who cut the moment short and looked straight down at the ground. I was starting to ignore him straight away. I couldn't deal with any more of his disgusted looks right now. I could feel tears building in the corners of my eyes and I rushed into the tent. I scrambled into bed and let the tears flow freely as I pulled out my phone. I went onto the chain of messages I'd shared with Noah.

Me: *Look, I know you obviously hate me right now and I'm sorry for what I did. I guess maybe I just didn't like seeing you with that girl, but this is the last try. I get it and I'll leave you alone now, I'm sorry.*

I pressed send, and while I had my phone out, I checked my unread messages.

Mum: *Sweetie, please reply to me.*

Mum: *I just want to know you're OK.*

Jake: *Hey, you can't ignore us forever, we need to stick together.*

Dad: *How's camp?*

Lexi: *Hey, how are you holding up?*

I rolled my eyes – trust my dad to pretend like nothing had happened and not even tell me *anything.*

Me: *Sorry mum, I'm doing fine and I love you so much. It's just a lot to process still.*

Me: *Hey Jake, you're right, I just messaged mum back. Sorry for leaving stuff to you, that wasn't right.*

Me: *Camp is good dad.*

Me: *Hey Lex, I'm not too bad. Messaged my family but my dad is still trying to hide it all, I really miss you.*

Once I'd sent all the messages, I felt entirely drained, so I placed the phone under my pillow and, with a sigh, I turned over and closed my eyes. I let the tears fall freely this time, and soon I fell into a distressing sleep.

I woke up some time later. I wasn't sure how long I'd been lying there, but I could hear the front of the tent open and heard Emma creep in. She sat at the end of my bed and gently shook my legs.

"Hey Cassie," she gently whispered.

I turned over and looked at her. She looked at me with great worry.

"Your eyes, they're all red, are you feeling all right?" she said, her voice filled with concern.

"Yeah, I was just rubbing them after sleep – it can happen sometimes, I'm OK," I replied softly, "but I'm still feeling quite rough, so I think I'm going to go back to sleep, if that's all right with you."

I could tell she wanted to say something, but at that moment she thought better of it.

"Yeah, of course, I'll let Dan know you're still feeling rough. You get some sleep. I'll see you later."

I sat up slightly so I could give her a gentle hug, which she returned, and then I laid back down. Today had drained me so much I felt like I could sleep for days – it would make avoiding Noah so much easier. Emma rose from the end of my bed and left the tent.

I checked my phone one last time – no new messages. I felt a weight in my stomach grow heavier, but I knew I couldn't do anything. I had said what I needed to. Soon I could feel my eyelids drop once again and I drifted into a calm sleep. At last, I managed to relax, and I didn't wake again until the next morning.

Chapter 18

As my eyes opened the next morning to see the harsh light of the morning sun, I knew I couldn't hide from my problems forever, no matter how much I wanted to. With a groan, I sat up in bed and noticed that Emma had already gone from the tent. I checked the time. Damn! I was late for breakfast. Emma must have let me sleep in thinking I was still feeling ill. I knew I had no time to shower so I threw open my suitcase and poked around for something to wear, settling on my acid-wash denim shorts and a pale pink crop top with lace detail on the back. I brushed my hair through and piled it in a messy bun on the top of my head. I sprayed a bit of perfume, slipped on my Converses and dashed out of the tent. I stopped for a moment outside the food hall, preparing myself for the scene that would await. Once my breath had calmed, I started to make my way in. I noticed Dean look up immediately and flash me a wide grin. He jumped up and walked over to me.

"Are you feeling better?" he asked tenderly as he placed an arm over my shoulder. I just nodded in response and gave him a light kiss on his lips. He returned the kiss and smiled as I pulled away. He led me back to our table, where I was greeted with a chorus of hellos from Dean's friends, while Emma put her arm around me and gave me a tight hug. I then turned towards Dean and settled in next to him, leaning my head on his shoulder and extremely relieved to find that we were facing the door rather than looking towards Noah's table. I couldn't tell whether Dean had done this on purpose but at least it meant that I wouldn't have to see Noah every time I looked up. Even though my back was turned, I could feel the intensity of his glare on the back of my neck, but I refused to let myself turn around and look at him. After Noah ignored both of my messages, I decided it was time I ignored *him* completely. If he wanted to be like that, then fine – but two could play that game. I'd had enough of his attitudes and him blowing hot and cold with me. I would focus on them – I didn't need him.

We sat and chatted all through breakfast and I was finally at ease. After yesterday, I was worried how I would feel today, but seeing Dean's warm smile and having his arm wrapped warmly around me gave me hope that things would be OK. Breakfast passed in a blur, full of chatting and laughing, and soon Dan was telling us what he had planned for that day.

"OK, so everyone, we only have a few days left of camp." A chorus of boos echoed around the food hall. "I know, I'm glad you've all had a great time so let's make these last few days even more memorable." A cheer erupted from everyone. "Today we'll be heading to a trampoline park. Then, as a treat, we'll be having lunch while we're out!" Excited chatter filled the hall, and it took a few minutes for everyone to quieten down enough for Dan to continue.

"So, you'll all have half an hour to get sorted and then we'll head out. I'll see you all by the coaches in thirty minutes."

"Well, this is going to be great," I said to Emma, "I'm so happy that I'm feeling better today."

She smiled back at me. "Yeah, I missed you yesterday, acting all weird and ill. It wasn't good, I need my weirdo." She looked at me affectionately and I couldn't stop myself from leaning in and giving her a tight hug and a sweet smile. "OK, come on, let's go and get ready, I don't want to be late."

Emma nodded and we walked out of the food hall. I saw Noah rush from his table, but I kept walking. As we reached the door, Noah met us there. I wasn't going to give him the satisfaction of seeing my reaction, so I slid my arm through Emma's and held on tightly, laughing at her and keeping my head down to avoid any contact with him. I sped up to get out of the door. Success! I glanced at his face and he seemed disappointed. I was confused. *Why* was he disappointed? I mean, obviously he didn't want to talk to me. I got that message loud and clear when he ignored both my messages of apology. So what was he doing?! I brushed it off and me and Emma raced over to our tent, excited to get going to the trampoline park.

Within ten minutes we were ready and making our way over to the coach. Dean wasn't there yet so we stood and chatted for a bit. Emma kept asking if I was feeling OK after yesterday. I assured her I was absolutely fine, although I could tell she wasn't fully convinced. While looking around waiting for Dean I noticed Noah approaching with a pained expression on his face. I turned back to Emma.

"Emma, say something," I begged her, "and just start laughing."

"What! Why?" she asked quizzically.

"Just do it!" The urgency in my voice was unquestionable.

"Woah, yeah, OK, er." She was taking too long and I could see Noah getting even closer. I burst out laughing and leant onto Emma's shoulder. She laughed too and I felt her body straighten. She'd seen Noah approaching, immediately grabbed my shoulders and started laughing too. Oh, she was amazing! Once he saw Emma and I seemingly in the middle of something, he stopped. I looked down, with my head still on Emma's shoulder, and saw his feet come to a halt. He skirted around us and joined his friends standing at the end of the line for the coach. With a sigh of relief, I lifted my head.

"OK, now explain that one to me," Emma stated, "because there's no way you can lie about that and say that it's nothing, otherwise you wouldn't be so blatantly ignoring and avoiding him like that." She crossed her arms and looked at me with such an accusatory stare.

"Ugh OK, so nothing happened, but Noah came up to me after the water fight and attacked me, saying how I was shooting him disgusted looks. I wasn't, but he just spouted all this rubbish. Since then, it's been weird and I just want to avoid him. I don't know what he wants to say to me but I just don't want to be around him." It all poured out of my mouth and I couldn't stop it.

Emma looked at me, stunned.

"Wow, that's... wow! Well, OK that's cool, I'm here to save you," she paused, "he looked really upset when he saw us laughing."

I looked at the floor. I didn't want to make Noah feel like that but had no idea what else to do! I'd attempted to apologise, but he hadn't accepted it. I didn't know what would happen if I was around him. When I saw him, my body reacted in ways I couldn't even comprehend, and I was happy right now. I didn't want to mess that up over some guy that was still a mystery to me.

"Yeah, but I don't know what he wants me to do!' I pleaded. "I mean, he can't be so on and off with me and then expect me to be fine with him. I've had enough of his chaos."

"Oh Cassie, I'm so glad you actually said that and you're not just being pushed around by what he's doing," Emma said.

"It's good Em. I feel good, slightly guilty but good."

"Oh, it's about time. It has been different this week or two with Noah being around and you being off. I'm glad to have you back," she said with a smile.

I was about to respond to her when, luckily, Dean approached and our conversation was cut short.

"Hey," he called out. As he got closer he dipped a kiss on my lips. A few of his friends followed behind and joined us as we waited to board the coach. I smiled up at Dean.

"Are you OK?" I asked.

"I am now," he replied. I blushed and smiled at him.

"You guys ready for today?" one of Dean's friends asked us. "Apparently, there's like this dodgeball court made up of trampolines."

Dean and Connor high-fived and they all launched into a conversation about how they planned to beat each other in dodgeball. I just stood there smiling and watching them debate who would be the winner. I could see Emma glancing at me from the side and I knew that our little chat was far from over. For now, though, I would just enjoy the day and have some fun.

We all piled onto the coach and set off, chattering excitedly about the trampoline park and the fish and chips we'd have for lunch. After about thirty minutes we reached the trampoline park, anxiously waiting to get in there. Finally, Dan got us all checked in and distributed those funny paper wristbands that always seem impossible to remove. We walked in – it was incredible. This enormous hall was covered in trampolines, across the whole floor and angled against the walls. There were large ones, small ones, a running trampoline for flips and even a foam pit! There was a second floor, too, which included the dodgeball arena and an obstacle course. It was awesome and I couldn't wait to get jumping.

"OK, so I know you're all itching to get on the trampolines and don't want to stand here listening to me," announced Dan, "but there are some quick little things you need to know. We have two hours here and our own room for you to leave all your shoes and bags. There's a quick safety video to watch and then you're free to go." There was a soft groan, but we all sat and watched the video.

Noah glanced in my direction a few times through the video, but I kept my eyes glued to the screen – it was safest. Although the looks didn't go unnoticed by Emma, she stayed quiet, although I could see her shoot daggers at Noah. Soon the video ended and we were free. Everyone dropped their stuff in the room and raced out to leap onto the trampolines. It was amazing! Me and Emma bounced around while Dean and his friends ran straight over to the foam pit and started taking turns doing back flips. I felt free and so weightless. Me and Emma bounced about and switched trampolines, doing twirls and different tricks, and laughing uncontrollably when one of us fell over. Ten minutes later, Dean bounced over and joined us.

"Hey, shall we go and check out the dodgeball arena?" he asked. "It looks pretty good and we can get a game going." I looked at Emma and simultaneously we turned to him and grinned, nodding enthusiastically. Dean motioned to his friends, and we all headed upstairs.

"OK, let's do teams – Cassie and Emma on opposites because you're the girls here – and we'll split on each side." Dean bounced over and grabbed my waist. Two more of Dean's friends joined us, including Connor, and three others went over to Emma. I could see a mischievous glint in her eye when she noticed Connor was on my team, and I began to worry for his safety. The balls looked soft, but Emma was evil when she wanted to be. The game began and everyone got ready. We raced to the middle line, grabbed the balls and started dodging. We were doing really well. Emma grabbed one of the balls and immediately fired it at Connor. He'd been celebrating his previous hit and hadn't been paying attention to Emma. The ball hit Connor straight in the head. He was knocked over by the impact and immediately fell down.

"Yes!!" Emma cheered. "Revenge is sweet."

"Hey, nice shot Emma," Dean called.

"Dude, I'm on your team. Why are you commending the enemy?" Connor protested as he lay on the floor.

"Hey man, you're my friend and everything, but that was a good shot, plus you did kind of deserve it," Dean replied.

I laughed and agreed, and slowly Connor made his way out of the arena. The game continued, and there were now three on Emma's side, with only me and Dean left on our side.

Emma grabbed another ball and set her eyes on me, but in no time, Dean swooped in and a ball hit Emma right in the stomach. She narrowed her eyes at him and stalked out of the arena. It was me and Dean against Jeremy, one of Dean's friends, now. I jumped between the trampolines and grabbed a ball. Jeremy had Dean in his sights and didn't see me creeping to the side. He launched the ball at Dean, and as the ball left his hand, I threw my ball in his direction. It whacked him straight in his arm and he was out.

"Yes!!" I jumped up and down. "Victory is mine!"

Jeremy grinned at me and bowed. Dean grabbed me and picked me up, but the two of us toppled over and fell to the ground, with Dean landing on top of me. I erupted in giggles – I felt happy.

"Whoops," I said, through the giggles.

"If only there weren't so many people around," Dean murmured. My cheeks grew red and I raised my eyebrows at Dean as I leaned up to kiss him. His friends began to cheer and soon I felt dodgeballs being pelted at us from every direction. Dean laughed and looked up at all his friends surrounding us. Emma was smiling along too, but her face seemed to be laced with sadness. I could tell she wasn't happy. Dean soon rolled off me and stood up, pulling me with him. The circle that had formed soon dispersed and we began another game.

We had a few more rounds of dodgeball, where we all switched sides. Me and Emma were never on the same team as the boys had deemed us the team captains, but Dean swapped over to Emma's side for one of the games and she smiled widely, high-fiving him. I felt like she held her hand there a little longer than needed, and through that game she seemed to spend more time looking at Dean than she did the other team. I watched her carefully but didn't say anything. I wasn't going to become the psycho girlfriend that didn't even trust her best friend!

At the end of the contest, we'd won two more rounds and the other team one. Thoroughly sweaty and tired, we headed back down to our room to grab some drinks. Dean downed his drink and headed out to get a refill, while the rest of his friends filtered out of the room and went over to the foam pit. Emma told me she was going to the toilet, so I sat there on my own and pulled out my phone.

Lexi: *I'm glad you're not shutting out your family.*

Lexi: *Any updates on the whole Noah thing. ;)*

Me: *There could be, I'll fill you in later.*

Lexi: *Oooo, it requires a full phone call; it must be juicy.*

Lexi: *And Cassie, it's good that you're talking to your family, I promise that. It might seem difficult but I'm proud of how you're dealing with this.*

Ah, of course, Lexi was missing her dose of gossip. I thought I'd call her later and tell her about Noah's outburst.

Her encouragement and support were always some of the best things I loved about Lexi. If I said I wanted to kill someone, she'd volunteer as a getaway driver. That was what I needed right now, and even if I wasn't near her, I knew she'd still do everything she could for me. With her talking about my parents, it reminded me I needed to contact my mum, I continued to scroll through my phone for a few minutes longer and seeing as my mum hadn't answered my messages, I thought I'd give her a quick ring. She picked up almost immediately.

"Hi sweetie," she said. I could already hear her exhaustion through the phone.

"Hi mum, how are you?"

"Well, I've been better, but I'm OK... I miss you," she told me.

"I miss you too, mum, I wish I could be there with you," I confessed.

"No, no sweetheart, I want you to have a good summer. Me and your father still have some things to sort out and you'll be home in less than a week."

My heart leapt at that. I was excited about going home, but it also meant this amazing summer would be over.

"Have you talked to dad?" I asked her.

"A little. He's been staying with Gary, so I haven't seen him much."

"Can I do anything?" I asked her, feeling desperate and useless.

"No honey, just enjoy your holiday. How has it been anyways?"

"It's been really good, mum, I... ." I stopped, not knowing how to tell her about Dean and Noah while her and dad were in such a bad place.

"Go on sweetie," she encouraged.

"Well, I met someone," I said.

"Oh, that's so wonderful! What is he like?" she asked.

"Well, his name is Dean and he's so nice – very chatty and so sweet. I really like him, mum."

"I'm so happy for you," she said and I could hear her smile through the phone.

"But there's someone else too, mum."

"There's two people?" she asked me, rather shocked.

"Yeah, there's another guy who arrived late. He's called Noah and I think I like him too. He helped me through a panic attack, and he's so easy to talk to."

"Honey, when did you have another panic attack?" she asked, concern lacing her voice. I explained what had happened and how Noah had helped me through it all and checked up on me.

"Oh sweetheart, it sounds like you do really like this other boy too. But remember, you can't keep both of them. You have to choose."

"Yeah, you're right mum, it's just really difficult and I don't know what to do!"

"Just trust yourself, what you really want will show itself. But, as someone that's been messed about before, it isn't nice."

"Oh mum, I'm so sorry about what has gone on," I told her with tears stinging my eyes.

"It's OK, your father and I both still love each other, but life has started to change and we just need to find out how we fit into each other's lives now things are different."

"OK mum. Well, I want to do what I can – please don't keep me away from this," I begged her.

"I won't sweetheart. Now, go back to your activity, or whatever it is that I can hear. I love you so much."

"I love you too, mum."

And with that I hung up, placed my phone back in my bag and rose from my seat. Turning to the door I noticed a shape standing there – Noah. My heart was beating so quickly I felt like it was going to leap out of my chest. I wouldn't let him see how I was reacting to him.

"Hi," I grumbled, desperate to get out of this situation as quickly as I could.

Noah looked at me for a moment.

"Hey," he replied softly. He ran his fingers through his hair, and I felt my heart flip. "Look, I'm sorry about what happened before. I don't know why I said that. I just… I… well, I don't know," he looked down, "I just don't know how to act around you it would seem," he said with a chuckle.

"Oh, um, it's OK," I stuttered, "no worries." I shot him a soft smile.

"Was that your mum?" he asked and took a step closer, lessening the gap between us.

"Er yeah, I hadn't really talked to her so I thought I should see how she was doing."

"And how is she?"

"She isn't doing great, obviously, with everything considered, but she's doing better than I expected," I told him.

"Is there anything I can do?" he asked, reaching his arm out towards me to comfort me. I stepped back before his arm made contact and it fell to his side as if he had been burnt.

"Not at the moment, I just need to assess it all. My mum seems to be doing well, which is good to see," I said with a brief smile. "But thank you," I added.

"Of course, I just want to make sure you're OK. You shouldn't go through it alone."

"Well, I have Lexi. She's been checking up on me," I replied.

"And I assume wonder boy, Dean, has been helping," he said bitterly.

"Well…" I trailed off.

"He doesn't know," he murmured, "you haven't told him?" I shook my head, and a grin began to grow on his face, "But you told *me*."

"Well, I didn't tell you. You found me crying my eyes out and I just blurted it out," I said defensively.

"Ah, but I gave you the option to keep it quiet, and you still told me," he said smugly.

"Well, I… ." I was stumped. He was right, I could've just lied about what was wrong, but I told him, I chose to confide in him. I just stared and his smile grew even more.

"You know I'm right Cass," he told me with an even wider grin and he took a step closer to me. His smell started to drift towards me, the sweat of the activities magnifying his delicious scent. I shifted my gaze to the floor, trying to relax my racing heartbeat.

"Well, I should... ," I began, desperate to break the spell I was under.

"I just... ," he jumped in at the same time, looking like he was about to burst.

We muttered at the same time. I looked up and our eyes connected. I felt I could've been knocked off my feet with that one gaze. I had to get away. There was no denying what he did to me but I couldn't deal with that right now.

"You first," he joked.

"Oh well, I was just saying that I should probably go and find Emma," I said as I turned towards the door and pointed in the direction where Emma had wandered off. He looked displeased at what I said. I didn't understand. A couple of days ago he was attacking me and basically saying that I should just stay away from him, but here he was trying to talk to me and get me to stay. I couldn't understand it – what did he want from me? I wasn't the one that made it weird between us.

"Oh, um, yeah, of course, I'll see you later," he responded. He moved to the side hesitantly and I needed to turn my body to slide past him. His proximity as I walked past was disorientating. I could smell him – his distinct smell that lit up my entire body, that made me desperate to be pressed close to him. It was intoxicating. At that point, all I wanted to do was close the distance between us and show him what he meant to me, but I had to stop and wait. I was just hoping that he couldn't hear my thumping heart. I escaped as soon as I could and raced away to find Emma. I could feel the burning heat of his gaze on the back of my neck as I sped away.

Emma looked up and noticed me heading her way.

"Hey, you took a while. Are you ready to get back on the trampolines?" she asked with an excited giggle.

"Of course, sorry I took so long, I was on the phone to my mum," I responded with as much enthusiasm as I could muster.

"Is she all right?" Emma asked.

"Yeah, she's doing OK," I replied, "there's some stuff going on with my parents and I just wanted to check in with her."

"Wait, what's going on? You haven't told me anything," she said.

"Well, they're separating. My mum is at home with my siblings and she isn't great."

"Oh Cassie, I'm so sorry!" Emma exclaimed and wrapped her arms around me and hugged me so tight.

"OK Em, I need… to… breathe," I said and she loosened her grip.

"Oh, I'm so sorry Cassie, I just wish you'd told me, I would have helped you and checked in!"

"I know you would Em and that's kind of the part I wanted to avoid. I wanted to have a good summer and not think about the problems at home. I knew if I told you and Dean then you'd constantly worry about me and I didn't want that, I didn't want to be the girl with the crumbling family," I pleaded.

"OK I understand that and I won't push you, but you know I'm here for you, right?"

"Yes, of course I do Em – thank you, that means a lot," I said and hugged her tightly. "Does Dean know?" she asked me, and I shook my head.

"I didn't tell him for the same reason I kept it from you, plus I haven't known him for that long and it's a lot to burden someone with."

"Cassie, Dean does really like you and he'd want to know," she told me. There was an odd tone to her voice but I smiled at her.

"I guess you're right. it's just... The more you let someone in, the more likely you are to get hurt," I admitted.

Emma nodded and I assumed that was because she understood. There was a guilty look on her face, and I couldn't tell if that was out of sympathy or whether there was something she was holding back from me. I was puzzled but didn't want to push it. This conversation had already lasted too long.

"Now come on," I said, "enough serious talk for today, we can talk later, let's go and have some fun. I don't want to spend the day moping about when we have a whole hall of trampolines!" Emma smiled at me and nodded.

"Let's go!" And we were off. We ran over to the trampolines. We tried some awesome flips in the foam pit and it was so fun. But that foam is really difficult to get out of, and after three attempts at flips, Emma and I were thoroughly worn out so headed off to find Dean.

We found him with a group of his in the dodgeball arena. To my dismay, Dean's group had split into him, Connor and a couple others, while the rest, I assumed, had found something else to try. As I looked over, I saw Noah with three of his friends making up the other team. Oh no! Both teams looked over as me and Emma approached. Noah looked shocked at first, but soon his shock turned to pleasure at the sight of me. Dean seemed irritated, but his expression quickly softened when he saw me looking over at him. I gave Dean a timid smile to encourage him. He was my boyfriend and I wanted him to win, regardless of who may have been on the opposing side. The whistle blew, the boys raced to the middle to snatch up the balls and the game commenced. I stood at the fence, watching anxiously as the balls flew between each team, slowly eliminating team members, until there was just one on each side. I'm sure you can guess who. Yep! Dean and Noah against each other. Wow, I couldn't have planned this even if I tried. I stood there anxiously watching the interaction, as they both grabbed a ball and bounced it, watching each other and calculating what their next move would be. This was starting to look like a Wild West cowboy standoff. Ugh, boys! I mean, honestly, what was this all about? Well, that was a stupid thing to say, I had caused it – I just didn't get it. Dean and Noah stared at each other for a minute and then simultaneously threw the balls. I froze, holding my breath. I knew Dean would be unhappy if he lost and Noah would love winning so he could prove something, as if dodgeball was this major thing. Dean got hit square in the chest and Noah dodged the ball hurtling towards him. I let out the breath that I'd been holding and saw the smugness plastered over Noah's face. As I turned to Dean, anger exploded over his face, his cheeks turning so red I almost expected steam to pour from his ears. Dean had been so worried about Noah, and I knew that this event wasn't going to help the situation. I stepped into the arena, made my way over to Dean – while completely ignoring Noah – and made a spectacle of throwing my arms around his shoulders and giving him a kiss on the lips. Previously, I'd been reserved about kissing him properly in front of others but not this time. I slid my arms around his neck tighter and looked up at him. He slowly bent his head towards me and our lips touched. I could feel everyone's eyes watching us, but Dean needed this. He moved his hands from my hips and slid them round my waist, pulling me tighter to him. I giggled as we started to lose our balance on the trampoline. Dean pulled away from me and grinned.

"Well, if that's what I get when I lose something, maybe I should start losing more often," he whispered with a mischievous glint. I whacked him on the chest and he just laughed at me. We pulled away from each other and stepped towards the exit. Dean's friends broke into hoots and hollers as we walked out, and I could feel the blush creeping up my neck.

"Shut up," Dean laughed and shoved Connor, the instigator of the cheering, as he passed. I forced myself to keep my eyes away from Noah – I couldn't bear to see his expression, whether it was one of anger, annoyance or, god forbid, sadness. I knew I couldn't deal with it. Both me and

Dean left the arena with his friends and neither of us looked at Noah once.

Soon after the dodgeball incident, our two hours were up. We'd left the arena and our group hung around on the trampolines for the remaining time. Dean and Connor had a competition and I can proudly say that Dean *definitely* won. Dan soon called us over and our groups slowly filtered from the trampoline area down to our room to grab our stuff and out to the coach, where Dan was waiting for us. I made sure that I avoided any interactions with Noah – I just couldn't face him, not after the display with Dean. Yes, Noah had been nice and checked up on me about my parents, but the whole dodgeball stunt was clearly just a way to bait Dean. I made it onto the coach and slid into the window seat, but my relief was short-lived as Emma overtook Dean and swooped in next to me.

"Well, that was… interesting", she said.

I turned to her. "Oh please, let's not even get started on that," I begged.

"Cassie, you should've seen Noah's face when he saw you kiss Dean. It was clear that his dodgeball victory was short-lived, his whole face just dropped."

"Really?" I asked her, hoping she was just joking.

"Oh yeah, it was insane, he looked like a hurt puppy, I almost felt bad for him."

I was shocked when she told me. I looked down at my lap and wished I could speak to Noah or just do something to make this better. I just missed being around him. Ignoring him had proved harder than I'd expected. I had no idea what I could do, but I felt like I needed to do something – I was restless!

"Are you sure nothing is going on there?" she asked me.

"I'm sure, there's nothing going on," I assured her. "He's made that clear a lot and so have I, plus I'm happy with Dean and I don't want to change that."

"OK, that's good. It's good that you're happy and it's good that you're with him and... that's good."

"Yes Em, it *is* very good," I responded.

"And nothing at all with Noah, even with all the little moments you seem to be unable to avoid?" she asked, with slight bitterness in her voice.

"Look, it doesn't matter," I told her as I brushed aside her change of tone. "Things are weird with me and Noah but we only have a few days left of camp. I want to enjoy them and relax."

"That makes sense Cassie, but are you happy?" Emma asked. I paused for a minute and thought about what I was going to say.

"I am," I said, but my thoughts drifted to Noah and how I felt with him, the happiness he made me feel.

"Well, as long as you really are sure that you're happy," she said, looking a little unconvinced by my response. But she nodded and sat back in silence.

I slumped down in my seat – I was exhausted just by this conversation let alone everything else that had gone on today. Emma turned to face the front of the coach, letting the subject drop. She then turned to the side and started chatting to

Connor and Dean, who were sitting on the other side of the aisle.

After about ten minutes, we stopped outside a fish and chip shop.

"So," Dan started, "we're getting fish and chips. I'll do a quick count of what you all want. There are four choices – fish, saveloy, sausage or pie. If you don't want any of those then you can just have chips, so when you hear what you want please raise your hand. If you don't raise your hand for anything then you're going without, so listen up."

Everyone raised a hand and Dan made a note of them all. I chose a saveloy, while Dean went for cod and Emma had scampi.

"Great, thank you," said Dan. "Now, if you all don't mind going and finding a spot on the beach, we'll bring your food down to you."

Everyone piled off the bus and set off to the beach, laying down jumpers, towels and blankets.

"Hey, I'm just going to pop to the toilet," I told Emma as we stepped off the coach. She nodded and ran over to join our group where they'd settled on the beach. I strolled over to the toilets but just stood outside for a while – I wasn't desperate and needed time to think. I felt like I'd spent more time thinking this summer than when I was at school. I leant on the wall, closed my eyes and took a few deep breaths to calm myself. After a few minutes, I pushed myself off the wall and stared out over the beach, watching the waves crash against the shore and hearing the seagulls flying above. I watched as they slowly hopped towards people, waiting for a chance to steal their food. The beach was full of families and friends walking around and laughing – the sight made me smile. I started back down the beach, but before I could get very far, I felt an arm grab me and spin me around. I hadn't walked very far and was still hidden by the wall of the toilet. It felt like an electric shock had run through me, lighting up my insides. I shot my head up and connected with those milky chocolate eyes.

"We need to talk," Noah stated. He yanked me back next to the toilets so that we were completely hidden, and we stood staring at each other for a moment. I was breathless and overwhelmed by his intensity.

"OK, what do you want to talk about?" I asked him naively, deciding it was best to avoid the topic for as long as I could.

"Look, I know I snapped at you and made it weird, but I was hoping we could go back to being friends. I can't bear this cold-shoulder attitude. You were the first friend I made here and regardless of what has happened between us I don't want to lose that completely," he said softly. I just stared back at him.

"Oh um. I'm sorry too, I guess. I know there was a reason you snapped at me, and you've really helped me with all my family and things. We do really get on well. I know I was a little mean about you and *that girl*. I don't know why – just seeing you two, I guess," I explained, with a slight edge in my voice.

"Oh, come on, you don't need to use *that* tone," he muttered.

"What do you mean? There was no tone," I responded defensively.

"Don't lie, you know there was," he looked at me, "I just don't get it."

"Well, there's nothing to get," I snapped, "I just don't like her – that's why I responded like that."

"Ah, of course." He paused, looking away and then stepped closer. "It wouldn't be because you're *jealous*, would it?" He asked, raising his eyebrow in questioning. I scanned his amused face and my eyes focused on his lips. They teased me, looking so delicious. My immediate thought was to raise my head, lean up and show him what I really thought about him and *that* girl. But I didn't.

"What, huh… I don't… what are you talking about?" I stuttered.

He placed his hand on the wall just millimetres from my head, caging me in his arms and my breath caught in my throat.

"Well, from what I've seen it looks like you could be jealous – the dirty looks, the little comments. I mean, Cass, you did try to kiss me. You can't blame me." He leant closer to me until his face was just a whisper from mine and our breath mixed together.

"I don't know what you're talking about." I took a deep breath. "I guess I was just caught up in the moment. You were there, I confided in you and I felt vulnerable, that was all."

"Oh really, that was all it was?" he said, raising an eyebrow at me.

"Ye... yes, that was all," I stuttered. "Look, my friends and my *boyfriend* are waiting, so if you haven't got anything else to say then I should be going."

"Ah, but why would you want to do that?" he said, drawing his arm next to my hair and tilting his head to the side. "We're having a good time."

"No, it's not a good time because you're being crazy." I wasn't backing down.

"But is it crazy?"

"Yes," I insisted while trying to resist the pull I had towards him.

"Oh, I don't think so." His eyes focused on my lips.

"Hmm?" I was too disoriented for any coherent speech, my attempt to resist him had been unsuccessful. I had to get away, I couldn't do this. I shook myself and pushed him back. "OK that's enough, stop!"

Leisurely, he pushed his hands off the wall and stepped back, raising his hands in a mocking sign of surrender.

"If that's how you want to play it, you're free to go, but I know you don't mean it." Noah made it sound like the end of an interrogation, but I wasn't listening to it any more. The way he questioned me – his arms caged me in like a prison, but a prison I'm not sure I wanted to escape. Either way, I was getting away from him as quickly as I could. This wasn't happening when I was with Dean – I wouldn't do that to him.

I rushed back to Emma and Dean as they sat on the sea wall chatting and laughing. They were sitting closer than usual, with their heads bent together, and I was puzzled – they hadn't even noticed I was behind them. This was happening more and more often. I felt a sense of unease but I was still disoriented from the moment I'd just had with Noah. So, I forced down the business with Emma and Dean and made my way over to them.

"Hey guys," I called as I walked over to them. They sprung apart like opposing magnets. It added to my suspicions, but I still placed a soft kiss on Dean's cheek and sat down next to him.

"What are you guys talking about?" I asked.

"Oh nothing, we were just joking about the events of the trampoline park," Emma joked.

"Hey!" Dean laughed and turned away from me to face Emma sitting across the blanket, "I did great on the trampolines!"

"Oh, of course you did," Emma said, nudging him.

They both set off in a fit of laughter and quiet bickering. I turned out to the sea and set my eyes on the horizon. Dan started to hand everyone their meals. I received my food and ate silently. I wasn't prepared to get into any conversation with Dean and Emma, seeing the way things were going with them. I noticed Noah walk back down to the beach and sit with his friends. *That* girl handed him his food and he began to eat. I noticed him glance back at me a few times. He was looking sad and restless, but I didn't pay him any notice. It was just too much of a mess and I still hadn't recovered from the incident, so I just kept my eyes glued to my food and finished eating.

When everyone had finished, Dan herded us onto the coach. I sat at the rear, with Emma, Dean and Connor, and we set off back to the campsite.

I was quiet, my mind overflowing with the Noah situation as well as whatever was going on with Emma and Dean. I felt restless and needed to do something. I was overwhelmed and didn't know what was coming next. My feelings for Noah were only growing stronger and no matter how much I tried to avoid him, it seemed impossible. Maybe Lexi was right about this whole fate idea, but there was still no denying my feelings for Dean. I really liked him and he was so good to me. I understood I could never have things both ways, but I felt trapped. Whichever path I chose, someone would get hurt, and the way it was going... I'd be the one hurt the most.

Chapter 19

The evening passed quickly. Dinner was quiet and sped by. It felt like I was sleepwalking, watching everyone else go about their activities while I just sat there, alone with my thoughts. I finished dinner, cleaned up and went to bed. I was beginning to feel homesick so I grabbed my phone and hit Lexi's name.

"Hi," I said wearily.

"Hey girl, you sound tired, what's up?" Lexi asked, suddenly concerned.

"Ugh, I'm just exhausted, I guess," I replied.

"Well, you promised a top-up in the gossip – you want to start there?"

"Might as well – it seems to be where my madness stems from. So, Noah has been acting all kinds of weird with me – he snapped at me at one point."

"Wait, what?" she said, sounding shocked.

"Yeah, there was this girl hanging off him and I got a bit annoyed and apparently sent him some dirty looks, which I can't say if I did or not… but this girl was literally falling all over him, it was ridiculous."

"Oh girl, you were definitely giving him dirty looks."

"How do you know; you weren't even there?" I protested.

"Oh, I can tell by the way you're talking about him. You were shooting daggers at him because you like him and he was with another girl," she said smugly. I was about to protest again but she was right.

"He had a dodgeball situation with Dean today too. They had like this standoff thing in the trampoline park," I explained.

"OK, that's going to need more detail," she said.

"So, we went to this trampoline park today, like the one we went to at the end of school a few years ago, and there was the dodgeball arena and Dean and a bunch of his friends went against Noah and a few of his friends. Well, it got down to just Noah and Dean at the end and Noah hit Dean, which didn't help the situation."

"Ooo, a showdown for your affections, that's kind of cute."

"No, it isn't cute! Plus, there's more," I confessed.

"Go on."

"Well, we then went to get fish and chips for lunch and as I was walking to the toilets, he cornered me, claiming that I was jealous. And he brought up the almost-kiss."

"Oh god, I mean he was right – you were jealous," she teased.

"Come on Lexi, shush!"

"OK, OK, I'm sorry… just let me know when you two make out," she added.

"Hey! No!"

"Ugh, fine. Anyways, change the topic then… How are your family getting on?"

"Well, I spoke to my mum," I told her. "I called her today, just to check up on how she was."

"That's good, what did she say?" Lexi asked softly.

"She said she was doing OK, given the circumstances. She hasn't really spoken to dad – he's been staying with Gary from his work."

"Well, maybe having some space will help him."

"Yeah, my mum told me that they needed to work out how they fitted in each other's lives now. Things had changed, apparently, and they needed to work through it."

"Well, that's not terrible. They're calm and don't hate each other. There's a chance, Cassie, don't lose hope," she encouraged.

"I guess you could be right," I agreed, "but I won't be planning the second wedding just yet."

"Hmm, well we shall see what happens," she replied.

"Enough about me," I said, desperate to change the conversation, "how has your summer been?"

"Oh, it's been all right. I've been spending days at the pool mostly – there were a few cute guys around."

"Ooo, any new prospects?" I asked.

"No, not really, they were all right but none that caught my eye," she told me with a sigh.

"Oh, no one like Jake, right?" I teased. Lexi used to have this *major* crush on my brother when we were younger, and I have never ceased to mock her for it.

"Oh, shut up Cassie, that was ages ago, that would never happen now."

"Ugh, that's a shame. It would've been great to have you as my sister-in-law," I continued.

"Oh Cassie, I hate you," she moaned, but I could hear her laugh through the phone.

"You never know," I teased.

"OK, let's stop this conversation now!"

"Hmm, fine," I sighed, "well back to me then. I think Emma has been a little weird – you know that girl I made friends with here?"

"OK, go on," she said steadily.

"Well, she's been getting suspiciously close to Dean. I mean, leaning in close but jumping as soon as I approach. She seems disheartened when I talk about Dean and miserable when I'm around him, but so much happier when it's just her and him. I don't know if they're just close or if I should be worried."

"I'm not sure to be honest with you. They could just be close, I guess. Then again, she could just feel bad because she doesn't want to seem like she's going for your man. She could just be harmless."

"Yeah, you're probably right, I should stop worrying."

"Honestly, with everything else going on, there really is no point in worrying – just enjoy your summer, enjoy the last few days you've got left."

"Yeah, I will. Thank you, Lex."

"Of course, Cassie. Now, I need to go, I've got my food."

"Bye Lexi, I'll talk to you later," and with that I hung up. Emma joined me in the tent five minutes after I was settled. I heard rustling and she settled into her bed.

"Night Cassie," Emma whispered. I grumbled in response and shut my eyes. I started to wind down but saw a small light flash from under my pillow – my phone.

Noah: *Hi. :)*
Me: *Hey Noah.*
Noah: *Sorry about today.*
Noah: *Are we OK?*
Me: *Yeah, sure.*
Noah: *OK, good.*
Noah: *I was worried.*
Noah: *Sorry, I was just joking.*
Me: *It's fine.*
Noah: *Did you enjoy today?*
Me: *Yeah, it was a good time.*
Noah: *Yeah, the trampoline park was pretty cool.*
Me: *Well the dodgeball was rather interesting.*
Noah: *Oh right, that was a little awkward, yeah.*
Noah: *Sorry about that one too.*
Me: *Well, that's good and it's OK.*
Noah: *Good.*
Noah: *So, friends?*
Me: *Yeah, why not. Friends.*
Noah: *OK good, otherwise I'd feel terrible.*

It was odd that he was trying to continue normal conversation, particularly after the stunts he pulled this morning, but I admired the attempt. I turned my head and looked over to see if Emma was still settled. I could hear her quietly snoring and knew that I was still safe. We chatted for a while longer, but my exhaustion from the day was getting to me and I knew I needed sleep. I shut my eyes, allowing sleep to take over.

I woke up the next morning, blinking my eyes to adjust to the brightness. I was ready for a new day – hopefully a day with less drama. It was the final countdown of camp – three days left. The end was coming fast and it was crazy. I wanted my final days to be calm and to be able to enjoy them, before I was hurled back into reality and the family mayhem waiting for me. My feelings about leaving camp were conflicting. I was excited to go home, to see Jake, Hailey and Bradley, to see Lexi and spend time with her and Connie and Lottie. I hadn't spoken to them much this holiday so it would be good to finally get together with them again. But while home had its perks, I'd been in a bubble for so long that I wasn't sure if I was ready to jump back into the real world. But it wasn't the idea of leaving the camp that upset me so much – I wasn't sure if I was ready to say goodbye to Noah. Despite everything we'd gone through, his presence had become a comfort to me and I wasn't sure if I was prepared to let that go.

I eased myself into a sitting position and turned to Emma. She was still snoring away and I needed to do something about it. A few ideas ran through my head. I'd already jumped on her recently, so I turned to my second option – a bottle of water sat next to my bed so I thought an early shower might do her good. I twisted off the top of the bottle, dipped my hand in and splashed Emma with a few drops. She stirred but didn't wake. I tried again with a little more but there was still no movement. There was only one choice – with a wicked grin on my face, I tilted the bottle slightly over her head and let a small trail dribble down onto her face. Soon enough, she sat up and looked around dazed. I shot away from her.

"Jesus, Cassie, what the hell was that?!" she spluttered.

"What are you talking about?" I asked innocently.

She sat there staring at me while she wiped away the water trickling down her face and shot me a glare that told me I was going to regret what I just did. With a giggle, I fled from the scene and finished getting ready.

"I know what you did, Cassie, and there's no getting away with it," she called after me.

"You have no evidence," I called back towards the tent as I made my way over to the toilets for a shower. I was walking over and saw Noah across the campsite. I shot him a quick smile and continued on my way. Before I jumped in the shower, I checked my phone quickly.

Mum: *Hey sweetie, enjoy your last few days, we're all looking forward to seeing you soon, Bradley and Hailey are really missing you.*

Dad: *Hi Cass, hope you're OK and enjoying camp.*

I replied to mum quickly and let her know I was OK and that I was looking forward to coming home. I ignored dad's message – I mean, he didn't even have the guts to tell me about anything going on between him and mum and then he decided to message me as if nothing was wrong. With him behaving like that, there was no way I was responding and ruining my final days. He could go through a few more days of radio silence from me and see how he liked it. I've suffered plenty of silence from him!

I shoved my phone under my towel and hopped in the shower. I quickly washed my hair and hopped out again. I dressed in my favourite denim shorts and a black bodysuit, ran a brush through my damp hair and put on a little mascara. Once I was happy, I walked out of the showers and dumped my stuff in the tent. Emma was just finishing getting ready too, so I waited for her. As soon as all my stuff was sorted in the tent and Emma had finished getting ready, we dashed over to the food hall to join the others for breakfast.

As we were coming to the end of camp, Dan had promised a special breakfast on each of the final days. This morning it was a selection of waffles, pancakes, bacon, eggs, sausages as well as all the usual stuff. Honestly, I wasn't sure what else he could do to beat this. Me and Emma shot each other a mischievous grin at the heavenly sight that was laid out before us and in no time we dived into the array of delights. With great precision, Emma grabbed everything she wanted and walked away.

"See you at the table," she called over her shoulder.

I stood there and deliberated about what I was going to take, my mouth watering at the sight of it all. I had no idea how I was going to pick, but I soon decided on a waffle with a side of bacon. As I reached for the tongs to grab the waffles, another hand reached forward simultaneously, and as our hands touched there was that feeling that had become ever so familiar to me. A shock ran up my arm and my breath caught in my throat. I hadn't spoken to Noah – god, I hadn't even looked at him – since that moment at the beach. I tried to ignore the pull, but as much as I willed them not to, my eyes couldn't resist glancing up at the gorgeous face that was just inches from mine. As soon as I looked up, our eyes connected and a sense of calm came over me. My erratic breath eased, despite my heart beating a thousand times a minute. Noah stirred up feelings that I'd never felt before.

"You first," he grinned.

I leaned towards the waffles that were, of course, near him and I was quickly surrounded by his scent, as it danced around me, hugging and taunting me, my hand itching to grab his and pull him closer to me. I knew I couldn't, but that didn't stop my desire. I reached for the waffles and grabbed two, placing them on my plate.

"Er thanks," I mumbled.

"No problem, Bailey."

I almost dropped my waffle at that. It was new but coming from his mouth my last name sounded incredible. I'd never been a fan of it – it sounded like another first name, which I always thought was weird. But the moment my name left his lips I knew I would never get enough.

"So, you switch up the nicknames, huh?" I queried.

"I thought I'd try something different, keep you on your toes, you know," he said grinning as he reached for the syrup. "What do you think?"

"Hmmm," I pondered for a moment, "well it's not the worst. First time my last name has been used like that but at least it's not the boring name everyone calls me."

"Well then, I'll keep on using the different names, they're just like you," he said.

"What, odd and weird?" I joked.

"No," he said, seeming almost offended, and then whispered, "incredible and unlike anyone or anything else." He finished drowning his waffles in syrup and offered it to me. I nodded silently and smiled at him. Then he drizzled a generous amount over my pancakes and went to put the jug of syrup back where it had been. In the process, he brushed my hand. From the way his eyes leapt to mine, it seemed as if he was as equally affected as me.

With that, I cleared my throat, sent him a faint smile and turned to my table. Neither Emma nor Dean had seemed to notice the interaction I'd had with Noah, which for Emma was a surprise as she was usually an eagle-eyed watcher when it came to anything between me and Noah. She and Dean seemed too engrossed in their own conversation to notice me. I sat down and shrunk into the background as everyone continued their conversations, staring at my food. Stirred up by Noah's words, I couldn't bring myself to eat any of it. The way he looked at me, the intensity of his gaze, burning a hole straight through me as if he was seeing into my very soul – I could've lost myself in those eyes, diving deep into their chocolatey glory. But I didn't. Instead, I sat there at the cold, hard table, fixed on my food and lost in a fantasy while the world carried on around me.

I soon finished my breakfast. I hardly ate anything but knew Dean and Emma would worry if I didn't, so I ate the bacon and half a waffle. Once everyone had finished, we walked out. Apparently, we were going to be collecting wood today for a bonfire tomorrow. At the sound of the word "bonfire" Dean looked at me and grinned.

"Where it all began," he whispered. I kissed him on the cheek and smiled.

"That was one heck of a night," I agreed.

"So," Dan continued, "we're all going to head to the woods and play some games. We'll have lunch in the woods and then we'll split up and find some firewood, OK? We're taking a truck with us to load it all on to and then we'll head back here for dinner."

There was a low murmur of excited conversation. The woods stood just on the outskirts of the campsite and there was an unspoken rule that we weren't allowed to venture in there alone. Of course, me and Dean had kind of ignored that one, so it was quite an exciting time today, having permission to actually go into the woods without sneaking around. I was looking forward to what I hoped would be a great day.

I was soon gearing up for the woods. I put on my welly boots in case there were any stinging nettles and grabbed one of my checked tops to protect myself against chilly weather and some of the sharper branches. Once we were all sorted, me and Emma linked arms, heading for the woods. We talked and laughed as we walked in a carefree and relaxed way – a good start to the day. Time with just the two of us was really nice but recently it had been a little less common, so this was good. It was so relaxing and calm around her. We were halfway to the woods when I felt arms grab my waist. I jumped and spun around. I saw Dean laugh at me and thumped him in the stomach in mock anger. But I couldn't stop from showing my laughter, which just caused him to laugh even more. I rolled my eyes at him but accepted his hand. He nodded in acknowledgement to Emma, who seemed a little distant, and we continued to the woods.

As I stepped under the canopy of green, I was amazed. Living in a city, I never saw proper nature, but this forest was amazing. The array of emerald, lime and mossy greens was extraordinary.

"Right," Dan announced as we all gathered around him in the woods, "we're first going to play 'capture the flag'! I will split you into two teams and the first team to get the other team's flag wins. If you're tagged you're out and soon, you'll pick it up as you go," he explained.

We all split into our teams, with me, Emma and Dean all on the same team, and Noah on the other. I'd just avoid him, stay by the flag and hopefully I wouldn't see him. After this morning I didn't want to get into any situation with him. He seemed increasingly confident and I was pulled to it, an irresistible tug. He was dangerous and I wasn't sure how long I'd be able to resist him.

Dean, Emma and the rest of the team fled into the woods while me and a couple other people stayed to guard the flag. My heart was restless as I saw the coloured bibs of the other team racing through the trees. I wondered if any of them were Noah and if he would even come up to me. I shuddered with excitement just at the thought of being face to face with Noah in the woods, hidden under the emerald canopy – the secrets that would blow through the branches. I was intrigued to see what the allure of the forest could bring.

The game was full steam ahead and I could see reds and blues running through the trees. It was hectic but the energy in the woods was incredible. I could see some blues sprinting towards us, but our defence soon sprang into action and cleared them from our path as quickly as they appeared. I realised that I'd picked a good position when I noticed how worn out the rest of the team were, some of their faces matching the redness of their bibs, which made me chuckle.

As I looked out around the forest, I noticed a blue colour flash in and out of the trees. None of our red team seemed to be close enough to get them away so I set off. They seemed to be edging around the flag trying to find a point to attack, but as I darted in between the trees I managed to sneak up and capture them. It was one of Dean's friends I noticed as I neared them.

"Ha, better luck next time," I cheered as they turned around and slumped back to their base. "I got you," I muttered under my breath with a sense of triumph.

"You may have got *them*," a voice called smugly, "but it looks like I have *you*." I whirled around – it was Noah.

"W-W-What!" I choked out.

"In your own time," he called as he waved, crossed his arms and leant cockily against a tree waiting for me to get a coherent sentence out.

"Where did you come from?" I uttered.

"In general? Or from the woods?" he answered.

"The woods," I stated.

"Oh well, I was over there," he said, pointing to the general area of his base. "Then I noticed one of my teammates unaware of this sneaky red," he gestured to me, "so I thought I'd become sneakier and save my team member. Clearly I got here too late," his eyes connected with mine, "by maybe I got here right on time."

A confident grin stretched, drawing my eyes to his lips, and he took a step closer to me.

"I mean, if I'd gotten here earlier then we might not be alone right now." His smirk widened.

"Hmm, well I think I'll just be going now, seeing as you were clearly late in your task and I have a flag to protect," I said.

"Woah, woah, woah!" Noah said, lifting his hand to stop me and blocking my path. "Now, why would I let a member of the opposing team sneak away? What will make it worth it? I'd hate to go back to my team with empty hands," he murmured.

"Get over yourself Noah," I tried to say with confidence, but clearly it wasn't believable. "Come on, people will wonder where we've gone."

I stepped forward again, but this time he placed his full body in the way, stepping closer to me, his smell once again surrounding me. I glared up at him, but my breath caught when I realised how close we had become – my chest was mere inches away from his and I had to turn my head up fully to see him. I could feel the heat of his body and without realising what I was doing, I leaned closer to him. The space grew smaller, his head started to lower to mine and I could feel his breath on my face. His eyes started to close – he wasn't stopping me from kissing him this time. But rather than lean in any closer, I used that moment and his unawareness to skirt around him and dart away, back to our base. He stumbled forwards and his head whipped round suddenly as he became aware of my disappearance.

"Better luck next time – now we're even," I shot at him and with a mock salute I set off back to our flag.

As I started walking back to my base, I looked over my shoulder and Noah was standing there, still in slight disbelief and shaking his head at me as he leisurely leant against the tree trunk. With a giggle I turned back and ran, my cheeks blazing with what almost happened. That was the second time I had almost kissed him, and it was getting harder and harder to resist those lips. But this wasn't the moment, so I pushed it away and continued to our flag. When I got to the base, I noticed a little group was gathered.

"Hey!" I said when I saw Emma and Dean were among the group. They were both panting hard with rosy cheeks and grins that stretched from ear to ear.

"Hey," Dean responded, looking confused and a little worried, "where have you been?"

"Oh, there was a blue trying to sneak up to our flag so I took care of him," I said and shot him a wink.

"That's my girl," he said proudly, slinging an arm over my shoulder.

As Dean said that I noticed Emma's smile didn't reach so much to her ears any more. I put it down to tiredness – I mean, she hadn't mentioned anything more about her brother so I hoped things were OK. We were having a good time now so it wasn't right to bring it up, but I might ask later if she still seemed a little down.

"So, what's going on?" I asked.

"Oh, we're just grouping together. We've nearly got the flag – most of them are in prison but we have to move quickly!" I noted how seriously Dean took all of this and laughed to myself – so competitive!

"OK, so what's the plan?" Emma chimed in.

"Well, I'm thinking, if we storm the place, they can't take us all at once," Dean said.

There were nods and it seemed that was what we were going to do. I volunteered to stay by the flag with Connor just in case any rogue blues decided to try stealing ours.

With the plan all agreed, it commenced. The others all spread out and charged for the flag, a whole line of reds running through the forest leaping over fallen branches. As I stood there, looking around for any blues, I heard a collective cheer. I really hoped that was our team and not the blues. My hopes were fulfilled when our team came marching through the woods, holding the blue flag high. I smiled at the excitement on Dean's face as he walked over to me.

"Now, as I remember correctly, the kiss after dodgeball for losing was rather good. But what do I get now, seeing as I've won?" he asked me.

With a grin I looked up at him and wrapped my arms around his neck.

"Well, how about this?" I said to him and kissed him as deeply as I could manage. His arms slid around my waist and linked at the back, holding me close. The rest of our team started cheering, I broke the kiss and giggled at the audience that had seemed to gather.

"Yep, that was definitely worth the win," Dean chuckled.

"Well, it's obvious we have a winning team," Dan announced as we walked over to him.

"As for the losers, staying in line with the punishments, you'll be clearing up after dinner tonight."

There was a collective groan. "Woah, woah, don't blame me – you guys lost," Dan joked.

He glanced down at his watch. "But on that note, lunch will be served. Everyone go and find a space, settle down, and we'll hand out the food."

Soon the lunches were dished out and we all sat down on the forest floor and caught our breath. Many people were still red faced from the game, a lot of them had grabbed their bottles and started gulping down water. I sat back, soaking in the sun and loving the summer warmth and how it felt filtering in through the trees and onto my face. I looked around, admiring the scene of friends sitting and smiling, with not a care in the world, surrounded by all the incredible scenery. This is what I'd miss when I went back home.

As I continued looking around, my eyes landed on Noah and his locked on mine, desire burning in a gaze clearly troubled by the kiss we'd almost shared. I immediately let my eyes drift away from him and continued to look around. I rejoined the conversation – some crazy debate about which superhero was the best.

"Hold on, how can you say it's Batman, he's just rich, really," Bradley protested.

"Oh, come on, you could use that same argument about Iron Man," Connor retorted.

"No way, Tony Stark is a genius, and you can't tell me otherwise," Dean declared.

"OK, but what about Thor? He's a literal god," Connor added.

"Nope – Thor is good, I'll give you that, but I mean, Iron Man started it all," Dean argued.

"Well, if we are going chronologically, it was actually Captain Marvel, *then* it was Black Widow – both amazing women," I added.

"No way, Black widow is just a good fighter," Bradley chimed in.

"Well, she could take *you*," Emma muttered.

"OK, but I think we're all forgetting an all-important one… Scarlet Witch!" I said, almost yelling. "And if any of you try to tell me that either Scarlet Witch or Captain Marvel aren't the strongest, then I will have to take you down!"

Everyone looked at me with complete amazement.

"Wow, you seem passionate about this, Cassie," Connor commented.

"You bet I am," I replied, "Marvel is the greatest, so please try and fight me, I would love to hear your crazy notions."

I was greeted once again with stunned silence for a moment, but in no time the conversation was up to full blast again. Emma and I shared a glance and laughed, deciding to give up trying to follow what the boys said and just return to laying back and enjoying the sun.

An hour later, we'd all finished and it was time for the next part of the day – bonfire wood collecting. It all seemed a bit mundane and boring to be honest. I would've much rather played a few more games, but at that moment I had no idea how *un*-boring the afternoon was going to turn out and the truths that were waiting for me…

Chapter 20

"Right, this doesn't need much explanation," Dan announced. "Wood on the floor, pick it up. Take it to the trailer and repeat the process. There we go!"

We stood around expecting something else, but Dan soon flapped his arms and we took that as the sign to begin, and slowly groups spread around the forest and started gathering big bits of wood and taking them back to the truck. I set off with Emma. It was just the two of us as Dean had split off with a group of his friends and gone in another direction.

Me and Emma started a slow amble around the woods, looking for good pieces of wood and just relaxing and enjoying the sun. As we walked in silence, I noticed how peaceful the woods were, with birds singing, little creatures scurrying past by my feet and the trees swaying like they were waving to me. I felt calm.

"So," I asked Emma, "have you enjoyed camp?"

She turned to me with a smile plastered on her face. "You know what? It's not been the worst," she joked. "There was this annoying girl, but after I put up with her it was OK."

I playfully shoved her and we carried on walking.

"Favourite part?" I asked.

"Hmm," she paused for a minute, "I would have to say the trampoline park, that was great!" I nodded in agreement, my mind flashed back to that day, the moment with Noah, the problematic dodgeball game.

"Yeah, that was great, except for that little incident in the dodgeball arena," I commented.

"Oh, but that was hilarious, that whole Western standoff on trampolines thing!" she added.

"Ugh, you laugh at my pain, you wound me," I said with mock sadness.

"Oh, come on, you have to admit it was a good day!" she protested.

"OK, OK fine, I think that's fair, it was pretty good," I responded. "Now, the worst part?" I asked. She turned to me and looked me straight in the eye – I could tell she knew straight away.

"Definitely the water games in the lake," she said without hesitation, "I did *not* enjoy being soaked by that gross water."

"Oh yes, that was not fun at all, that water was disgusting," I agreed.

"Ha!" Emma burst out, "I forgot about your little dip in the water."

She smiled at me. "That was an interesting day for the both of us there – the start of the Noah and Dean rivalry."

I just rolled my eyes. She was right, that was the start of it, but I couldn't think of it that way. Instead, I thought of how that was the day things started with Noah – the way he saved me, the feeling of being pressed against him, they were memories I could never get out of my head.

"All right, come on," I said, trying to steer the topic away from any problematic topics, "we need to actually find some firewood, otherwise we'll probably get in trouble. No doubt Dan will be watching us and have some sort of punishment for those who get the least amount of wood." Emma agreed and we kept walking, stopping every once in a while to gather wood that we thought was best suited for a fire. It was pretty easy and we kept light conversation going the whole time.

"Right," Emma huffed with a hand full of wood, "I can't carry anything more, so I'm going to head to the truck and dump this lot before I drop all my hard work. You going to be OK on your own?" she asked, I nodded and smiled.

"I'm sure I won't get attacked in the woods on my own for like five minutes – now go before you drop any of it," I told her as I could see some branches start to sway.

I assured her I'd be fine. She was hesitant at first but soon nodded and turned to walk away. I kept on walking through the forest looking for more wood, my arms only half full. I heard a snap of twigs behind me and swiftly turned my head to see if it was anyone – nope. I carried on, with the calls of the other campers seeming quiet and distant. It was so relaxing to be on my own and have a moment to breathe without anyone else around. Sure, I had had some moments to myself at the campsite but there was always the chance of people being around. But here? Here, I was all alone and felt free.

A snap of the twigs again. I ignored it this time, thinking it would either be an animal or the wind or something stupid.

But my predictions were soon proved wrong when I heard a voice, Noah's voice.

"You know, you probably shouldn't be out all this way on your own," he said.

As I turned round, I saw him leaning gracefully against one of the larger oak trees that stood tall in the woods.

"And why is that?" I asked him, my heart thumping at the idea of us being alone once again.

"You don't want to bump into any creepy weirdos now, do you," he replied

"What, the ones that may kidnap me from the safety of a summer camp?" I asked, slightly exasperated by his constant appearances with no warning.

"Well, you never know," he joked.

"Fairly sure I'm looking at a creepy weirdo right now," I joked. He raised his eyebrows at me. "Well, definitely a weirdo," I added.

"This one might want to steal you away from that boyfriend," he murmured under his breath. I was shocked by his answer, there was no way he thought I wouldn't hear him. He was becoming more confident in what he was saying and it was starting to make me nervous. My arms slackened at his words, I was shocked. I never would have expected him to say anything like that. Unsure of what was happening, I forgot about the wood in my arms and it crashed to the forest floor.

"W... what?" I stuttered.

"Nothing," he grumbled, looking angered that I was questioning his words. He seemed to want to challenge my relationship with Dean but each time he did, he then got worried about the repercussions. I nodded and let it go. Glancing over at him I saw the intensity and the hurt in his eyes – it was a painful sight. I knew I was the cause of that pain even if I hadn't meant it. I couldn't deny the way I felt and what he seemed to feel towards me.

Averting my gaze, I rushed to pick up the wood – I needed to do something! Being alone with this boy always felt dangerous. He rushed over to help me and soon I was overwhelmed by the proximity and intensity of his body, his warmth radiating towards me. I was hopeless. We both knelt in silence for a few minutes, reaching for sticks or anything to detract from what had just happened. The silence of the forest seemed overwhelming, and I was scared that Noah would hear my thumping heart. Soon it was clear that neither of us were actually picking up any wood. We slowly rose to our feet, and with Noah standing this close to me I had to turn my head up to see him properly. He smiled down at me, and the pile of twigs was discarded at my feet.

"Hi," he said. My face blushed at the look on his face.

"Hey," I whispered back.

I could feel myself leaning closer towards him, that irresistible pull. This was intoxicating, the proximity was intoxicating, he was intoxicating. He leant closer to me too, and I was soon stumbling back at the pressure of his body, falling over the branches. But Noah slid his arm around me, keeping me upright and guiding me backwards. I was pressed against a tree, and he stood in front of me with one arm still around my waist, the other pressed to the side of the tree. His head moved closer and closer, leaning down to meet mine. Soon, his mouth was less than an inch away from me.

"I'm going to kiss you now," he told me, "and I want you only thinking about me."

I nodded vigorously – with him so close to me and overpowering my senses, I don't think I had the capacity to think about anything else. I was powerless. I tilted my head and the hand that was on my waist came to rest just under my chin and lifted it closer to his face.

His lips grazed mine…

Like a whisper on my mouth, I could feel myself falling into a state of euphoria. Even with that whisper of a kiss I was undone. Noah moved his head back and looked me in the eyes – he seemed to be asking for permission. He seemed suddenly unsure, but my eyes must have shown him that I wanted this, because soon he was closing the space between us again and this time his lips were more confident and far from gentle. My arms slid around his neck, and I pulled him closer. I didn't realise a person could feel this way, that a person could make you feel this way. With just one kiss, Noah had stirred up a storm in my stomach. It was bliss! His lips pressed hard on mine and I was worried that there would be a bruise there later. But I didn't care, he could mark me as his – I *was* his, I had been for a while and hadn't even realised. At that moment I knew he was mine. His tongue slowly trailed across my lips. and I opened my mouth. The kiss deepened – this was nothing like anything else I had ever experienced. As his tongue entered my mouth a whole new sensation burst inside me and I could feel a moan escape at the sensations he aroused. I worried that I'd never again experience anything like this. His hands explored my body, caressing my sides, clutching my head and smoothing down my hair. Soon my arms were running all over his back. I ran my hand through that delicious chocolate brown hair, and I smiled against his lips, knowing that I had wanted to do that since the moment he drove into the camp. Now, at last, I could and I knew I wanted to keep doing it for a long time.

The kiss became a frenzy. I couldn't get near enough to him, and he felt the same. We were pulling at each other and becoming desperate. I had wanted this for so long – each moment I'd seen him, been around him, and all the words we'd shared. I had wanted to kiss him, and here I was now, doing exactly that.

I knew I should feel guilty. I was with Dean for goodness' sake – he was my boyfriend and I was cheating on him! But at that moment guilt was the last thing on my mind. I knew I should be pushing Noah away, stopping him, but it felt like I was coming home. It was the first thing to feel perfectly right in so long. It was crazy, but it was the truth.

Noah pulled away from me, both of us panting and gasping for breath.

"Wow, Cass… you have no idea," he panted, "how long… I have wanted to do that," Noah said with a grin. I smiled back at him. "Me too."

This had been one of the most heavenly moments in my life, but I was brought back down to earth by the thought of Dean. He had been so good to me, and here I was with another guy. I pushed Noah back.

"Oh god, oh god, oh god," I said as I stood further upright, "what have I done?!"

I stumbled away and he tried to reach for me, but I pushed him away. I couldn't do this. I had a boyfriend! I didn't know what to do. I started pacing. He tried to reach for me again.

"Hey Cassie... ," he started.

"No! No! I shouldn't have done that. No matter how much I wanted to, it was wrong. I have wanted to do that for ages, but this is all wrong."

The words streamed out of me and I couldn't control it. He just looked at me, pained, and I felt horrible. Whatever happened, someone was going to get hurt. While I liked Dean, there was no denying the connection with Noah and the way he made me feel. Something I thought only existed in fairy tales. I knew what I needed to do. Noah made his way towards me again.

"Cass, there are things you don't realise. Things you need to know," he told me, but I couldn't listen to one second more. I knew that whatever he'd say would make it impossible to go, because as soon as he started speaking I'd become powerless. At that moment I *needed* my power to sort things out with Dean.

"No! I need to go!" I almost yelled and set off. I ran through the forest as quickly as my legs would take me. Every inch of my body protested as I ran away. My desire to be near him was overwhelming, but I still carried on, willing my body to move forwards and not turn back. I knew it was what I had to do. I knew now that there was no way this could continue. And with only two more days at camp, I had no other choice.

"Cass, wait!" I heard Noah yell. He shouted something else, but I was too far away and his words became muffled by the sounds of the forest.

I had to find Dean! I needed to talk to him, explain things, sort this all out. I couldn't be with him any longer. I was meant to be with Noah. I knew that would kill him, but I couldn't lie any longer. But I needed to clear my head, first. There was no way I could speak to Dean coherently in this state. I knew where I could go to be alone, the place only me and Dean knew about, so I headed to the lake. Technically, I wasn't breaking the rule of not leaving the woods as it was all connected, but it was far enough away so that no one would see me or be around there collecting wood, and I knew Dean wouldn't be there because he was with his friends. At this point, I really missed Emma. She would've calmed me down and we could've sorted it together. After she said she was going to drop the wood I hadn't seen her, but I could find her later, although right now I needed to be on my own to try and understand what had just happened. I slowed slightly as I ran – I needed to catch my breath. I could see the lake glistening through the trees and knew I was getting close, safe in the knowledge that I was too far from the rest of the campers to be seen. I'd become pretty good at navigating these woods over the past few weeks so I knew where to find the clearing by the lake.

As I got closer, I could've sworn I heard giggling dancing in the breeze. I brushed it off, thinking it must have just been the wind playing games on me, but as the clearing came into sight I noticed it wasn't as empty as I was expecting. There were two people standing there. The sun was reflecting off the lake and shading their faces so I couldn't make them out. By the shape of their silhouettes and differences in height difference and build I could tell it was a guy and a girl, and a couple, judging by the affectionate way he seemed to hold her. Crazy that another couple had found the same spot as I did with my boyfriend. I paused and slowly backed away. Just because my life was in tatters, didn't mean I had to ruin what seemed to be a special moment for another couple. I turned away and thought I'd just head back to the tent.

But I recognised that voice – it sounded like Emma's. And that giggle was definitely hers. But who was the guy? Maybe she'd finally got it on with one of Dean's friends and that's why she never came back to me during the wood collecting. Oh, that would be so cute! They leaned closer and shared a sweet kiss. Emma had certainly kept this quiet. Oh wow, that's really cute! This definitely wasn't new love, seeing the way they were relaxed around each other. I hid myself behind one of the bigger trees and spied on them. But as they pulled away, Emma clearly whispered something. The boy threw his head back with laughter, causing the sun to light up his face. I saw who it was… oh my god!

Chapter 21

I was frozen... A whimper rose in my throat, but I couldn't keep quiet. A cry tore from me, and the couple – hands still clasped – looked over, startled, wondering where the noise had come from. Dean's eyes landed on me through the trees, so I quickly hid, hoping he hadn't seen it was me. I was going to approach them about it, but on *my* terms. Emma followed Dean's gaze and she finally saw me too. They looked like two rabbits caught in headlights. Anger tore through me.

I couldn't bear this. Here I was, racked with guilt about me and Noah while my apparent best friend and my boyfriend shared a loving moment together. I ripped through the forest and straight to the campsite. I heard footsteps behind me, but I didn't care, I couldn't see either of them. I ran as fast as I could, leaping over fallen trees and bursting into the campsite. My lungs were burning and I could hardly breathe, but I didn't care – I needed to get away. I looked around the campsite, thinking about where I could hide. I had an idea – I sprinted to the first aid tent and said I was feeling sick. It wasn't a lie. Clearly, the nurse saw how green my face was and sat me down with some water and a bucket. I sat and clutched my stomach, trying to regain my breath and calm my heart, but it wasn't working. I could feel my chest tightening and my heart beating faster. My breath was catching in my throat and I couldn't get anything out.

I scrambled for my phone, my hands shaking so hard I almost dropped it. I found Lexi's name and called her. She picked up immediately.

"Hey girl, what's up? You got an update for me?" she said cheerily. But I couldn't respond, my breathing was still too erratic.

"Cassie, what's going on?" Lexi asked again, and that was when the tears burst from my eyes.

"Help!" I choked out in a sob.

"Ok, OK, I'm here, this is going to be OK," she started. "Cassie, just focus on my voice and listen to what I'm telling you. Focus on my words and on what I tell you to do."

"Mmhmm" was the only reply I could manage. I closed my eyes.

"OK, we're going to do this together. Now, we need to control your breathing first so I need you to take a deep breath in. I'll count with you, OK? So, deep breath in. Yep, that's it, that's amazing. Now hold it – yep like that, well done – and now release. Yes Cassie, that's it, keep going."

She repeated this with me a few more times.

"Mmhhmm," I mumbled again.

"Now, what's around you Cassie? We need to distract you – tell me what you can see," she said calmly.

"Uh, um, I'm in the… the first aid tent," I stuttered, opening my eyes.

"OK, good, good, what colour are the walls?" she asked.

"The t… tent is blue," I said.

"OK, good. And what are you sitting on?" she asked.

"A… a plastic chair, it's grey and… and got a cushion on it," I managed

"Yes, well done, that's great. OK, now clench your fist and focus on how that makes you feel."

"Mmhmm," I said as I lifted my hand from where it was clutching the seat and squeezed it into a fist.

"Good, and now curl your toes," she said. I followed what she was telling me and focused on the sensation as the toes curled in my shoes. I took a few more deep breaths and calmed down.

"Thank you, Lexi," I murmured.

"OK good, you're welcome, you know I'm here any time. Now, are you going to tell me what that was all about."

"I… I kissed Noah." I confessed.

"Oh my god, Cassie, does Dean know?" she asked.

"No, not yet – I was going to find him to sort things out."

"Okay…?" She encouraged.

I took a deep breath. "I saw him kissing Emma."

"What the hell?!" she exclaimed.

I peeked out the window of the tent and saw Dean emerge from the woods with Emma close in tow.

"Yeah, it's a little bit of a mess," I agreed.

"A little bit? Oh hun, this is a whole state!" she added.

"Thanks Lex."

"What are you going to do?" she asked.

"Obviously, I'm breaking up with Dean and I guess I'll see about Noah."

"Well, that seems smart – piece of trash!" she commented.

We talked for a bit longer and Lexi got my mind slightly distracted asking about my parents. I told her I was blanking my dad, which she supported. She then told me a little more about her summer, and it was good to talk to her, although I was feeling so drained it was hard to concentrate on her words.

"Hey Cassie, I'll leave you alone for a little while. I can hear the distraction in your voice from here."

"Ha, ha, yeah, OK," I agreed.

"And I'll check in with you later, OK?"

"Yeah, thank you Lexi," I said once again.

"You really don't need to keep thanking me – I'll always be here to help you," she promised.

We quickly said goodbye to each other and with that I hung up.

I peeked out the window once again and noticed Dean walking around looking concerned, probably worried that he and Emma had been caught and that their dirty secret was out. Well, I'd let him worry a little longer. He scoured the campsite but couldn't find whoever he was looking for – me, perhaps. He found Emma once again, and they stood together, talking momentarily before they split up and continued to look around. I turned back and peered down at the bucket.

"I'm sorry, is it all right if I move to the corner, I'm feeling pretty faint and the sun is really hot?" I asked the nurse. She nodded, clearly worried by my state, and moved me over. Sitting here meant I was less likely to be seen by Dean and Emma if they came over to the first aid tent. I had no idea how long I sat there, the last few hours playing through my mind – my kiss with Noah, Dean and Emma, Noah, Dean, Emma. It was endless. I noticed the rest of the group returning to the campsite, and the nurse ran out to let Dan know that I was with her. He nodded, and I could see Noah crane his neck towards the first aid tent to try and see me, having obviously overheard what the nurse had just told Dan. Noah looked like a wreck and guilt filled my stomach. I shrunk down in my chair desperate to avoid any contact with him.

I eventually tried to close my eyes and give myself time to think, but when I did, the memory of seeing my- apparent-friend and my boyfriend kissing kept replaying in my mind. The sight of them together, the fact that they'd been going behind my back for so long – no wonder Emma always seemed more odd when I was around and sprung apart from Dean any time I got close. I sat up and stared down at the bucket, feeling nauseous and dizzy. The nurse came to check on me a few times but clearly she was still unhappy with my appearance – and I couldn't blame her. I felt light-headed and pale, and she could see it, giving me a sympathetic look. I wondered if she'd heard any of my conversation with Lexi, and maybe that was why she was being so nice and sympathetic now. Wow, not only was I the girl with the crumbling family life, but I was also the girl whose boyfriend cheated on her! This just kept getting better.

"Hi sweetheart, do you fancy any food," the nurse asked sweetly.

I shook my head weakly. I couldn't even manage words let alone any food, the thought alone made me sick to my stomach. She nodded and walked away. I sat there and watched the sun disappear behind the trees and wished for this day to be over.

In the evening the nurse told me I had a visitor.

"Who?" I asked – my voice was a hoarse whisper.

"He said his name was Noah," she replied. I sighed – I'd run away from him, and yet he still came to check on me. He never gave up, even after everything I put him through.

"No thank you, I still don't feel well" was my response. "Do you think you could tell him I'm not doing well?"

I glanced out the window and saw the nurse walk over to him and shake her head, probably telling him I was still ill. Slowly he walked away, looking defeated and glancing back multiple times. A desperation to run out to him and finish what we started washed over me, but I knew that I couldn't, no matter what Dean had done. He was still my boyfriend, if only in name, and I needed to end things with him before I even started to think about Noah. I felt tears sting my eyes and I looked back down at the bucket. This was not how my days were meant to go.

I asked if I could stay in the sick bay overnight, in case I had a problem. The nurse allowed it, clearly seeing that I was in no fit state. I didn't know what she thought was wrong with me but if it meant I could stay here then I wasn't complaining. I released the tense breath I'd been holding. I knew I couldn't be in close proximity to Emma, not after everything that had happened and all the lies. I'd told her about my parents and she stood there, pretending to be such a great friend while snogging my boyfriend behind my back. I'd had enough duplicity for one day – Emma could sit and worry about me for a little while. I hadn't seen her or Dean again since they emerged from the forest, but at that point I didn't care any more. They could do whatever they wanted. Clearly they were too wrapped up in themselves to even notice I wasn't there.

I laid down on the hard, uncomfortable bed, missing my soft sleeping bag, but I'd take this gross bed any day if it meant I didn't have to see Emma. My eyes grew heavy from the constant flow of tears, and I couldn't fight sleep for much longer. I closed my eyes and tried to get some rest, worried about what the next day would hold. Relieved that I now only had two and a half days left, I drifted into a deep and restless sleep, wishing tomorrow would never come.

The morning arrived too soon. The sweet bird song and shining sun gave the impression of a pleasant day, but I knew it was far from that.

"How are you feeling?" the nurse asked me sweetly.

"OK, not the best," I answered.

"I think some food would do you good. Do you want to go to breakfast?" she questioned.

"Not really," I said, "I don't want to be around people really in this state." The nurse nodded and understood.

"I'll go and get you some toast and bring it back," she said sweetly.

I laid back down and within five minutes she was back with the food. I ate the toast slowly, while the nurse watched to see if I could keep it down. It was just plain buttered toast, but I was thankful for the sustenance.

After around ten minutes, the nurse came back and said that Noah had come back again. With a deep breath I stood up and left the first aid tent to walk over to him. He looked so rough. His hair was a mess but not his usual cute mess. His eyes were dark and swollen, like he'd hardly had any sleep, and I knew that I'd caused this. The desperation to leap forward and embrace him in a tight hug was overwhelming. His eyes glued to the floor, as if he was scared to look at me. I couldn't blame him. I kissed him and then fled looking for Dean. The moment he looked up at me, I was taken aback by the misery in his eyes. The intensity and sadness, it was worse than when I pushed him away in the forest after our kiss. I almost couldn't bear to look at him, but I also couldn't turn my face away – I was addicted.

"Hi," I said weakly.

"Hey," he responded, "I saw the nurse bring out some food and realised you wouldn't be at breakfast so I thought I would come and see if you would speak to me." His voice was weak and exhausted, and I could feel my eyes filling with tears.

"Let's go outside," I said to him.

I needed some fresh air and hoped the summer breeze would make me feel less faint. We silently walked out into the sunlight and stood by the side of the tent.

"How are you feeling?" he asked.

"I'm OK – I just started to feel sick and dizzy yesterday," I answered.

"Is it because of", he paused, "you know... what happened with us?" he asked hesitantly, almost afraid of what the answer would be. I just shook my head, not trusting my words. He let out a breath.

"OK good, because I was really worried that I'd messed up everything and I didn't want to lose you and make everything horrible and awkward."

He stepped towards me and took my hands in his. I was quickly warmed from head to toe, just by his touch.

"I really like you Cass."

"Wait Noah," I interrupted, pulling my hands away from him and feeling immediately cold. "Look, there's some other stuff that came up yesterday and I need some time to think."

"Wait, what happened? Did someone do something?" he asked rapidly.

"Look there was something with Dean and Emma and I need to sort some stuff out."

"Oh" was all he said. He didn't seem shocked. "But I don't want to forget what happened."

He came closer and reached out for my hand, I let him take it gently.

"Cass, that was the best kiss I've ever had!" he told me. I just looked up at him, unable to formulate a response.

"What?!" I heard from behind us. "You two kissed? When?" Dean had just appeared from the food hall as breakfast was finishing. His face was full of rage and confusion.

"I knew I should never have trusted you!" he spat at Noah.

Dean lurched forwards towards him with a face of pure anger, his fist raised in the air, ready to come crashing down into him. I stepped in between them and in front of Noah to make sure no one was hurt.

"Hey!" I yelled at Dean, "you have no right to get mad at him, seeing as you've been sneaking around with my best friend."

That shocked him, he stumbled back.

"You knew?" he asked.

I nodded. But as soon as the words had left his mouth, he shot a glare at Noah.

"I can't believe you told her! I told you to keep it quiet – it was none of your business, you had no idea what was going on," Dean growled.

"No, I... ," Noah started.

"Hold on a minute!" I jumped in, "Noah didn't tell me, I saw the two of you in the forest yesterday! Wow, no wonder you were so good at cheating Dean, obviously you've had plenty of practice!"

"That was *you*?" he whispered.

"Yes, that was me. So don't talk to Noah about keeping things quiet. Try and explain to me how my boyfriend and my best friend kissing isn't *you* cheating on me and *her* lying." Dean was silenced by that. "Come on, I'm waiting. What kind of sad excuse are you going to give to try and worm your way out of that?"

At this point Emma appeared, clearly disturbed by the mayhem outside. As her eyes adjusted to the sun, she looked around and saw us. Her face broke into a look of horror. Dean turned back towards her.

"Oh, and look, here comes my best friend," I said, poison dripping from the words.

"She knows," he mumbled.

Emma walked over, her face a mix of regret, sadness and relief.

"Cassie, I'm so sorry, I didn't think Noah would actually tell you," she said.

"He didn't," I told her.

"She saw us yesterday," Dean filled in for her. Emma's face went white.

"How could you do that to me, Emma?" I pleaded.

"Look," Emma began to explain, "you and Dean had been uneasy for ages, since you started speaking to Noah really, and each time you got weird and disappeared me and Dean started to spend more time together, just the two of us." She looked over at Dean and sent him a weak smile. "And we just realised how well we got on and that we just... made sense. I'm sorry you had to find out this way, Cassie, but I'm not sorry that it happened."

"Oh, so it's my fault for leaving two people that I trusted alone for a while!" I spat out. "Well, you know what Emma, each time I wasn't around was not about Noah, it was more about my parents splitting up. But sorry, next time I'll remain happy all the time just to make sure my next boyfriend doesn't cheat on me with my friend."

"Come on Cassie, you're not exactly entirely innocent here either," Dean responded and Emma looked puzzled.

"OK, me and Noah kissed yesterday," I confessed.

Emma looked shocked, but also slightly happy too.

"So, you can't act all innocent, Cassie," Dean continued, "look, we just clearly aren't meant to be together."

I stared at him, shocked by his matter-of-fact tone. But I knew he was right. I sighed and nodded.

"Look Dean, maybe you're right, clearly we weren't meant to be together, but that doesn't excuse the lying. I may not be entirely innocent, but me and Noah kissed once and I pushed him away and immediately went to find you to talk about it, and where are you? Making out with my friend in our spot Dean, our spot!" I was almost yelling. Dean and Emma were both silent after that, and I was glad I'd finally got to them.

"Look Cassie……" Dean started, but I wasn't prepared to listen to anything they said.

"Dean, I'm sorry but I can't talk to you two right now. It's one thing for my friend to be with my boyfriend – well my ex-boyfriend now, just for the record – but it's another thing for you to have lied about it for so long." I took a deep breath. "If Noah knew about it then clearly the kiss that I saw wasn't just a single moment. And that makes me wonder how long this has all been going on."

They both shook their heads and looked down.

"And at that spot Dean? Really?"

He looked as guilty as he had ever been.

"Look I can't do this," I continued. "Dean, I know you're right and I know I'm not innocent either but I just can't bear the idea that I've been around you two for so long, thinking things were OK, and all the time you've been away with each other every time I haven't been there. Sneaking around and thinking how stupid I was, mocking me while I wasn't there because I didn't know that the people I had become closest to me were together the whole time!"

I couldn't stop myself and the words just flowed as the tears streamed from my eyes. I knew I wasn't innocent, but for my *friend* to do that to me was just too painful.

"Please Cassie……" Emma tried to speak.

I just shook my head at her – I couldn't bear to hear one more word from them. I turned to walk away, and Noah followed me.

"Cass, look," he grabbed my shoulder to turn me around. I spun to look at him.

"How could you have known? How could you not have told me?! How am I supposed to trust you!" I wept.

"Look I didn't want to hurt you, and it wasn't my place to say. I didn't want to mess things up. I was hoping they'd tell you first! I told them that, they needed to tell you."

"When?" I asked him.

"W… what?" he stuttered.

"When did you find out?" I asked him again.

"Just before the trampoline park," he mumbled.

"So *that* was why you tried to fight him in dodgeball and why you cornered me at the beach?" I asked, accusingly.

"That wasn't the only reason, but I thought that after I saw the things with Dean and Emma he'd tell you so you could dump him and you'd finally stop denying what was between us," he explained.

"But how can I? You knew my boyfriend cheated on me and you kept it to yourself!"

He responded with a look of shame.

"I know Cass, but I didn't know how to tell you and I didn't want to be the one to break the news to you. it was down to them quite frankly! "

"Noah, my parents split up because they always argued, and they argued because they never told each other anything, and now here I am face to face with a boy I really like but not even sure if I can trust him. How can we build a relationship from that?" I asked and waited for a response.

"But Cass, that was one of the reasons I wanted *him* to tell you! You already had so much with your family, and you told me I was the only one that you had confided in. I didn't want to break that. I was hoping he, or even Emma, would actually do the right thing and tell you."

"I understand that, but my dad would lie to my mum. That's what started pushing them away from each other in the first place. This relationship could be doomed before it even started if I'm constantly worried that you could lie to me in the future!" Noah looked at me and I could see him feeling defeated once again.

"I never wanted to hurt you Cass. I did all of this to try and protect you."

"I know you wouldn't want to hurt me, but I'm still standing here hurt. I just can't do this right now Noah. That kiss was amazing, honestly it was, but right now it's just too hard." I turned away and walked towards my tent.

"Cass, please," he begged as he tried to reach for me.

I recoiled from his touch. "I just can't talk to you. Maybe later, but I can't now. Noah… please understand, please just give me time."

Noah looked to the ground, as if he wanted to say something but knew he needed to bite his tongue. He stepped back and accepted what I had said. I ached as I turned away from him, but I needed to. Every fibre in my body was telling me to go back and stay in his arms, but I couldn't. I needed to understand things before I could go to him. If I stayed with him for too long then I wouldn't be able to leave.

I needed to think this through. Every part of my body wanted to be with Noah, but I couldn't ignore the fact that he had avoided telling me for so long.

And then there were Dean and Emma. Maybe Dean was right and we didn't belong together. But I couldn't deny the fact that they lied. Emma had asked me constantly about Noah, and every time I asked *her* about any guy, she brushed it off. Of course, she couldn't exactly say she liked my boyfriend, but she stood there constantly and lied to my face. Clearly, she only asked about Noah to see if there was a chance that things might happen, so that I could break it off with Dean, allowing her and Dean to be together without having to tell me anything about them cheating. I had to admit, they did seem happy together but they still lied to me. I knew I'd been turning away from Dean, but the lying was the part that hurt the most. They were the two people I had become closest to over this summer and now… well, I didn't even know any more.

As I walked around the campsite on my own, trying my best to avoid anything to do with Dean or Emma, Dan called us all over.

"So, our activity for today is a trip to the zoo."

Some people groaned, but there was a general murmur of excitement. The zoo would be good – it was a big place, which would make it easy to avoid talking to Dean and Emma or even bumping into them. I stood to the side on my own. This trip seemed like an easy win.

"We'll be leaving in about twenty minutes," Dan announced, "please go and get your stuff ready and we'll meet back here and get going!"

He clapped, and with that the group began to disperse. Emma and Dean hesitated, glancing over at me. But as soon as I noticed them, I turned away. I walked back to the tent, hoping they wouldn't follow me. I quickly shoved everything in my bag and walked out again. As I left the tent, I walked straight into a big wall of a chest. Arms flew out to stop me tripping over and I saw straight away who it was.

"Woah, you OK?" a deep voice asked.

"Thanks, Noah," I coughed. His scent was dancing up my nostrils and I was having difficulty ignoring what it was doing to me.

"I just wanted to see how you were doing," he said sweetly.

"I'm not the best, but I know that Dean was right – we weren't right for each other and now he has the chance to be happier with Emma, I guess." I shrugged.

"So, what does that mean for us?" he asked me, a hint of hope lacing his question.

"Look Noah, I understand about Dean and Emma being together… but I can't ignore all of the lying." He looked deflated. "I just need some time," I continued.

He nodded and backed away.

"I meant what I said about us, though, Cass. I don't want to forget what happened – it truly was one of the best kisses ever," he told me with a sad smile and turned and walked away. I watched him go, and when he was further away, I fled from the tent, desperately trying to avoid any interaction with Emma.

Chapter 22

My desperation at avoiding Emma and Dean was exhausting but also a success. When I got to the coach, I rushed on and sat at the front, knowing that they'd sit at the back – the way we always had – and Noah would sit in the middle. Emma and Dean boarded the coach and soon noticed me at the front. I faced away and she looked deflated. I turned to look out of the coach window and could see their reflections vaguely in the window. They looked helplessly at each other but soon seemed resigned to the fact I wouldn't speak to them and walked to the back of the coach. I didn't want to be mad at them forever and part of me knew that I'd be able to talk with them at some point and maybe we could become friends again sometime. Maybe things would be better as friends. But not right now…

Noah soon followed suit onto the coach and saw me sitting at the front. I quickly placed my bag on the seat next to me to make it perfectly clear that I wouldn't speak with him. But instead of looking disheartened, he raised an eyebrow as he looked down at the bag and grinned. With a little shake of his head, he chuckled and continued to the middle of the bus to sit with his friends. He seemed as if he didn't even care any more, rather he found it humorous, I don't know which one I hated more. My head fell against the window, and I stared into the surrounding fields as the coach pulled out of the campsite and we set off for the zoo.

It felt like one of the longest drives I've ever had. It was in fact only fifteen minutes but sitting there- on my own- with the pressure of Noah's stare and the thought of Emma and Dean at the back of the coach was too much to handle. I shut my eyes, wishing my thoughts would subside, but no luck.

It was a huge relief when we arrived at the zoo – at least there I'd have something else to focus on. As we stepped off the coach, I shoved my earphones in and stood with the group as Dan explained when we'd be leaving and where to meet. I saw Noah's worried glances. Emma looked over too, desperate to catch my attention it seemed, hoping for some unspoken communication. I couldn't give her the satisfaction. I was remaining strong after all she'd done to me – the lying, the betrayal – it wasn't right. I knew I couldn't blame Dean – we'd been drifting apart for a while now and I'd been crushing hard on Noah. But with Emma? I hadn't exactly known her a lifetime, but she'd become closer to me in these few weeks than other friends had over a number of years. She'd sat there and listened to each moment with Noah, encouraged me with Dean and tried to comfort me– and yet she was going behind my back all this time.

Dan finished his instructions and we were all free to go. I turned quickly and shot off in a random direction to get away from the group and avoid any interactions. When I was happy that I was far enough away, I slowed down to a walk and enjoyed my surroundings. I looked around and realised that, despite the mess, this was a pretty cool place. I couldn't remember the last time I'd gone to a zoo, so it was nice to be able to enjoy this trip. I grabbed one of the maps they were giving away and decided what I wanted to see.

I made my way over to the meerkats first. They were great, but, as I stood there, I started feeling empty. A hollowness I haven't felt since before camp. I knew what it was – it just sucked that I couldn't do anything about it. But I wouldn't let this ruin the day!

I shook myself and started over to the aviary. It seemed cool so I decided to go and find somewhere to sit. It was a short walk and I stopped to grab a drink. I waited in line for a while and as I was looking around, I noticed Dean and Emma walking in the other direction, holding hands and leaning close together. Emma's face was turned to the side. I couldn't make out much against the sun but I could tell how happy and relaxed she was. I hadn't seen her that happy for a while, really at all since I'd known her, and it was good she had found something that made her feel like that.

Seeing here like that, things started clicking into place. The way her face would drop each time I was with Dean and when Dean and I held hands or kissed. How disheartened she seemed when I walked up to them when they were together and she knew she'd have to hide her feelings once again. I knew how hard that was – when all you wanted to do was shout it from the rooftops. She had loved Dean but didn't want to do anything because of me. I wondered what the deciding factor was that made her take the leap and kiss him. Maybe it was me and Noah – only a matter of time. I couldn't hold that against her, being with who she wanted. Something

I wish I could do. I hadn't treated Dean right either, and Emma seemed to really care about him. If they could make each other happy the same way that Noah made me happy then I wouldn't stop them or make them feel guilty. She'd gone after what she wanted, the same way I'd wanted to do with Noah. The only difference was that she did it without fear.

With that thought, I turned to look at Dean. He seemed comfortable with Emma and maybe he seemed happy with me, but with Emma it looked right. They made sense and I was glad that he was in a better relationship. I'd wronged him. I knew I had feelings for Noah long before I finally admitted it to myself, and for me to stay with Dean for so long was wrong. I smiled as I looked at them – they were happy, and I knew I would be too… eventually.

The people in front of me got their drinks and I moved up the queue and ordered my drink. Once I played I walked towards the aviary. It was a grand glass dome and I was surrounded by glorious, towering emerald trees and a collection of colourful birds. I was in awe as these beautiful creatures flew about my head. After a few moments of taking in the amazing scene, I noticed a bench in the corner, which seemed like a good place to hide for a while. I walked over and sat down. I pulled a book from my bag and began reading as the birds chirped away above me.

The drama of the previous day started to wash away. It had been a while since I'd properly sat down and read. Over the past few weeks, I'd been so swept up with the new romance and the excitement of camp that I'd forgotten about my friends at home and the things I love, like reading. At that moment, I grabbed my phone and dropped Lexi a message.

Me: *Hey, how have you been?*

Lexi: *Oh, hey stranger, I'm good!*

How's your lover boy?

Me: *Well… that's a bit of a long story.*

Lexi: *Tell!*

Me.

Everything!

Me: *It's a little complicated.*

Lexi: *I got time. ;)*

Me: *Hmm OK, call?*

No more than ten seconds later, Lexi's picture flashed on my screen, and I answered.

"OK, come on, talk to me!" Lexi stated.

"Oh, and hello to you too," I laughed.

"Yeah, yeah, we're best friends. There's no need to say hello when there's gossip. Now, talk to me!"

"Ugh fine!" I conceded. "So, first of all, me and Dean broke up."

"Wait, what?! That was quick, what happened?" Lexi started.

"Uh, come on, you can't be surprised. He kissed Emma. And don't play dumb – you know how much I like Noah. I mean, you knew way before *I* even did," I told her.

"Well, that's true. I could've told you to stop messing about a long time ago," she said. I sighed, knowing she was right.

"Well why did you Lex?" I questioned.

"Cassie, I love you but you have always been too independent for your own good. You wouldn't have accepted it if I had told you, you needed to work it out yourself. And you did!" She confessed.

"OK, but I've calmed down now after my little meltdown phone call yesterday, so how about I fill you in on the whole thing." I took a breath.

"Yes, yes, go on," she said.

And with that I told Lexi everything about yesterday – the close call in "capture the flag", the whole story with the kiss, me finding Dean and Emma kissing in *my* spot, discovering that Noah already knew… everything.

"Are you still there, Lexi?" I asked. Still nothing. "LEXI!"

"Woah, sorry there, Cassie, that wasn't what I was expecting to hear at all. Man, that sounds hot!"

"Yep," I agreed.

"And you caught Dean kissing Emma? In *your* spot?"

"Yep," I said again.

"Well, first of all," Lexi said, "I totally called it for you and Noah. I mean, I could hear how much you liked him in your voice the first time you told me about him." I could hear the smugness in her voice.

"Ugh, yes thank you Lexi."

"OK, and this whole Dean and Emma thing," Lexi continued, "they're like, together now properly? How do you feel about that? Because yesterday… you were a pretty big wreck."

I took a pause.

"I'm not mad, really, or upset. They seemed good together, and honestly part of me was relieved when it all came up because I had a reason to end things."

The minute the words left my mouth I felt guilty. I meant it but not in a malicious way.

"Oh," Lexi said.

It dawned on me at that point that I didn't care about what Dean had done because I didn't love him. I was fine with him and Emma because *I* didn't want to be with him.

"Is that crazy?" I asked Lexi. "I mean that I'm not bothered by them being together."

"No, I don't think so," she replied, "I think that you had never had a cute guy who liked you and hadn't had a relationship before, so you convinced yourself that you wanted to be with him. I'm not saying you didn't *like* him, but it seemed that as soon as Noah came along you were completely taken with him. He was the right guy for you Cassie."

She stopped for a minute, and I took in what she was saying. She was right.

"Cassie, I really think that as soon as Noah came along, there wasn't a chance for Dean."

"Yeah, I think you're right. But,'' I took a deep breath, "Noah knew about Dean and Emma days before I found out and he didn't tell me. How am I meant to ignore that? Dad did the same thing to mum and look at their relationship now!"

"Oh god, come on, Cassie," Lexi started, "what do you expect? He'd just seen the boyfriend of the girl he liked with her friend and had no idea what to do! My bet is that he wanted them to tell you themselves. You might see that as a lie but actually Noah was just giving them the time to do what was right!"

I knew she was right.

"Yeah, that's what he told me." I sighed.

"And Cassie? Noah is *not* your dad, and you're only starting out. He didn't lie to you on purpose – he was giving Dean and Emma a chance to do the right thing."

"You're right, thanks Lex, I just don't know what to do! I want to be with Noah. Damn, I really want to, but I don't know what to do!"

"Cassie, only you can decide what you want to do. Either realise he didn't want to hurt you and wanted Dean and Emma to do the right thing or keep thinking that he was lying – and that's it. But Cassie…"

"Yeah?"

"From what you've told me about him, I can't imagine he'd just blatantly lie to you or want to hurt you purposely. If you keep pushing him away, he'll give up and you'll be the only one left miserable – and you deserve to be happy, Cassie."

As she spoke, I heard footsteps and the rustling of the trees. I stood up to get a better view and stepped closer to the noise. As I turned the corner, around the bushes and plants, I came face to face with Noah. My breath caught in my throat.

He looked at me with a tentative smile and raised his hand in a timid wave.

"Look Lexi, I need to call you back."

"Wait, what?" she asked.

"I... I just need to go," I told her as my eyes held Noah's.

"Cassie, you're sounding..."

Lexi's last words were cut off as I hung up and put the phone back in my pocket. My eyes were still glued to Noah's face.

"Fancy seeing you here," he joked.

I could tell he was trying to hide his feelings, but his distress showed through the cracks in that delicate smile.

"It seemed like a good place to escape to," I told him with a gesture down to my book, which rested open on the bench.

"Ah," Noah replied.

We fell into an odd silence, just staring at each other. I was unsure what, and even if, I should say anything.

"I just," Noah started, "I just wanted to see how you were doing."

He made a step towards me. My eyes were drawn to the movement of his feet.

"I'm O... OK," I stuttered.

"Well, that's good to hear," he replied, taking another step closer to me. I looked up to see that delicate smile replaced with a mischievous one.

"Yeah, I guess so," I said, "I just wanted to hide out for today. I'm getting used to things, just not there completely yet."

"Well, it's a start," he whispered.

With one final step he was dangerously close. I looked down and noticed his boots were pressed right up against my

Converses. He gently placed his index finger under my chin and brought my head up so he could meet my eye.

"Hi," he whispered to me with a smile. He leant closer and I could feel his lips come near. My eyes fluttered shut and I started to lean closer to him. I began to melt into his touch, his embrace.

Then I remembered him keeping the secret from me, the way he knew about Emma and Dean and let me remain ignorant. I froze, my eyes flew open and I pushed him away.

"I can't right now, Noah. I'm sorry, but not yet." I could feel tears begin to sting my eyes. "I'm not saying never, but I need a little more time."

I couldn't bear to look at him for one minute more. I turned back to the bench, grabbed my book and shoved it in my bag, and ran out of the aviary, not looking back once.

I checked the time and realised I still had another hour before we had to meet at the coach. I pulled out my map and checked what kind of places I could go and see. The penguins looked sweet, so I started making my way to their enclosure. As I got closer, I could see Dean and Emma standing together, his arm was around her and her head resting on his shoulder. It seemed like such a natural action. I had never really had that with Dean. When we sat together like that I felt uncomfortable or weird, and when his arm was around me I just felt odd. My head had never properly fit or my arm felt odd around his waist. I stopped and looked at them for a minute. As Emma raised and turned her head to talk to Dean, she spotted me out of the corner of her eye. Guilt flooded her face as she stepped away from Dean. She seemed to want to come over to me, but I shook my head at her with a little weak smile. She stopped in her tracks and made no further move towards me.

My mind was racing. Emma probably still thought I was upset at her about Dean, but the truth was, those feelings had passed. I didn't mind about her and Dean any more – in fact, I didn't really care at all. They did what they felt was right, although they could've told me sooner. Then I realised that I should've told Dean about Noah sooner. We'd both rushed into this summer fling, swept away by fleeting feelings, and I don't think either of us had been truly happy while we were together. Mistakes happen and it wasn't like this was a lifelong relationship. I'd still had fun and met some good people – it had just gone a bit differently than I'd expected, which was OK. But part of me hoped that my summer wouldn't end with just that summer fling. This time, I wanted the summer *romance* and I knew what I had to do.

Chapter 23

After the penguin enclosure, I made a swift move to the food area and sat down to read my book – the safest option for avoiding other people. I put my earphones on at full volume while I sat there reading for the final hour. I'd seen what I wanted to and I wasn't going to enjoy the trip if I had to look over my shoulder every thirty seconds for any unwanted company. Sitting down in a corner, where no one could sneak up on me, seemed like the best option. Or that's what I thought.

As I sat at my table, I noticed a figure approaching. I had my head in my book, which meant I could only see his trainers. I prayed that he wouldn't sit with me, but he settled opposite and, despite my attempt to ignore him, placed his hand on my book so I couldn't read. I lowered the book and glared at this intruder. A wave of surprise washed over me when I saw who it was... Connor. I hadn't really spoken to him since the trampoline park, and even then, he'd only said a few words to me.

"Hello?" I asked more than said, looking quizzically at him.

"Hey," he said with a grin.

"Can I help you with something? I'm kind of busy," I said, with a nod down towards my book and getting slightly irritated. I mean, there weren't tons of people at this camp, but by the way they kept popping up today, you'd think there were hundreds of them.

"Yes, it looks like a real page turner," he joked. "Get it?" he added goofily.

I looked at Conor blankly.

"Because you know… it's a book," he explained, with a stupid smile on his face. I stared at him blankly again and he opened his mouth to continue.

"Yes, I got it Connor," I told him flatly.

"It was funny, right?" he asked, fishing for something.

"Absolutely hilarious," I deadpanned, "can I actually help you with anything Connor because I would really like to get back to my book."

"Oh, yeah right. Well, I mean I realised I haven't spoken to you properly for a while and things with Dean seem a little… awkward if you know what I mean."

I rolled my eyes. There it was, the last thing I wanted to talk about at that moment.

"Um OK, thank you for the reminder. Your point being?" I asked, looking back to my book, getting bored.

"Well, you know, if you ever want to make him jealous, here I am!"

"Wait, what?" That was the last thing I was expecting Connor to say and my head shot up.

"You know, he's apparently all lovey-dovey with Emma now and you're here on your own. I'm just offering my services if you ever want to annoy him or whatever. I can help," he said as he leant back in his chair smiling at me cockily.

"OK Connor," I started and placed my book on the table staring right at him, "I'm sure that whatever crazy idea you have going on in your mind right now seems great to you… but what you're saying right now, well it just sounds crazy. I don't want to make Dean jealous. I don't like him any more, and I don't know how your *girlfriend* would appreciate you going around all summer trying to get with other girls."

I looked at him, but he just sat there smiling back at me.

"So, I'm going to put my book back up and my earphones back in and pretend this conversation never happened, OK?"

"Whatever you say," Connor responded with a wink, as he stood up, pushed the chair back and flashed me a smile, before turning and walking away.

This day could officially not get any weirder, and it wasn't even over. A day and a half left here, then I would be home. The thought of seeing my friends and being back home in my safe zone filled me with joy. But I couldn't shake off the nagging feeling that part of me didn't want this precious camp bubble to pop.

The fateful hour struck… It was time to head back to the coach. Now, dear reader, don't roll your eyes at me for being dramatic – this was how I felt. Thoughts flying around my head a hundred miles a minute. Would Noah try to kiss me again? Could I resist him a third time? Would Emma try to talk to me? What was she thinking at the moment? What about Dean? I mean, I didn't know what he'd do, and I didn't want to find out.

I made sure I hung back silently as the coach was boarded. As soon as I saw Noah, Dean and Emma get on and get settled I felt it was safe for me to board and find a seat a good distance away from all of them. Once again, I decided to sit at the front of the coach, away from Dean, Emma and Noah. As I jumped on, I saw Noah. He was sitting next to *that* girl again. I'd completely forgotten about her since Noah blew up at me about her. After everything that had happened with me and Noah I'd almost hoped that he would be done with her. But here she was, settled in next to him and laughing about some stupid story. I rolled my eyes at her, knowing she was just being ridiculous.

That was until she leaned over and stroked his arm. Envy and anger flared up in my stomach, and it took all my strength not to yank her hair right there and pull her off her seat. Then I remembered that I was the one who had rejected Noah in the aviary today – and many times before that. He wasn't mine, he could do what he wanted. Not that being mine seemed to stop others from doing what they wanted, as my mind drifted to Dean.

At that moment, I realised I had been staring for a while and had almost burned a hole in *that* girl's head. He glanced up and our eyes met, although 'met' is an understatement. Every single time I'd laid eyes on Noah since we'd first met, I'd felt that jolt. No matter how many times it happened, the connection was overpowering.

I quickly forced my eyes away from him. I looked out of the window, I shoved my headphones on and closed my eyes. Noah was confusing me. I'd rejected him a lot now and maybe he was tired of waiting around for me. Maybe Lexi was right and he was now fed up with me, trying it on with that other girl now, seeing as *she* hadn't rejected him constantly and been horrible. I pulled out my phone to shoot a text message to Lexi.

Me: *I need to forgive Noah, don't I?*
Lexi: *Wow she's finally cracked it!*
Lexi: *Yes, you do, you stupid girl!*
Me: *You do know how to deliver things sweetly don't you!*
Me: *No sugar coating here.*
Lexi: *Oh, come on, you've been acting crazy.*

The time for sugar coating is over.

I rolled my eyes at her message. It was a tough way to tell me, but I knew I needed it.

Me: *I don't know how, what do I do?*
Lexi: *Cassie, think about what is more important –*
being happy with the guy that clearly loves you
or keeping hold of this crazy idea about him hurting you
Lexi: *It's up to you.*
Me: *Argh, OK.*

I put my phone away and looked out of the window. Lexi was right, Noah made me happy, and *I* was happy and comfortable when I was around him. I had never felt this way before and couldn't push away and deny my thoughts. I couldn't just throw it all away because I wanted to be stubborn. It was crazy for me to ignore and attack him for giving Dean and Emma the time to tell me themselves. It isn't him I should've been mad at – I knew that now.

I sat back in my seat, knowing I had to do something, but what? I wanted to do something proper for him, not just go and talk to him. Stuck on this coach, there was nothing I could do, so I closed my eyes and drifted away with the music. My mind floated back to our kiss in the woods, the way his lips felt on mine, the feel of his hands running over my body, the ghost of his touch dancing over my skin. Every memory was burnt onto my body. It was a feeling I couldn't get rid of, and didn't want to get rid of either.

I drifted off for longer than I realised because in no time the coach came to a halt. We'd arrived back at the campsite. It was mid-afternoon and we still had a few hours before dinner. As I stepped off the coach, my eyes adjusted to the blazing sun. It was glorious, and I started walking aimlessly. I wasn't sure what to do or where to go, but I was happy. I noticed Dean and Emma walking over to the food hall and she glanced over at me. Her face was still full of worry and guilt, but I sent her a weak smile and kept walking. I decided I'd make my way to the lake – not to *the* spot – just to sit. Hiding away serenely, it seemed like a good place to be right now. I ambled through the woods and found a nice spot – a short little pier that jutted a few feet into the lake. I discarded my Converses and dangled my feet over the water.

I looked over the lake and realised something – I felt calm. There wasn't this sense of missing anything or emptiness. I can't lie and say that there wasn't a part of me that wanted Noah, but that's exactly what it was – a want. I didn't feel like I needed him or anything else to complete me. Then it dawned on me, the feelings I used to have of a missing piece of me or the sense of hollowness weren't due to me not having someone... It was a loss of myself. Over these past few weeks, I've become more comfortable with myself. Maybe that was in part the way that Noah made me feel, but I finally felt happy with "me". I didn't need a guy or anyone to compete with me, I just had to accept who I was.

Noah had let me do that. He hadn't pressured me or tried to make me choose. He sat back and let me do what I needed to do. He had liked me for how I was and hadn't attacked me for anything. This is why I loved him!

I looked up from my book. I knew I was just speaking in my head, but I'd finally realised I loved him! He had done so much for me. He kept his distance, he respected what I said, he cared about me – and I loved him. That was why I couldn't be with Dean properly and that was why it didn't work well with him. Lexi had been right – ugh, god, how could she see it before I did? Dean really did have no hope when Noah was around. I was taken by *him* and I wasn't complaining.

I didn't need anyone else, I understood that now, but I wanted my friends back and I wanted Noah next to me. I wanted to be in his arms – I wanted that! I knew that whatever I was going to do had to be done tonight. I only had one day left after this and I couldn't miss my chance, or have to say "I love you" and "goodbye" in the same conversation! It would be too hard. I grabbed my phone.

Me: *I love him!*
Lexi: *You what girl?*
Me:
I!

Love!
Him!
Lexi: *OMG, finally!*
Lexi: *What are you going to do about it?*
Me: *I don't know yet.*
Me: *But I'm doing it tonight!*
Lexi: *Yes!*
Lexi: *Tell me how it goes. ;)*

I put my phone back and laid down on the pier. Looking up at the clouds, I drifted into a blissful feeling of calm, happy on my own. I grabbed my book and dived into the fantasy story. I was so calm that I lost track of time and soon enough noticed it became a little colder and the sun a little dimmer. It will be dinner time soon. I pulled out my phone to give my mum a call.

"Hi sweetie," she said as soon as she picked up.

"Hi mum."

"How are you doing?" she asked. She seemed less tired than she had the last time I spoke to her.

"I'm doing pretty well actually, mum."

"Oh, that's lovely sweetie, what's happened?"

"Well, Dean and I broke up," I told her.

"Oh no, honey, what happened?" she asked, and I took a deep breath and told her everything about seeing Dean and Emma.

"Oh sweetie, that sounds horrible."

"But mum, it's good. I finally realised how I felt about Noah, and Dean is much happier too."

"Well... that *is* an interesting turn of events," she said hesitantly, "so are you with Noah now?"

"No, I'm scared mum. It turns out he knew about Dean and Emma for a few days, and he didn't tell me anything and... I'm scared mum. I'm worried that if he's already lied, or at least kept things from me, then he could do it again."

"Oh sweetheart, that's silly," she started.

"Mum, it's what dad did," I interrupted, and she was silent on the other end of the line. "That's what happened between you two – he kept things from you and look what's happened now!"

"Oh honey, no! Your father and I did have some issues and we soon became distant from each other, but it wasn't him lying. We kept things from each other and we both needed to – need to – change and learn. But sweetie, please don't let what's happening with me and your dad stop you from being happy or from being who you want to be with."

"Mum, I'm scared, scared to let him in," I confessed.

"Everything that's worthwhile will be scary – that's what shows it's worth doing. You can't let your fear push you away from things that could be great."

"I guess you're right," I sighed, "I'm just scared mum, I really like him."

"That isn't a bad thing, sweetie. Opening your heart for new people and possibilities can be good, and me and your father will sort things out, we won't be like this forever."

I could feel the tears begin to sting my eyes.

"I don't know what to do mum," I whimpered, my emotions now overwhelming.

"Sweetie, it doesn't matter what you do, as long as you follow your heart. Just show your feelings, and if it's right, then it will be OK." I could hear the sympathy in her voice. "I love you, sweetie, and I know you'll be OK."

"What do you think I can do?" I murmured, desperate for advice.

"You need to talk to him. From what you've told me, he seems to really like you. It's time you told him that, honey," she said tenderly.

"OK, I know what I need to do. Thank you, mum, I love you."

"I love you too, sweetheart."

"I can't wait to come home," I added.

"I can't wait to see *you*," she told me.

We said goodbye and I hung up the phone.

With a groan, I sat up and put my shoes back on before heading to the campsite. I saw Noah walk into the food hall as I stepped out of the woods, and my heart filled with joy at the sight of him. He seemed weaker, though. I wanted to run over and kiss him right there, but I knew he deserved more than that. He deserved an explanation more than anything. I just needed the right time to talk to him, and right before dinner, as he was walking into the food hall, wasn't the right time. I joined the rest of the campers and went to get food.

As I walked in, Noah already had his dinner and was at his table with his friends – so I knew this wasn't the time for a declaration of love. He was sitting down, playing with his food and not paying any attention to the things around him. *That* girl was sitting next to him and constantly talking, but

Noah clearly couldn't care less. Just thinking of me finally confessing my feelings and not having to hide it made my heart burst. This was all so new. I'd never been in love before. It was wonderful – my heart warmed and I was thrilled at the prospect of what could be waiting for me. I grabbed my food and sat down at a table on my own – which felt a little weird. I had forgiven Emma and Dean but I wasn't ready to jump back into friendship and slip into our old ways. I needed to talk to them properly and get my thoughts out. I glanced over at Noah a few times, and each time his eyes were already on me. It made me blush and I couldn't wait to talk to him. I wanted to walk right over and kiss him but knew I wanted to wait until I would have time to enjoy the moment. I ate my food in peaceful solitude.

Chapter 24

"So, I'm sure the keen-eyed among you have noticed that no dessert has been served," Dan announced as dinner came to a close. "This is because tonight we'll be having a bonfire. There'll be s'mores and hot chocolate." A cheer erupted from the campers. "We'll start it up in about thirty minutes. That will give you time to grab warm clothes and blankets or whatever will keep you from getting cold. I know there's a fire, but I can assure you that it *will* get cold. So, when you're ready, make your way to the field, past the first aid tent. Leaders will be waiting with the hot chocolate and s'mores."

My heart filled with hope when I heard the plan. This will be my moment – I could do this and finally be able to stop hiding my feelings. As soon as we were dismissed, I rushed out and went to get ready, stylish but comfortable was what I wanted to go for. I grabbed a soft woollen jumper and I threw it on over my crop top. I changed my shorts to leggings as my legs started to get cold and switched my Converse for some thick socks and my wellie boots. Checking my hair in my compact mirror, I brushed it through and left it straight and soft down my back. As I was adding a final layer of mascara to my eyelashes, Emma walked in.

"Oh… hi," she said, unsure of herself.

"Hey," I said to her with a quick smile, "can we talk later?"

Emma's face turned to a mixture of happiness and concern. I assumed she was worried about what I'd say after I'd been avoiding and ignoring her all day.

"Oh, yeah, yeah, of course," she said, stumbling on her words.

"Great," I said as I stood up, "I'll see you later."

I made my way out of the tent and almost raced over to the field, where the flames of the fire were starting. Emma followed me with her eyes, clearly confused by my sudden change of attitude.

I started towards the site of the campfire, where I could see the flames of the fire getting taller and taller. As the sun went down, the dancing flames seemed even more prominent. Excitement bubbled up inside me at the thought of being face to face with Noah, but as I neared the campfire, I noticed he wasn't there. I sat down on one of the benches and watched the flames leap into the air. After a few moments, I grabbed a hot chocolate and sat back down. A few minutes later, I felt the bench dip beside me.

"So?" Emma asked, expectantly.

I turned to her and saw worry on her face. I glanced over her shoulder and noticed Dean sitting on a bench further down with his friends. He tried not to make it obvious, but I could see him look over occasionally, to try and see what was going on.

"Right," I started, "I wanted to tell you I'm fine with you and Dean." Emma gave me a relieved smile.

"Dean seems so much happier with you," I explained, "and I'd been hiding my feelings for Noah for so long."

"Oh god, Cassie, that's so good to hear!" She leaped up and tackled me into a hug. I laughed.

"I can't blame you and I can't blame Dean," I said. "I wasn't good to him or with him and we can now both obviously admit that I was crushing hard on Noah… a lot longer than I cared to admit." She laughed at that and agreed. "All I want to say is that I forgive you and I want you to be together. When I saw you at the zoo you seemed so happy together."

"You weren't mad at that point?" she asked me.

"What? No, of course not. I saw you two and how happy you looked. It was nice to see, and you both seemed much more comfortable with each other than Dean and I were," I smiled.

"Oh, that's a relief – you just seemed mad, your face seemed…" she paused for a moment, "troubled".

"Ah right, that. Yeah, something had just happened with Noah in the aviary while we were at the zoo, and I was mad at myself really. I'd been hiding things and lying to myself and it was horrible. But I've realised that it was all crazy," I told her, and she nodded.

"Does this mean I have my friend back?" she asked. I nodded back at her with a smile.

"Oh, thank god! Don't get me wrong, I love Dean, but I need my girl," she said.

I gave her a shocked look, and she must have been confused because she tilted her head at me and continued, "What's wrong Cassie?"

"You said you loved him!" I replied.

"Well… yeah. I mean, I may have only known him for weeks, but we've gotten really close, and I guess when you know… there's no point in hiding it. I'm happy and I love him, I don't want to pretend." She looked over at Dean and waved at him. I looked over at him too.

"Do you think Dean will forgive me for all the mess with Noah?" I asked. She looked at me sympathetically.

"Oh Cassie, Dean could tell that you and Noah had feelings for each other – that's why he got so jealous. But then I started talking to him and we got closer, and I think he understood the split feelings more because that's how he felt too, when he was with me. I think, like you, he wanted to ignore the feelings, but neither of you could deny it. That was what drew me and Dean closer and that's how we started." She smiled at me.

"On the topic of Noah, what's going on with you two now?" she asked. "I mean it's obvious you're mad about each other and both of you are in the clear – so what's stopping you?"

I didn't answer her right away, I just looked at her and smiled.

"Maybe at some point," I said, "there could be", and I glanced around again for any sign of Noah. But no luck.

Emma and I began talking about anything and everything and realised we'd missed so much. Even before I'd found out about the cheating, I'd become so distant with Emma. She was hiding things from me and I was so distracted. But, as we talked now we became so relaxed, with no secrets or discomfort. She told me about Dean, and the look she had when she spoke about him – so full of love – was so right. She was happy now, and it was about time. I only wished the same fate awaited me.

Once Dean saw the smiles and laughter, he deemed it OK to come over. He sat with Emma and placed a gentle kiss on her cheek, which she returned with a sweet kiss on his lips.

"Now I'm starting to realise how you felt with us all summer, Emma," I joked, "but this is worse for me because you two actually love each other." They both laughed.

"Are we good, Cassie?" Dean asked, slightly worried. But before I could answer he continued, "I know that I seriously messed up with all the relationship stuff and I should've told you sooner and not got mad at Noah because I thought he told you. It was all just really messed up, but… I'm really sorry Cassie and I don't want to stop our friendship."

"Look Dean, it's fine. I wasn't right either and I seriously messed you around. I'm just happy that you're with who you're meant to be with. I'm so sorry for the distress I caused you and the pain I put you through. I hope you can forgive me too."

"Course I can Cassie. Things were just a little mixed up. I'm glad it's all OK," he told me with a smile.

We gave each other a brief, tight hug and continued with what we were saying. Dean started going on about fires, and me and Emma just looked at each other trying not to burst out laughing at his sudden bonfire enthusiasm.

I was looking into the flames, when I felt a sharp jab in my ribs. I looked to my left and realised that Emma had elbowed me.

"Hey Cassie," she said and tilted her head over my shoulder.

I was confused for a second and then understood what she was trying to tell me. Over my shoulder I noticed Noah making his way towards the fire. In an instant, I jumped up.

"I'll be right back," I announced and was gone before I could even hear what they said, although I heard a brief whisper followed by Dean's boisterous laugh. I shot them a glare and then turned my attention to what really mattered – the gorgeous boy coming towards me, the one I was completely in love with. I walked closer and we stopped a few feet apart.

"Hi," I said weakly, my heart beating fast.

"Oh, hey," he replied. "Look I wanted to say I get it and I'm sorry for what I did and I'll leave you alone now, if I didn't get it before then I totally get it now and I will leave you alone." He told me, but I held his arm to stop him from moving away.

"No, that's not what I want. Look Noah, I really need to tell you something." I said moving closer to him.

I took a deep breath, looking down at my feet, and went to speak. But Noah started talking before I could.

"Cass, I love you!" he declared.

"W… what?" I stuttered.

"I love you," he said again, "I've tried to deny it, hide it, ignore it, but I can't. And you know what? I don't want to any more." He moved closer to me. "The moment I saw you I knew you were something special and I had to know who you were. I didn't care how I managed it, but I needed to talk to you. From the moment you looked my way, your smile was in my thoughts, and as soon as I spoke to you, your voice was in my head and *you* were in my heart. Look, I'm not great with this emotional stuff but I had to tell you. I've spent too long being afraid and I'm tired of it! Afraid to tell you and Dean and Emma, afraid to tell you how I felt, afraid to lose you. But that ends now, so I love you! I'm completely and utterly head over heels in love with you," He exhaled. "So there it is. I'm sorry I've been bombarding you but I've said my piece, so I'll go now and I'll leave you alone."

I just stared at him for a minute, and he started to turn and walk away. Then I realised that this was my moment, the moment I'd been looking for all day, and I wasn't about to let my hesitation and fear spoil this once again. It was now or never…

Chapter 25

"Hey, wait a minute, don't I get to say something now?" I called as Noah was walking away. He turned back to me with a look full of worry, clearly concerned about what I had to say.

"The only thing I'd change about that whole speech… is that I didn't get to say I love you first." Noah processed my words, and a huge smile broke out on his face.

"Noah, I loved you the minute I got to know you. Your smile ran through my head constantly. My first thought of the day and my last thought of the night was of you. When I'm with you I feel calm yet excited. You've shown me how to love myself and that I'm enough on my own. I don't need you, Noah," his face dropped slightly, "but I want you. I want you so much that my heart hurts when you're not around. I just want to be near you every possible moment." He looked at me dazed for a minute. "Look Noah, I was just too scared to admit it to myself before. I'm not used to having someone love me for who I am and want me the way you do – I got scared! Scared of how much I felt for you, scared of being vulnerable with someone. I felt guilty about Dean and didn't know what to do. But I know now, and I know I need to be true to my heart, and my heart wants you, Noah."

He stood there in stunned silence.

"Well please say something!" I begged as he stood there staring at me with a shocked expression. He stayed silent. Then he decided to do something else, something better. He took one large stride, closing the distance between us, grabbed my face in his large hands and showed me clearly what he thought about what I said. His tongue explored my mouth, and I threw my arms around his neck to keep me from falling. His strong arms wound round my waist and pulled me closer to him and he lifted me off the ground. My legs flew up behind me and I smiled against his kiss. On my last night of summer camp in the light of the bonfire I had the best kiss of my life and confessed my love for the boy I couldn't live without. As Noah's arms wrapped around me, I knew that this would only get better. I heard whooping in the background and could tell it was Emma.

"Finally!" she called. We broke apart and laughed.

"Emma really knows how to keep the romantic mood alive," Noah laughed, and I agreed with him.

"Can you blame her? I'm pretty sure the whole camp was waiting for us to finally get together, and the nurse won't have to deal with me hiding away in the first aid tent any more."

I laughed and pulled him back closer to me. Spending so long being stubborn and foolish, I'd nearly missed out on someone that made me the happiest I'd ever been. I wasn't going to make that mistake again. Noah smiled against my lips and kissed me twice as hard. I knew I was never going to get tired of this boy or those lips – it was heavenly.

When we broke apart this time, we were both gasping for air. I hadn't wanted to give the whole camp a little show, so instead I grabbed his hand and pulled him over to the bench. I sat down next to Emma, and Noah pulled me in against his legs. I think now I'd told him I loved him, he was never going to let me go – and I was OK with that. I leaned back against his chest and let out a happy sigh. Sitting here with him, his hand trailing a soothing pattern on my thigh, was the most comfortable I'd been all summer. I desperately wanted to drag him away and kiss him senseless, but there would be time for that. Right now, I needed time with all of them so we could enjoy our last nights. Noah and Dean began talking and they shook hands.

"So, you guys are friends, huh?" I joked.

"Hey, this guy is fine when he isn't trying to steal my girl," Dean laughed, "just don't steal this one, all right?" he said with an affectionate kiss on Emma's head.

"Oh, no need to worry mate," Noah replied, "I've got the girl of my dreams right here in my arms," he said as he squeezed me tighter.

"Wow, cringe much!" I joked.

"You love it," Noah whispered in my ear. And the truth was, I did… but I wouldn't give him the satisfaction of knowing that.

I sank back into his arms and watched the fire as Emma rattled on about us and them and fate and other bizarre things. I didn't care what she was saying. I finally had the boy I loved and I sure as hell wasn't letting him go.

The evening's end came all too soon. We'd already indulged ourselves with s'mores and hot chocolate as we sat together and chatted. Noah went to grab a blanket when it got colder and he draped it over my shoulders and held me closer to him, placing the sweetest kisses on my forehead, cheeks and lips. After such a day, I was ready for the best night's sleep of my life. It was crazy to think that the zoo trip was only this morning. Dean said he was going to walk Emma back to the tent, so Noah and I took a leisurely wander around the outskirts of the campsite to give them some time to say their final good night of camp – and allow Noah and I a little longer together.

We began to slowly stroll around the campsite. I wasn't looking forward to finally saying goodnight to Noah and then leaving to go home and so burst our wonderful bubble. I'd wasted so much time this summer being stubborn and ignorant, missing out all the time I could've had with Noah just because I was scared. I'd been such a fool. We walked with our hands clutched, each desperate for some type of touch. I don't think I ever wanted to let go of him now.

"So, this has been an... *interesting* day," he joked.

"Oh, you can say that again," I laughed. He opened his mouth, and I knew what he was thinking.

"Don't actually say it again, you weirdo," I scolded him, and he let out a deep laugh.

"Just this morning you were shutting me down and running away from me." I rolled my eyes at that. "I mean, it was kind of funny. I could see how flustered I made you...

and I may have overheard your conversation with Lexi a little bit."

"How do you know it was Lexi? You don't even know her."

"You said her name, so it wasn't exactly rocket science to work it out. A friend from home, I assume?"

"Yep, I've been keeping her updated on all of the goings on with you and me."

"Oh no, how did I come off in that conversation?" He flinched.

"Well, she was moaning at me mostly about how stupid I was to stay with Dean when I was so clearly in love with you this whole time and that I should've stopped wasting my time being an idiot basically. So, actually, you came off rather well."

"Hmm, well I think I'll like this one when I get to meet her," he teased.

"We shall see about that," I said, teasing him right back. I couldn't help but smile when I heard him talk about meeting my friends, knowing that he was already thinking about fitting into my life after we left camp.

"Do you regret anything that's happened between us? I mean how it all happened?" he asked me. "Would you change anything?"

He looked anxious about my response, but, as I looked at him, I realised how much in love with him I really was. I stopped us walking and turned to face him.

"Hey Noah, listen to me. I know we took a little longer to get to this point than we might have liked", he nodded in agreement, "but I wouldn't change anything. We got to know each other in a better way than we would've done otherwise, I'm sure. Without the stress of a relationship and its expectations, I felt like I could be more myself and actually talk to you as my friend rather than thinking I needed to be this perfect girlfriend for you. I'm so sure that I love you and want to be with you."

His face glowed and he leant in to kiss me.

"Oh, I wish we had more time," I told him as I pulled away from him, knowing that Dan would be coming round soon to make sure we were all in bed.

"Come on,'' Noah said as he coaxed me towards my tent, "we can have more time, there's still tomorrow."

I leant my head on his chest and he placed a tender kiss on my forehead. While we were standing there, I noticed Dean walking from our tent towards his own. Noah draped his arm over my shoulder and we continued towards my tent. As I got nearer, I knew I had to say goodnight but I wasn't ready. It was such a bittersweet moment and I felt a weight at the bottom of my stomach. I turned to Noah, grabbed the collar of his shirt and pulled him towards me. I'd already used plenty of words today, so I decided to show him how much I loved him another way. Our lips collided and this was no gentle kiss. I put all the passion that had been building up these past couple weeks into it to show him how much he meant to me, and Noah returned every single bit of love. I melted against him and knew I'd be happy in his arms for the rest of my life.

I heard Dan's voice a little distance away, so I knew I had to go. I unwillingly pulled away from Noah.

"Well, I guess this is goodnight," he told me.

"Goodnight," I said, "I love you." A grin broke out on his face.

"I don't think I'll ever get tired of hearing you say that," he said.

"For the rest of our lives?" I asked him.

"Well, for as long as you'll have me."

"For the rest of our lives, then," I confirmed.

"God, I love you so much," he exclaimed.

With that, he slowly walked away, keeping his eyes on me for as long as he could and only turning away once he had to look where he was going. I walked into the tent and Emma was sitting on her bed waiting for me with a smug look on her face.

"What?" I asked her.

"Oh nothing, just seeing how *in love* you are," she smiled.

"Well... I'm happy," I confessed, "happier than I've been in a long time. And *you* can hardly talk, I thought your eyes would turn into heart shapes with the way you were looking at Dean at the bonfire tonight. But it's good Em, we're finally with who we're meant to be with."

She squealed and rocked back on her bed. "Ah, I'm so happy for us, you deserve it so much! I'm glad things are working out."

I nodded at her. "And you and Dean are so sweet, you fit well together, better than me and him ever did."

"You think so?" she asked.

"Oh yeah," I assured her, "honestly, looking back I think me and Dean didn't make sense at all. I'd always felt a little odd and uncomfortable around him. I mean, things make so much more sense when I'm with Noah."

I laughed thinking about how it was only yesterday that everything exploded, but here we were. Emma looked relieved at what I'd said.

"So, how do you feel about us going home on Saturday?" Emma asked.

I paused for a moment and thought about it – the idea that I wouldn't see these guys every day and that I'd have to be back home. I was excited about finally seeing my mum and being there to support her, but it would be so weird not seeing Dean, Emma and Noah every day.

"Don't get me wrong," I said, "I'm excited to see my friends at home. I miss Lexi like mad and I've hardly spoken to Lottie and Connie. But I've gotten so used to being here with you guys every day that not seeing you is going to be so weird."

"But hey Cassie, it'll be fine. At least we only live an hour away from each other so we can try and get together as much as we can," she said, trying to be hopeful. But I knew that things would change when we left, real life would have to continue. The thought scared me. Things worked here, in this summer camp bubble. But at home? Would it be OK? I knew it wouldn't be the same, but Noah was worth the risk. I'd felt something with him, something new that I was willing to fight for.

"What about you?" I asked her.

"I think the distance is going to be weird, but I want to try with Dean. He's made me feel so much happier." She paused. "I think he feels the same too, or at least I hope he does!"

"Oh, he *does*," I assured her.

Me and Emma stayed up another hour just talking. Even before I found out about

her and Dean, I hadn't spent much time with Emma and I had missed it. Over the past week or so I'd become preoccupied and began to ignore her – it was a shame. As we sat in our beds, Emma spoke openly about things with Dean – even some bits from when we'd still been together. It was a little odd, but I didn't mind. Dean didn't feel like an ex – in all honesty, we hadn't had much of a relationship.

I told Emma I needed to call Lexi. I knew she would've been waiting for me to call her all day and fill her in on what had happened. I laid back in bed and grabbed my phone, Lexi answered after the second ring, sounding breathless.

"Talk to me," she panted.

"Why are you so out of breath?" I asked her.

"Well, when I heard the phone ring, I rushed over to see if it was you. Do you realise I've been waiting all afternoon for you to call me and tell me what happened?"

"Oh… ."

"Soooo? Tell me! What happened? I'm hoping this call is a good one and you're telling me some exciting news." She waited in anticipation. "Cassie!" she blurted out impatiently.

"Oh wow, OK, I'll tell you before you burst! So, after I texted you on the coach on the way home, I got back to the campsite and went to the lake."

"And Noah went with you, you confessed your love and made out at the lake?" she asked.

"No," I replied, "shush."

"Ugh fine, hurry then."

"So, I was sitting at the lake and realised I had to do something and do it quickly. I stayed there for a while trying to get my ideas sorted. I gave my mum a call to see what she thought, and she helped me see the reason about Noah keeping things from me and so I knew I'd need to do something that night. I was running out of time already, then there was dinner, so I made my way to the food hall and…"

"And you saw him at dinner, grabbed his face and made out with him in the food hall?" she asked breathlessly.

"Lexi, would you chill with this whole making out stuff and just let me speak!" I laughed.

"OK, go, go!"

"So, I didn't do anything at dinner. I wasn't going to make a scene in front of the whole camp, come on! I just sat on my own thinking about what I could do – but, trust me, I was waiting to make out with him the whole time through dinner. Then it was announced we were having a bonfire for our last night, and before you ask about me kissing him at the fire… I did, " I told her. I heard a squeal on the other end of the phone and rolled my eyes at Emma's enthusiasm.

"TELL. ME. MORE!" she said.

"OK, so basically, I patched things up with Dean and Emma – that was all good. Then I noticed Noah walking over to the fire – he came late – so as soon as I saw him, I went over to him and he came up with this massive speech about how he loved me and was tired of hiding things away and that he wanted to be with me." Another squeal down the phone. "Then I told him that I loved him and that I'd been scared about the lie and worried because of what had happened with my parents. He'd been so understanding and accepting of me, and I couldn't wait any longer. So, after all *that* happened, we spent the rest of the night hanging with Dean and Emma, just sitting together. Weirdly, now that Dean wasn't worried about Noah stealing his girl, they got on pretty well, at least for guys that were about to have a fight like only two days ago. I've never been happier – honestly Lexi, I can't believe my luck that I met him." As I finished speaking, I released the breath I hadn't realised I'd been holding.

"Wow Cassie, that's amazing. You deserve it so much. And don't be stupid, it's not luck. You deserve happiness and that's what he's given you. I can hear how much you love Noah just from the way you speak about him, and I'm so proud of you for that – the fact that you opened up and let him in and showed him that side of you. I know it's a difficult thing for you to do and you did it for him – that's so incredible! It tells me he's worth it, because you wouldn't open up like that to just anyone. I really can't wait to meet him."

To hear that from Lexi was such a relief too.

"That means a lot, Lex, I can't wait for you to meet him too. He needs to pass the friends test, see if he can survive being interrogated by *you*." She laughed at that. "I'm kind of worried about not being at camp and going back to real life."

"Oh Cassie, it's going to be different. You're in your own little world now, but that doesn't mean the change is going to be bad. You'll be fine. Plus, how far away from each other are you?"

"Thirty minutes," I told her

"Oh, that's nothing, you're going to be fine," she reassured me.

But I knew only time would tell. I'd have to see what happened when we both got back to real life and how we could fit into each other's lives.

"All right, I need to go because I'm exhausted," I told Lexi.

I was so happy, but this had been a long, hectic day and I was ready for sleep.

"Yeah, I probably should get some sleep too," she answered, "you've got to keep me up to date with you and Noah, OK? If anything happens before you get back home, OK?"

"I will, of course."

We said goodbye and I put my phone under my pillow. I could already hear Emma softly snoring in her bed, and soon I felt my eyes start to grow heavy. I quickly fell into a peaceful sleep as my dreams filled with thoughts of Noah and our time together – all those little moments. It felt right and I couldn't wait to see what was going to happen and what life had in store.

Chapter 26

I was woken up by a vibration under my head. in my sleepy haze I didn't know what it was at first and I shut my eyes again desperate to go back to sleep, that was until I felt another vibration under my head and realised it was my phone, ugh who was messaging me right now?! I lifted my head and grabbed my phone. It took me a minute for my eyes to adjust to the screen, which read five a.m. I was going to kill whoever was messaging me! When my eyes finally accommodated the brightness of the screen, I saw Noah's name. I reflected on my mission to kill the sender – maybe I'd just be mean for a little while. It all depended on the contents of the message.

Noah: *Hey, loser. ;)*

Noah: *Get ready, I'm taking you somewhere.*

Me: *And where are you taking me at this ungodly hour?*

Noah: *Somewhere magical.*

Me: *Consider my interest piqued.*

Noah: *Quick, get ready and meet me by the food hall.*

Me: *Give me ten minutes. :)*

Noah: *Hurry x.*

It took me ten minutes to get up and get dressed. I was careful not to wake Emma – I wasn't going to sit there and listen to the stream of questions that she'd have for me. Another five minutes and my face looked presentable and my hair tamed. It was still early and pretty cold so I just shoved on some leggings and a crop top. I might be a little cold at first, but I knew I'd warm up in no time as soon as the sun was up.

I quietly put on my Converses, but as I did so my phone vibrated with another message. I glanced over at Emma, making sure the noise hadn't woken her up. She made a small sound but turned over and continued snoring away. I checked my phone.

Noah: *Oi, hurry up!*

Me: *Ah, such a loving message.*

Noah: *Love you.*

I laughed as I put my phone in my back pocket and snuck out. As soon as I left the tent, I could see Noah on the other side of the field, leaning against the wall of the food hall. When he saw me, he stood up straight and waved at me. I ran over to him, and he started walking towards me. When he got close enough, he wrapped his arms around me and lifted me off the ground, pulling me into a tight hug. I inhaled his scent, and a great big smile broke out on my face.

"I missed you," he whispered in my ear.

"Me too," I told him.

He put me down and leant closer, giving me a sweet kiss. I wrapped my arms around his neck, and he tightened his grip against my waist, breaking away before it could become too heated. I groaned in protest and leant forward to try and kiss him again. He leant his head back further so I could only manage a light touch on his lips – a whisper of a kiss, which made him chuckle.

"So, why did you drag me out of bed so early?" I asked him.

"Like I said… something magical," he replied.

"Is that seriously all I get? You're not going to tell me anything else?"

"Now, where's the fun in that?" I shot him a grumpy look. "Hey come on, it's a surprise, I want to be romantic. We've missed too much time already, so I'm making up for it. Don't ruin it, woman," he scolded.

"Fine, let's go. You lead the way," I said, "as clearly I have no idea where I'm going, apparently."

Noah looked at me once more and with a quick nod of his head walked away. He stopped for a moment and looked back at me.

"You coming?" he asked.

I nodded and walked towards him. He reached out his hand and I eagerly took it, loving the sensation I had the moment our hands connected. He wrapped his fingers around mine as my hand slid into his and he rubbed soft circles on my palms. It was something he'd often done, and I was becoming a real fan. We walked over to a small black car with a convertible roof. He pulled out a set of keys, walked round to unlock the passenger door and signalled for me to get in. I stopped for a moment.

"Wait, whose car is this?"

"Eh, I have my connections," he said ominously. I looked at him for a moment.

"Well, what are you waiting for? In the car!" he demanded and once again gestured for me to get inside. I happily slid into the leather seats. The interior was lovely.

"Well, as long as whatever we're doing isn't illegal," I said to him with an apprehensive glance.

"Gasp, how could you think I'd do anything like that?' he said woundedly. "Have some faith in me. I promise that when your parents come to collect you it won't be from a prison".

"OK, I trust you, but I need to ask you one thing." He waited to see what I was going to say. "Did you just say the word 'gasp'?" He laughed.

"Why yes, yes I did. Is that a problem?" I shook my head with a cheerful smile. It was little things like this that made me love him that tiny bit more.

I dipped into the car, and he shut the door behind me. Running round to the other side he opened his door, got in the car and started the engine.

"Are you going to tell me where we're going yet?" I asked as I sat impatiently in the car, my leg bouncing in anticipation.

"Nope, my lips are sealed, and you shall not be finding out until we get there!" he proclaimed.

I shook my head and let him drive. My eyes started to droop but I tried to keep them open.

"Hey, it's all right if you want a nap," he said, "I did drag you out of bed rather early."

"Wow, you read my mind!" I told him. "Wake me up when we get there." I let my eyes close, and I soon drifted off.

It must have been no more than thirty minutes later, when I felt a butterfly-like touch on my cheek. I smiled with my eyes still closed. Noah placed another kiss on my forehead, then another on my other cheek. I tried to stifle a giggle. He went to place one more kiss on my nose but I tilted my head up instead and his lips came to touch mine. He let out a low chuckle and added a firm pressure to the kiss, holding his hands to my waist. His tongue pressed against my lips and involuntarily I opened my mouth and welcomed him. The kiss deepened and I smiled. I don't think I'd ever tire of kissing him or the feelings that these kisses ignited in my chest. I pulled away, with a blissful look on my face.

"So, where have you taken me? Will you finally tell me or is this still all secretive and romantic?" I asked.

"We aren't quite there yet, so you'll be remaining clueless… for now. We need to walk the rest of the way and we better get going," he said as he glanced down at his phone. I narrowed my eyes at him, wondering what was so time sensitive. Obviously, Noah was unimpressed by my speed, or lack thereof, as he ended up grabbing my hand and pulling me to follow him. I had to walk almost twice as many steps to match his long strides, but it seemed we had to stick to his schedule and I happily obliged.

We started walking along what looked like a nature trail. The surrounding forest was rugged terrain with towering banks packed full of trees. I could hear the morning bird song and the rustling of trees – it was a heavenly noise, one that I could never tire of. The day was getting lighter, and the woods were starting to come alive. I quickened my step to be in line with Noah rather than having him drag me along. He intertwined his fingers with mine and we continued our walk. The path began to climb and excitement bubbled up inside me at what Noah might have in store for me. A comfortable silence passed between us as we kept walking and took in the wonder that was around us, the natural beauty I never appreciated when I was at home. As I walked up the path, I felt relaxed in the knowledge that we could be in silence with each other and there would be no awkwardness between us.

Another ten minutes passed, and I was becoming too impatient to wait much longer. I kept on asking Noah and nagging him, hoping that if I annoyed him enough, he'd finally tell me.

"Ugh, when will we be there?" I asked exasperatedly.

"Will you just have some patience, you crazy lady!" he told me.

I huffed at his response and all this secrecy. I was far too impatient for surprises, but it was incredible that Noah loved me so much that he wanted to do all of this for me and had planned it all in less than a day. This will definitely be something I remember from camp and entirely unexpected.

To my delight we stopped five minutes later in a clearing on top of the hill – a small flat area of land, called 'Hosey Hill'. The space had been clearly dug out as a resting place for hikers. It was so freeing. Noah unzipped his backpack and removed a soft checked blanket and laid it on the ground. He sat down and beckoned me over, shifting himself around on the blanket as I sank down between his legs with my back resting against his chest. He put his arms around me, rested them on my chest and ran comforting circles over my arms.

"So, this was your master plan, huh?" I asked him. "A romantic getaway picnic."

"Oh, well after we wasted so much time, I knew I had to think of a great plan that would get you alone for a while, so we could actually be together without the watchful eyes of the leaders and the looks of Emma and Dean."

I turned around and looked at him over my shoulder.

"So, in a matter of hours, you managed to craft and carry out a whole plan to hijack a car, kidnap me to the mountains and have a picnic?"

"That would be correct," he said, "I wanted to do something great for you."

I stared at him, utterly stunned. I was at a loss for words – he'd done all of this for me, going through so much effort just for us to spend some time together, after everything I had done to him. I moved closer to him and couldn't think of anything better than to kiss him right there and then. I planted a quick and soft kiss on his left cheek and then I kissed him once again on the right cheek. He closed his eyes and smiled. I then moved to kiss him lightly on the forehead and trailed my lips down the bridge of his nose, placing a ghost of a kiss there. Before, finally, I moved my lips down to his lips and he returned the kiss keenly. He placed his hand behind my head, his finger became entangled in my hair. He tugged gently and I let out a soft moan, at which he chuckled softly.

I'm not sure how it happened, but in no time I was turned around and my legs were locked around his hips, with his arms wrapped tightly around me. Noah's hands moved from my hair and down my back, exploring my body. They skimmed up and down my thighs and I rocked against his hips. He laid down and my legs soon straddled him, our lips never once breaking connection through the whole movement. After a moment, he grabbed me tightly and rolled over. I was now laid underneath him while he hovered over me, kissing me senseless. I could feel every inch of his body pressed against mine. His weight became a comforting pressure along my body, and he placed his hands flat on either side of my head, caging me in. He moved back slightly and looked down at me, a smile playing at the edges of his mouth.

"What?" I asked him, breathlessly. Becoming suddenly nervous.

"Nothing," he laughed, "I just can't believe that you're mine."

"Well don't you forget it," I returned.

A look of true love filled his eyes and he leant back down and kissed me once again. His lips left mine and travelled slowly down to my neck, pressing a path of light kisses down my cheeks and over my collar bone. My hands slowly explored his chest, feeling his muscular abs underneath his T-shirt. I found the bottom of the top and slowly ventured underneath the soft cotton to his hot skin. A soft growl escaped his mouth as my hands moved across his body and he added pressure on my neck. I could feel his teeth nibbling and knew this would leave a mark tomorrow. But I didn't care – he was showing the world that I was his and I'd happily oblige. I could think of nothing other than me and Noah on this blanket together, far away from any pressure or people. As he kissed me deeper, the rest of the world fell away and I was transported to a world of bliss. He pulled back and glanced in my eyes – his gaze felt electric. His tongue slid out of his mouth and moistened his lips, an action that made me draw my bottom lip between my teeth. His hand reached out and gently pulled my lip back.

"That lip is going to get you in trouble," he murmured, a new passion burning in his eyes.

"Oh really?," I started (excited by the prospect), I was about to continue but the rest of my words were silenced by his lips crashing against mine once again. The feelings that he stirred in me were the things of fantasy, only felt in books and corny films. But here I was with the boy of my dreams. This was what I'd been waiting for, the addictive feeling that we were the only ones in the world. Even the bird song faded into silence as I laid here with him, the trees all stilled at the ferocity of our kisses.

We broke apart, both panting for breath. I looked at Noah with such a look of love, trying to show him all that he meant to me. Words weren't enough right now, and honestly, after that kiss I wasn't sure if I was capable of formulating proper words.

"There's something I need to ask you." Noah said after a few moments of silence, raising his eyebrow suggestively.

"OK, shoot. What's your question?" I replied with more confidence than I actually felt. He paused for a moment and just looked at me. My breath began to quicken and I immediately began to worry about the question. Had I done something? Did he now not feel the same? Did he want to end it as camp ended? I stayed silent and let him speak.

"Will you be my girlfriend?" he asked with an amused look.

"Ugh, I hate you," I said with a laugh, and he laughed too.

"You should have seen your face. You looked so worried. I was tempted to stretch it out, but you were just so cute."

"You're so mean!" I groaned, thumping him on the chest. He flinched, feigning pain but continued laughing.

"Aw, come on, you were just so adorable, I couldn't resist." I narrowed my eyes at him trying to pretend to be mad. However, he began tracing his thumb over my lips and there was no way I could stay mad.

"You still love me?" he asked as he smiled down at me, and I rolled my eyes.

"Ugh, well I guess so. I mean, it's not like I can go back to Dean or anything, so it looks like I'm stuck with you," I teased.

"Oh, ha, ha, very good one... so will you be my girlfriend?" he asked again.

Without hesitation I keenly nodded, a blinding smile on my face.

"Of course I will, you doofus, you didn't even need to ask."

His face broke into a smile as bright as mine.

"Well, I thought I'd mark the occasion, plus I didn't want to leave camp with an elusive 'are we official or not?' I want you to go back home knowing you've got a boyfriend who loves you, and a boyfriend that will beat up any guy that tries anything on with you… just for the record," he said.

"Oh, don't worry, now I have *you*, no other boy would stand a chance. So just shut up and kiss me," I demanded, pulling his head back down to mine so his lips were just a whisper away from me.

"Well, there's no way I can deny that request," he chuckled, and our lips connected once again. I don't think I'd ever get enough of Noah's lips, with their soft, kissable look. And they were all mine – I'd be the only one kissing these lips from here on out. His hands found my waist and tightened where they landed. They flexed as my top rode up and his fingers grazed my skin. I felt like it was on fire, even with the lightest connection, the slightest graze against my skin. I looked into his eyes and they began to darken with passion. I couldn't tell whether hours had passed or not, but I didn't care. I just wanted more time with Noah.

The final day of camp was becoming the best day of the whole summer. But as we lay there tangled in each other's arms sharing sweet kisses, the spell was broken by Noah's alarm. We finally pulled apart and shot each other a warm smile. He glanced down at his watch.

"What's up?" I asked.

"The surprise," he told me with a grin.

"So, this wasn't the whole surprise?" He shook his head at my question. "Wow, you do spoil me! You didn't have to do *all* of this Noah."

"I only did it because I wanted to. You deserved all of it, a day to just forget everything," he said sweetly. "Now, come here."

He turned me around and I sat back into his chest. I looked around confused while Noah pointed towards the horizon to direct me.

"What am I looking at?" I asked.

"Just give it a minute," he told me.

I looked back through the sea of lime and emerald trees flowing away from us and that was when I saw it… .The sun was rising over the trees, casting a glorious light, as if it was waking up the world. I was in awe – I'd never seen anything like this. The trees looked as if they were stretching up, basking in the sunlight and coming to life. My breath caught in my throat at the beauty before me.

"So? What do you think?" Noah whispered in my ear.

"I… I… it's breathtaking!" I managed to choke out.

"Yes, you are," he purred and his words danced over my body. I whacked his arm playfully and he let out a low grumble.

"Thank you for doing this," I said as I turned my head to him over my shoulder, "you've made this so special."

"It's not over yet," he told me.

Noah shuffled around and pulled a flask of coffee with two travel cups from his bag as well as some pastries. I looked at him with so much joy.

"I seriously can't believe you managed to pull this off, let alone do it all for *me*. And you even included caffeine – my dream guy," I said to him in bewilderment.

"Cas, I'd do whatever I could do for you, I love you." My heart warmed at his words – I was glowing. "But if I knew that coffee was all it took to win your heart, then I could have saved a whole lot of energy this summer."

"yeah, but I'm worth it aren't I?" I teased.

"you definitely are," he agreed.

"I love you so much," I whispered, my breath quickening with each word exchanged. We'd said we loved each other repeatedly, but every time my body warmed to the words. We were so close that his lips danced dangerously close to mine once again. I kissed him sweetly but didn't let it get too heated. I looked over at the pastries and my stomach let out a low grumble.

"I think I need to make sure you're fed before I have to deal with hangry Cass,'' Noah said jokingly. I eagerly nodded my head as my mouth began to water at the smell of the baked food floating over and overwhelming my senses. He passed me a fresh croissant and I realised it was still warm. Without hesitation, I nearly inhaled the delicate pastry. Noah smiled wistfully, his eyes full of yearning.

"Are you OK?" I asked. He simply nodded, so I waited for him to elaborate.

"I was just thinking of all the time I'd wasted with you when I was too scared to admit how I really felt," he confessed.

"Hey, it wasn't just you," I told him. "I was a complete fool for staying with Dean for so long... but we're here now and that's what matters. But we have time to make up for it, and that includes a whole bunch more summers," I assured him. I could tell by his gentle smile that he agreed.

"Please tell me my suspicions were correct and that flask contains caffeine," I begged, eyeing the steaming container.

"Of course, I know my *girlfriend* and I know you need your caffeine."

My heart glowed even brighter at his use of "girlfriend".

"May I?" he asked, while holding the flask the way a waiter would hold a bottle of wine. I grinned and nodded vigorously. This was an amazing surprise, but I needed my coffee and needed it soon, otherwise it would not end well. I held the cup steady, and he filled it up. Once Noah had his cup too, I leant back against his chest, grabbed another pastry, a chocolate one this time, and let out a sigh of relief.

I never wanted this moment to end, but of course the time to leave arrived all too soon.

Chapter 27

Noah's phone rang.

"Hi... yeah... yep... OK, great... see you soon," he said. I couldn't hear what was being said on the other side of the phone, so, for once, I decided to be patient. Noah at least deserved a peaceful phone call after everything he'd done.

"Come on, we need to get going," he told me.

I knew he was right – we couldn't stay hidden away forever. But with his lips next to me I'd have been content to spend the rest of my days living out in these woods. With extreme reluctance, I stood up and helped Noah pack everything away, sneakily grabbing a bit more coffee before he put the flask back in his bag. We headed down the hill, hand in hand. I'd moaned about the walk on the way up but now that we were leaving, I desperately wanted it to be longer – to have as much time alone with Noah as I could get.

In no time we were back at the car. Noah helped me into the passenger seat and dipped a light kiss on my lips. I couldn't decide which I loved more, these light kisses that sent a shiver through my whole body or the intense kisses that caused my whole being to burst into flames. As long as he was kissing me, I didn't mind.

I sank back into my seat with a sense of tranquillity washing over me. Noah walked back to his side of the car and got in. Starting the engine, he peeled out of his parking spot and set off for the campsite, taking the scenic route back. This was the perfect ending – sitting in the car with the boy I loved and watching the world pass by. I was going to miss being surrounded by nature.

We got back to the campsite just before lunch. I realised I wouldn't have much more time with Noah, just the two of us. I shot him a glance and he just grinned back at me. I saw Emma rushing over to me. She was breathless as she approached me and wrapped her arms round my neck.

"Oomph," I huffed at the force of her attack, "hello to you too!"

"I can't believe you vanished this morning and didn't tell me anything about what you were doing or even where you were going! I first thought you had died, then obviously Dean talked me down and said that Noah had disappeared too. So we assumed you were off together, and then you weren't here for breakfast – I covered for you with Dan by the way – and I couldn't even reach your phone!" she complained.

"I'm sorry, I didn't even know. Noah just messaged me and told me to meet him. I knew if I told you then I'd be suffering an onslaught of questions before I left, and I needed to sneak away. Plus, I left at like five a.m. which would have been way too early for you, and I wasn't in the mood for questions that early when there was no caffeine inside of me." I tried to reason with her, but I could tell by her face that she was still not convinced.

"Well, you need to tell me every single detail," she demanded, wiggling her eyebrows.

"Ew Emma, come on!" I said with a blush rising in my cheeks, remembering that Noah was still standing mere feet away, leaning leisurely on the hood of the car. Emma was still looking at me with a determined look and I knew I couldn't escape.

"Look I'm not getting out of this," I told Noah with a look in Emma's direction, "can I see you at lunch?" He nodded, with an amused smile and walked round the car to drop a kiss on my lips.

"See you soon," he whispered to me. "Don't be too crazy Emma, I want my girlfriend back in one piece," he called as he slowly turned and walked away. I watched him join some of his friends and then I turned to Emma as she waited expectantly.

"So, what happened? Where did he take you? And did I hear him call you his girlfriend?" she asked, her face excited and her eyebrows raised.

"Ugh, fine. OK, so at like five a.m. this morning Noah sent a message telling me to get ready and meet him at the food hall. I had no idea what it was about but I went to meet him."

"So that's what that noise was this morning," she interrupted.

"Sorry, I tried to be quiet," I said and winced. She waved her hand as if to say, "don't worry about it", and waited to hear more.

"It was in the interests of love, so I shall allow it," she said, and I continued.

"Well, I went and met him and he'd arranged somehow to borrow a car. He drove us to this nature park, we walked up a hill-type mountain thing called "Hosey Hills", and he had a blanket with a flask and pastries all in a backpack and had this warm breakfast for us. And as we were sitting there, he asked me properly to be his girlfriend."

Emma squealed but I just rolled my eyes and kept talking. I'd had practice with this behaviour from trying to tell a story to Lexi.

"He'd timed it so that we could sit there and watch the sunrise together." I looked over at her once I'd finished, and she was nearly red from holding in her reaction.

"Go ahead," I told her.

"OMG, THAT'S SO CUTE!! I CAN'T BELIEVE HE DID THAT FOR YOU!!!" Emma squealed again, and it all flowed out in a speedy stream. I shook my head at her reaction but smiled at the fact that I could once again talk to her about what was going on in my life and not be worried about being judged. It was so good to talk freely with her about these things now. She asked more about what happened, and I told her what had gone on and what we did. She was so happy for me and Noah, and then started spouting off about how we could all go on double dates and that she couldn't wait for the four of us to hang out together. I laughed at her enthusiasm but listened all the same.

Time before lunch passed quickly, with Emma going on and on about us and Dean and all the plans she had. Soon we were walking to the food hall. As we approached, I saw Noah walking up from his tent. I called over to him, and when he saw me his face lit up. He jogged over to us and threw his arm around my shoulder.

"Hey," he murmured in my ear. I smiled up at him and planted a small kiss on his cheek.

"Hi," I replied.

"How was the chat with Emma?" he asked with a grin.

"You know what, it was good… but next time you can sit through Emma's speech about us and all the double dates she has planned." He groaned at that, which made me giggle.

"Hey Emma!" he called.

"Oh hey, Noah," Emma called back.

"I heard you had a great time interrogating Cass."

"Oh yeah, I found out all the juicy information," she said with a laugh. Noah looked down at me and raised his eyebrow.

"All of it, huh?" he murmured to me, but I just looked up at him and shrugged my shoulders.

We continued our walk to the food hall and noticed Dean standing outside, waiting for us. Emma jogged over and he picked her up, giving her a great hug. We followed behind and walked over to them.

"Hi guys," he said to us.

"Hey, how are you?" I asked, giving him a quick hug.

"Yeah, yeah I'm good," he replied. Noah nodded in his direction and Dean reached out a hand towards him. Noah took it, and it seemed like a silent agreement passed between them – boys!

We all walked in together and sat at our usual table. Noah quickly went to say hi to his friends, and to fill them in, before heading back over to our table.

"You don't want to sit with your friends?" I asked.

"Why would I want to sit over there away from my gorgeous girlfriend?" he murmured. I glowed at his words and felt at ease as we all sat there together.

Others might think it could be weird sitting there with my ex, who cheated on me with my friend. Put that way I could understand the weirdness, but the thing is it works. Plus I was focused on Noah now and what had finally grown between us. I loved Noah, I had never loved Dean. Simple. I realise now that I didn't feel bad being away from him – but with Noah? Saying goodbye to him last night was bad in itself, even though I was seeing him again in eight hours. I had no idea how I was going to say goodbye to him and go home. But I wasn't going to think about that right now – this was my last day with him and I was going to savour every last moment.

Dan hadn't planned anything for the final day – apart from a few games – so we could all have time to finish packing and getting ready to go. I knew I still needed to pack some stuff but I could do that when I went back to the tent with Emma later. Right now, it felt impossible to leave Noah's side.

Lunch passed in a daze. The four of us sat and ate and chatted. I sat next to Noah and felt his hand find my thigh, giving it a tight squeeze before letting go and taking hold of my hand. It was like now that I'd told him I loved him, he was never going to stop touching me – not that I was complaining. We finished lunch quickly, and as we walked out, we noticed a game of volleyball starting by the lake. We dashed over and joined the teams.

"You remember our first run-in at that lake?" Noah whispered to me, raising an eyebrow. I blushed at the memory and nodded. I switched my focus to the game and started to play. We played a few games and by the end I was thoroughly exhausted.

"You fancy going down to the lake?" I asked Noah.

"You don't have to ask me twice," he replied.

I waved goodbye to Emma, but she was preoccupied with Dean, we left them to it and started to the lake.

We walked down to the pier that I'd found, and as I got there I sat down and took my shoes off, swinging them down on the edge of the pier. Noah soon joined me. I didn't have any places like this at home, so I soaked up every last moment. As I looked at Noah, I realised that I may have thought some guys were good looking before and maybe had crushes on guys, but I knew I'd never been in love before and part of me doubted that I could ever feel this way about someone else. It was like a perfect storm when I was with him. He did things to me that I couldn't explain, but never made me feel nervous or insecure. My body ached to be near him, and when he was gone, my thoughts were only of him. It was special.

"What are you looking at?" he asked. I hadn't even realised but while I'd been looking at him he'd noticed and turned to look at me.

"Oh nothing," I said, shrugging my shoulders, "I'm just happy to be with you."

"Well, I'm glad about that, otherwise the whole telling me you loved me and saying you'd be my girlfriend would've been rather misleading," he teased.

"Well, you never know," I replied with a grin, "could just be boredom, maybe I just fancy a summertime fling." He shook his head at me and placed a sweet kiss on my nose.

"Hey," Noah said, his voice sounding more nervous, "I wanted to check in about your family too. I know it's still a bit of a difficult topic, so you only have to talk about things if you want to, but I wanted to check up on how you were doing."

He played with a pebble as he spoke, avoiding eye contact, clearly worried about how it would affect me and not wanting to push anything.

"Oh," I sighed, "well, they're separating now, which I'm torn about. The arguing got so bad when I was at home and it just made things so stressful. I guess in that respect I'm happy that they're away from each other, but it's also hard. I always thought of my family as this close-knit unit – and now? Dad is staying with a friend from work and it's just going to be weird! getting home and him not being there. But, you know, maybe that's what they need, and hey, being separated isn't divorced. Maybe there's hope. They need to have some time away from each other to know what they're missing. You've made me quite the optimist, Noah, I think they'll be OK – they really do love each other."

I finished speaking and he was just looking at me. "What?" I asked, suddenly conscious of my outburst.

"You just amaze me," he said. I was bewildered by the sudden complement and waited for him to develop. "I mean, come on Cass, last week you had a breakdown when you found out the news, but look at you now – you're calm and reflective. Plus, don't even get me started on the way you handled the whole situation with Dean… You're so much wiser that you give yourself credit for. You just never cease to amaze me and I can't wait to see what is in store for us when we get back to our normal lives."

His smile was blinding as he spoke – I knew he'd meant every word and would be with me and support me. I wasn't used to trusting a guy in this way. Sure, I had guy friends but no one I spilled my guts to. Noah was different, he was special. I knew I would be strong when I got home because Noah wouldn't let me fall.

"Can we just stay here forever?" I asked, wishing this moment would never end.

"If only, but unfortunately there may be a missing person's report filed if we don't return back to the campsite," he answered, with a smile.

"But can we stay here a little longer?" I bargained with him. Noah's smile grew with that, and he nodded.

So that was what we did. I leant against him, and he put his arm around me, rubbing soft patterns up and down my arms while I dipped my feet in the cool, refreshing water. This was my safe space; this had truly been one of the greatest things from this summer (among others of course). I was happy.

Chapter 28

We stayed there for a while, but when we checked the time, we realised that we'd stayed a little too long and needed to head back to the camp. I dragged my feet out from the cool bliss of the delicious water and put my shoes back on. Noah was already standing, so he grabbed my hand, pulled me up and wrapped his arms around me, crashing his lips against mine. I giggled at his force but hooked my arms around his neck and returned the kiss. Noah's arms tightened as he picked me up from the floor. I wrapped my legs around his waist and his hands moved to the back of my thighs, stroking the bare skin below my shorts. I broke the kiss and moved my head back. Noah grunted in objection and tried to move my head back towards his lips.

"Uh huh, I thought you said we needed to go back to camp," I teased.

"I'm sure we won't be missed for five more minutes," he growled, and with that he grabbed my head back to his and kissed me. I was sure my lips would be bruised. It was so passionate – I felt I could combust at any moment.

When Noah was satisfied that he'd kissed me thoroughly enough, he reluctantly let me down. I smiled at him and we walked back to the campsite.

"Well, that was one fun trip," he said as we made our way back through the woods. I was still silenced from that kiss, my head whirling, so I just nodded instead.

We continued our walk at a gentle pace, talking about everything and nothing. I realised that through my stubbornness I had also missed out on discovering basic girlfriend (I still grinned at the idea of me being Noah's 'girlfriend'), knowledge – his favourite colour, TV show, place... He'd been so attentive towards me, but I'd been too busy running away from him every time I got scared. It was good to finally hear about his life in more detail.

We were soon back at the campsite, and I could see the sun starting to set – setting over the campsite as well as on our last day. We went to find where Emma and Dean had disappeared to – with no luck. I thought it would be better to just wait them out, instead of trying to find them and landing on something we didn't want to see. Noah agreed, so instead we sat down on one of the benches scattered around the campsite, watching the sun in its final hours.

"You know, I've just realised," I said to Noah.

"Hmm, what's that?" he asked.

"Well, this morning you kidnapped me so we could watch the sunrise together, and now here we are watching the sun go down too."

"Starting and ending the day with you," he said, "seems like the perfect day to me." I turned to him and smiled.

"You always know exactly what to say, don't you?" I told him as I tucked myself into the crook of his arm.

"Well, I need the best lines if I'm going to keep my gorgeous girl in my arms." I giggled at his corny lines and turned back to watch the sun.

Emma and Dean emerged from behind the food court and she made her way towards me with a blush creeping over her cheeks.

"Hey," I said to her with a smirk, "what were you two doing?"

"Oh, you know, just talking," Emma said with a glance over to Dean, who'd made his way over to Noah and was chatting with him.

I looked at her knowingly. If Emma's clothes were anything to go by, she and Dean weren't just talking over there. I shook my head at her obvious lie.

"Ah, how sweet," I said but leant in closer towards her. "Nice hickey, by the way," I whispered. With a squeal, her hand flew up and covered her neck, but trying to hide the evidence was futile. I laughed at her attempt, and soon Emma relaxed and laughed too.

"Let's just hope it's gone before the parents get here tomorrow morning," she replied.

"Or that you have some majorly impressive foundation," I joked.

At that moment, Dan walked out of the office and started to speak. We all turned our attention to him.

"OK, all you wonderful campers," he announced, "your final surprise as a final goodbye will soon be underway. So, if you all head back to your tents and change, the final night party will commence in fifteen minutes!"

We all erupted with anticipated chatter about the party.

"And," he continued. "As we had so much firewood left over last night, we'll be having another bonfire later on, with a chance for those over eighteen to sleep under the stars." There was a mixture of groans and cheers – clearly, the younger campers weren't too happy with that final part.

"Now, now. You'll all have your year, but for now if you're not old enough you're just stuck with the great party. Now go, get ready and be back here as soon as you can!" Dan had finished and I turned to Emma.

"Come on, let's get ready for the party," I said, and with a wave to the boys we started to wander back to the tent.

"You don't happen to have a turtleneck, do you?" she asked as she self-consciously rubbed her hickey.

"Unfortunately not," I laughed, "maybe we can find a subtle scarf or bandanna to wear if the make-up plan doesn't go well."

Laughing, we stumbled into the tent and started searching around for the cutest outfit we could find.

The next ten minutes were complete chaos filled with hilarity as we switched and swapped our outfits. In the end, I settled on a short white bodycon dress, decorated with small blue and pink flowers, and I wore my hair down – over this past month it had become lighter and now cascaded down my back. Emma helped me with some makeup and I added eyeliner and mascara with a little bit of blush and highlight. Emma herself had on a light blue denim skirt and a white lace crop top with a cinched detail on the front. She wore similar makeup to me, but added some eye shadow, as well as what she'd used to mask the hickey. Emma let out a sigh of relief as the mark was hidden.

Once we were both happy without our outfits, we made our way to the food hall. Noah had changed into a white polo shirt and a pair of black jeans – oh, it must have been illegal to look that good. I smiled at him and quickly made my way to where he was leaning against the wall of the food hall, waiting for me.

"Hey babe," he said when I was close enough, "you look incredible."

"Well, you're not looking so bad yourself." I leant in and gave him a kiss. "Come on, let's go inside."

I pulled him in behind me. The food hall had been transformed – benches and chairs had been pushed to the sides of the room and there were a few set up with food at one end. The floor was open and a portable dance area was in place. There was a table in the corner setup with speakers, blasting out music that filled the room. Some people already littered the dance floor, bopping and moving to the music, and a few of the seats around the room were occupied with friends and groups chatting. Laughter filled the place, waltzing between the music. It all looked incredible and was a great way to say goodbye.

"May I have this dance?" Noah asked me. As I turned to face him, I saw he was making a bow-like gesture and holding out his hand to me. I giggled and shook my head at his ridiculousness.

"Why of course you may,'' I responded, taking his hand. He led me to the dance floor, and we joined the rest of the campers. Emma and Dean soon followed us and joined in with the upbeat music. After a few songs, I'd become so tired that I went to grab a drink and sit down. Noah soon noticed I'd left the dance floor and came over to join me. His arm flopped over the back of my seat and he leant in close to talk to me over the roaring music.

"Are you having a good time?" he asked. He was quite out of breath from the dancing and had a thin sheen of sweat covering him, but he still smelled heavenly – in such close proximity it was hard to focus. I nodded my head silently and he laid back in his chair. The urge to climb onto his lap was overwhelming, but I stopped myself, knowing I couldn't exactly give the whole camp a show.

I sat there with Noah as we talked as best we could. Dean and Emma joined from time to time and we all sat together to enjoy light chats and jokes. It was a great way to say goodbye, and I had to commend the leaders for putting all this together. They had found a way to make this final night special and I knew I wouldn't forget it for a long time.

A slow song started to play, and Noah looked up.

"Ooo, we're definitely dancing to this one, a slow dance is a definite must for a new couple" he told me.

I started to shake my head, but Noah refused to let the topic drop and grabbed my wrist, yanking me out of my seat. I groaned, to no avail, so I just gave in and let him lead me to the dance floor. He spun me around and pulled me close, our bodies lining up perfectly. One hand smoothed down my back while the other held my waist tight, keeping me against him.

I swayed to the music and rested my head against Noah's chest, taking in his alluring scent.

"Are you enjoying yourself?" Noah murmured.

"Mmhmm," I replied, in blissful contentment.

"I'll take that unintelligible sound as a yes."

"Mmhmm," I repeated, and he let out a laugh as we continued to sway to the music.

A tear started to fall from my eye and seeped onto Noah's shirt. I lifted my head and chuckled.

"Sorry about that," I said nodding to the water mark mixed with blusher on his white top.

"Wait, why are you crying?" he asked worriedly.

"I'm just happy, so happy," I told him.

He grinned at my response. Letting go of one of my hands, he spun me out and dipped me right in the middle of the dance floor. With a kiss, I think I was addicted to his kisses now, he lifted me up and pulled me close to him.

"What was that for?" I giggled.

"Just making sure everyone here knows you're mine," he stated, "I might have to repeat the process when I meet your friends too, just to warn off all the boys."

"Oh, come on, I promise you, there are no guys for you to be worried about at home." I assured him.

"Oh Cas, you got here and had two guys crushing on you in less than a month. If you're trying to convince me that no one at home has a crush on you, then you're crazy."

"Ha, Noah, don't worry, either way I'm all yours."

"Oh babe, I know," he said, "I know how irresistible I am."

I laughed at his confidence. "I know, I know," I told him.

After the dancing, the evening started to wind down and there were clear signs of tiredness on everyone's faces.

"So," Dan declared, "it's getting late and it'll soon be time to head back to the tents. Your parents are going to be here between one and two p.m. tomorrow, so we're going to give you a lie-in, and we'll have a special breakfast again. When you're ready, please head to your tents – and I remind any of the eighteen-year-olds who want to sleep outside, me and a couple other leaders will be joining you round the campfire for a final night under the stars. So, feel free to grab sleeping bags and find some space on the plastic mats set around the fire.'' Once Dan had finished speaking, the campers returned to their excited chatter planning their last night at camp. Some of the younger campers had been scheming.

Me and Noah sat back and relaxed, as a small number of younger campers walked out. They looked slightly disgruntled but still chatted with their friends as they made their way back to their tents.

"Are you sleeping outside?'' Emma panted as she made her way over to me.

"Of course, are you crazy? It sounds awesome!" I replied to her.

I realised that weeks ago I would've completely rejected the idea of staying outside because I would have been too anxious, but this camp had changed me, Noah had changed me.

"OK, that's great! Can we go and grab our stuff?" Emma asked, "I'm already starting to get cold." and I nodded in agreement.

I turned to Noah. "Are you staying too?"

"Well, if you're staying outside, then obviously I'll be around with you," he replied.

"Well, great then. I'll go get my stuff and save you a spot next to me," I told him with a kiss.

I turned to Emma, "Let's go!"

She grabbed my arm and dragged me out of the hall. We made our way down to our tent and started getting ready. Switching into comfy clothes this time, I slipped on a pair of leggings and one of Noah's sweatshirts, which I'd stolen when we went to the picnic this morning. It still smelled like him, and I inhaled his scent.

Once we'd changed, we grabbed our sleeping bags and headed out of the tent. We could see the glow of the blazing fire. I glanced at Emma with an excited squeal, and we rushed over.

As we arrived, we picked out spots on the plastic sheets and left space on either side for Dean and Noah to join us.

I settled down inside the sleeping bag, and as I was getting ready, I noticed Noah walking towards us. He'd switched out of his jeans and polo shirt and now wore blue checked trousers and a white long-sleeved top. That boy could make anything look good! I waved to him, and his eyes landed on me. Even in the darkness I could see the smile on his face.

"Hey," he said as he made his way over, he changed into comfy clothes too.

"Hey, good to see you," I smiled at him.

"Hey, I've got a plan." I looked up at him, confused. "What if we zip our sleeping bags together? That way we can stay together." I nodded eagerly and unzipped my sleeping bag so we could connect them both.

"Hold on a second," he said, staring at me, "is that my sweatshirt?"

I froze and blushed, giving him a timid smile and nodded again.

"It looks better on you than it ever did on me," he said.

He bent down and kissed me. "*Far* better than it does on me," he continued with a murmured.

When we'd zipped the sleeping bags together, I slipped inside and Noah joined me. I laid on my back and gazed up at the sky.

"So, this is pretty special," Dan announced. "There's apparently meant to be a meteor shower tonight, so, if we're lucky, we should see something."

Excitement bubbled up inside me. I'd never seen a shooting star, and to get a sight of one would be the icing on the cake of this amazing camping trip. I rested my head on Noah's chest and we both looked up to the stars. The sky was so alive out here. At home, I never saw this amount of stars, thanks to the pollution of city lights.

"It's beautiful isn't it," Emma commented.

"I've never seen anything quite like it," I agreed, watching the stars wink and dance above me.

As I was staring up, I noticed something out of the corner of my eye. I let out a startled gasp.

"I think I just saw something," I told Noah in disbelief, "right over there!"

I pointed into the sky in excitement, but the flash of light had already vanished, gone in a blink of an eye. I laid back down with Noah, hoping to see another star shoot across the sky. My eyes didn't leave the sky for fear of missing anything, and after about five minutes of nothing another star shot past. Simultaneously, Emma and I let out a gasp at the beautiful happening above us. This was one of the greatest nights ever. I had my best friend back and my boyfriend – who I love so much – next to me. I smiled up at the sky. I might be miniscule compared to the whole universe, but right here? This was my world and what mattered.

"You know if you make a wish on a shooting star it will come true," Noah whispered to me. I looked at him. With my head still laying on his chest, I knew that this was where I wanted to be.

"Why would I need to make a wish, I've got everything I want right here," I told him. With a quick kiss, I settled against him, and my eyes started to droop. I didn't fight the sleep that overtook me and soon I was drifting off into a blissful dream, safe in the arms of someone I loved.

Chapter 29

I woke the next morning with the biggest smile plastered on my face. As I opened my eyes and sat up, stretching my arms, the evening before came flooding back to me – the memories of the warm fire, the spinning stars, my dream boy whose arms were still wrapped around my waist. With the sky above me instead of our old tent, I realised what day it was and felt a crushing weight on my chest – it was time for goodbye. Noah's head was tucked into my neck and his arms around my waist, his breath sending a small chill down my spine and tickling my hair. I turned over to look at his sweet face. His eyes were still shut, and he had the ghost of a smile on his lips. I pinched him on the arm.

"Hey, wake up," I whispered to him.

He stirred but his eyes stayed shut. I quickly poked his cheek – the smile grew but still his eyes didn't open.

"Oh, keeping me hostage are you?" I teased.

This made Noah laugh out loud. I shook my head at him and moved forwards to place a kiss on his cheek. But, as I moved in closer, he tilted his head and my lips connected with his.

"So, that was your plan," I said, raising my eyebrow.

"And good morning to you too," he grumbled.

There was an added deepness to his voice in the morning and my insides did a somersault at the sound. I wished it was the wake-up call I could have every morning.

"I guess we better get up," I groaned, "I still need to finish packing."

I tried to move Noah's arm again but he still kept me captive.

"Come on lazy, we've got to go."

"Well, no, because if we never wake up then we won't have to leave," he said like an excited child.

"I'm not sure that's how it works, so come on, we need to get ready. Plus, aren't you hungry?" I reasoned.

"Well, I guess so," he said, finally opening his eyes and freeing me.

I noticed the rest of the guys around the remnants of the fire were getting up too. There were about twelve of us around the fire – me and Noah, a couple of his friends and then some of Dean's friends too. I noticed there were a few people I hadn't spoken to before. Well, I was leaving today – guess I could talk to them next year.

Something in me clicked – it was time to say goodbye. I couldn't put it off or ignore it any longer. I knew I wasn't ready, but this bubble of sunshine and laughter would soon pop and it would be back to normality. This fantasy would have to fit into my daily life. I couldn't deny it any longer – and I wasn't even packed yet!

I gradually emerged from my sleeping bag with a groan and a stretch. Emma was just waking up too. We shared a sympathetic look, both knowing it would be "goodbye" very soon. Noah began to unzip the sleeping bags – I took mine and gave Noah a quick peck on the cheek, suddenly aware of the monstrosity of morning breath. My hand flew to my mouth, and I shot Emma a glance. Immediately she understood, so we linked arms and started back to our tent.

It was only at that point I noticed the mess in our tent. We sure had managed to make ourselves at home, and I winced at the work it would take to tidy all of this up. Glancing at my phone, I saw we didn't have long to get ready. Good thing Noah loved me because I could not be bothered to put much of an effort into my outfit today.

Me and Emma got ready. I dressed in my favourite high-waisted shorts with a black and white bodysuit and, of course, my trusted Converse, while Emma slipped on a sweet summer dress and a pair of black sandals. With one final glance at the wreckage that was our tent, we looked at each other, shrugged and started to make our way to breakfast.

As I approached the food hall, I caught the aroma of bacon, waffles and chocolate. I looked at Emma with wide eyes, and with a giggle we rushed inside, my mouth already watering. Dean was sitting at our table waiting for us. We joined him, and in no time Dan was signalling us to grab our breakfast. I had to stop myself running over there in my haste to get to the food. At the counter, I reached for the waffles, just as another hand reached out.

"Hmm, I'm getting a sense of déjà vu here," a voice murmured.

My head jerked to the side and my eyes landed on Noah's sweet face and his gorgeous brown eyes. I glanced down at our hands and instantly recalled the time, only a few days ago, when we stood in this same position.

"The only difference now is that I can do *this*," I whispered, leaning up to kiss Noah on the lips.

"I like that difference," he said through a mischievous grin, "come on, let's go sit down."

He flung his arm over my shoulders, as I grabbed a couple of bacon rashers and placed them next to my waffles, drizzled with maple syrup. I let Noah lead me back to the table and Dean and Emma. As soon as I hit that seat, I dived into my food. Noah chuckled at my enthusiasm, but he soon followed my lead and plunged into his waffles too.

Breakfast passed all too soon and in no time me and Emma had to face the state that was our tent and get packed. In around three hours, our parents would be pulling into the campsite, and it would be time to leave.

"Well, here we go," Emma said as we walked into the tent.

I pressed play on my phone to give us some music. I looked around at my mess and had no idea where to start. I soon decided it would be best to start with getting my suitcase sorted. I grabbed the case from the end of my bed and started folding the clothes that were already shoved inside. I couldn't be bothered to sort the clean from the dirty, so I just folded it all together. I mean, I was going home anyway so it didn't make much difference. Once all the clothes in the suitcase were in order, I started on the mess spewed all over the floor. Finally, after tossing each other's clothes around, accompanied by constant giggles and distracted conversation, the floor was clear and all our clothes were on our beds. We folded the final pieces, and soon our tent and clothes were all packed up and we were in much better order.

After much battling with my items, I eventually zipped up the suitcase. A sense of relief and finality washed over me, though seeing the emptiness of the tent was saddening.

"Right, now we need to get these sleeping bags away," Emma whined.

"We can do this," I assured her, "yours first."

We laid Emma's sleeping bag out on the floor and soon had it rolled up, folded and placed in the bag. It took the two of us a lot more energy and effort than I care to admit, but we did it. But the feeling of victory was short-lived as we soon realised we had to repeat the whole process with *my* sleeping bag. We shared a resigned glance and went to work once again. Five minutes later, we'd wrestled my sleeping bag away too. The tent was looking empty – and I knew what that meant.

We emerged from the tent and I checked my phone – twelve o'clock. With only two hours left until our families arrived, I knew exactly what I wanted to do. I hunted down Noah.

"Hey you," he murmured.

I looked up at him and he leant down and placed his hand under my chin. Bringing my lips to his, he kissed me sweetly. Then his hands moved to hold my face, deepening the kiss. I smiled against his lips and snaked my arms around his waist. This is what I'd miss, being able to kiss Noah whenever I wanted, instead of us having to plan when we'd see each other. Sure, I'd still see him but not like I can when we're here.

I pulled away from Noah and asked, "What's your plan for your final hours?"

"Aw, come on Cass, you make it sound like you're about to die!" he protested.

"Well, I might feel like it. I don't even know what kind of home I'm going back to! I've no idea what family members will even be *in* the household. Excuse me, if I don't want to leave here."

He looked at me sympathetically and embraced me in a warm hug.

"Look, it will be OK," he assured me, "plus I'll be around whenever you need me."

"I just don't want to deal with them," I confessed.

I could feel tears stinging my eyes. Noah held me tighter, and we stood there for a while. My tears came and I didn't try to hold them back – I knew I was safe with Noah and that he'd protect me. I pulled back and looked up at him, thankful that he was here with me.

With so little time left, I thought it best to just relax. Everything had been packed, leaders were beginning to gather up their stuff and I wanted to spend my final moments here in carefree bliss. I still had my blanket, so I grabbed it from the tent, spread it on the grass and laid down. Noah joined me, intertwined his fingers with mine and placed our connected hands on his chest.

"So, what are we doing?" he asked. "Cloud watching?"

"Why not?" I heard Emma chime in as her and Dean made their way over to where we were laying in the field.

"It's our last moments," she added, "let's spend it with the people we care about most and enjoy this incredible scenery before we're dragged back to reality."

They laid with us and we all pointed out shapes that we could see in the sky. Some were a bit crazy – like Noah spouting on about a witch on a giant bunny holding a flag – others weren't so ridiculous. After a while, I became sleepy, and with Noah stroking his thumb lovingly against my hand, I shut my eyes.

I felt a hand sweetly brush against my face.

"Cass... hey Cass", I fluttered my eyes open, "it's time to go baby."

I jolted up and looked around. There were already parents starting to pull into the field, and I realised that I'd slept through my last hour of camp.

"No, no! It can't be time to go!" I protested. "We were meant to have more time to say goodbye!" I could feel the tears that were starting to blur my eyes.

"Hey baby, it's OK," Noah reassured me, "I *will* see you soon, this doesn't have to be goodbye."

"But this is the end of camp!"

"It might be, but it's not the end of us," he insisted. "I'll see you and you'll see me. It'll be fine... and you know that I'll be right there whenever you need me."

With a quick kiss he continued, "Come on, let's get your stuff loaded in the car."

I was confused at first, then, as I scanned the array of cars, I noticed my mum stepping out of hers and looking for me. I could feel my breath quicken at the thought of facing her and what awaited me at home.

"Hey, it's OK," Noah said, clearly aware of my distress. His hand grabbed mine, "come on, I want to meet your mum before we leave, let's go."

We made our way over to the car, Noah carrying my suitcase and me holding my sleeping bag and blanket. As soon as I was close enough, my mum reached out and pulled me close to her.

"Oh, I've missed you so much sweetie! One month is too long," she said.

Once she let me go, her attention turned to Noah, "And who is this?"

"Mum, this is Noah, my… boyfriend."

He stepped away from me and reached out his hand to my mum.

"It's a pleasure to meet you, Mrs Bailey," he said. I shot him a glance at his use of a more mature voice.

"Oh please, call me Claire," she laughed. Turning close to me, she added, "I like him Cassie, you've done well!" I looked down as a blush grew over my face and smiled at her remark before looking back at Noah.

"I'll put your bags in the back, Cass, give you a chance to chat," Noah said with a smile. He walked around the back of the car and placed my bags inside.

"So, you did it sweetie? You went to him?" she asked, and I nodded.

"I really love him, mum."

"That's so good honey," she told me and asked, "How are you?"

"I'm OK, how are *you* mum?" I responded in a serious tone.

"Oh, I'm wonderful," she said in a cheery voice. I looked at her sceptically.

"Well, not great, I'm just trying to keep up with things. I know we'll be fine," she confessed.

I nodded and let the subject drop. This was neither the time nor the place for this conversation.

"Mum, I want you to meet the friends I made here," I said, gesturing at Emma and Dean to come and join us. They walked over and introduced themselves. Immediately, my mum and Emma were chatting away, like I knew they would. Dean was standing slightly to the side, looking slightly awkward – not that I could blame him. I imagined what he'd be like when he met Emma's parents and wished I could be around to see it!

"Well, it was lovely to meet you three. I'm so glad that Cassie has widened her horizons and met some new people – that's wonderful. We must have you all over for dinner when you're settled after camp. I'm sure Cassie's siblings and her father would love to meet her wonderful friends – and her boyfriend."

I looked at her suspiciously – she was talking about dad as if he hadn't moved out. I guess I wasn't the only person that didn't want to believe he was gone. Noah glanced at me too, obviously picking up on my mum's words. I just shrugged my shoulders.

I looked at Emma and saw tears in her eyes. I walked towards her and gave her the tightest of hugs. We'd been through so much in only a month.

"I'm going to miss you," she whispered in my ear.

"Me too" was all I could muster. We broke apart and laughed at each other, both with tears in our eyes.

"Come here," Dean said and gave me a hug too. "This has been one exciting summer Cassie, I'm going to miss you." I nodded to him, and he let me go.

"It won't be long, and I'll see you two soon, I promise," I assured them. "I mean, Emma is already planning a whole bunch of double dates".

They both smiled and nodded. Then, Emma noticed her parents enter the field and dragged Dean over to them.

Like all mums, my mum then hung around for another thirty minutes, speaking to Dan and Emma's mother too. To my delight, I was able to see Dean meet Emma's parents. He did well – despite his awkwardness!

"Hey Cass!" I spun around and saw Noah standing with the people I could only assume were his parents. Looking at the father, I could see the resemblance to Noah, and the mother looked at her son adoringly. I walked over to them, my heart was racing. As I got closer, Noah placed a reassuring arm around my waist.

"Hi, it's wonderful to meet you, I'm Cass," I said as I shook their hands.

"This is my girlfriend, the girl I was telling you about," Noah added.

"Oh Noah," said his mum, "you left out the part about her being so sweet. Cass, it's so lovely to meet you, we've heard so much about you!"

I raised my eyebrow at Noah, and I could see the blush creeping up his neck. My mum came to join us, the parents introduced themselves and soon they were talking like old friends. I wasn't complaining as it gave me more time with Noah.

"Well, it was splendid to meet you," mum said, "but I'm afraid me and Cassie need to be leaving." She checked her watch. "My goodness, we've been here too long already!"

Mum said goodbye to Noah's parents and walked back to the car, giving me and Noah a moment to say goodbye to each other. We walked a distance away from his parents for a bit of privacy.

"I love you so much!" I exclaimed. I didn't know what else to say.

"I love you too, and I'll be driving down to see you as soon as humanly possible, I promise," Noah assured me.

"It's going to be crazy not seeing you, I don't know how I'll manage," he confessed, moving in closer to me.

Any words I was going to say were soon silenced by Noah's lips. I kissed him back, summoning up every single thing I felt – the mix of sadness at leaving him, joy that I'd met him and relief at finally deciding to confess my feelings for him.

We broke apart, panting, and knew it was time. I said goodbye one more time and started to walk away. Noah grabbed my hand and walked with me to the car. When I reached for the door handle, he spun me around and brought me in for one more hug. My face rested in the crook of his neck and I inhaled his heavenly aroma one last time.

"I packed you one of my hoodies in your bag, baby," he whispered in my ear.

I looked up at him. He knew what that would mean to me, and it made my heart swell. I got in the front seat and did up my seat belt. Noah gave me one more kiss through the window and with that he walked away from the car and away from me.

"Wait!" I called out to him, and he spun around.

I reached down to my bag and rummaged until I found what I was looking for – my favourite pink scrunchie. I handed it to Noah and he slid it onto his wrist, smiling.

"In return for the hoodie, so you have something of mine when we don't see each other."

"Oh, I love you so much," he said once more and then stepped back from the car as my mum started up the engine. She reversed and pulled out of the car park. I stuck my head out of the window and waved goodbye to everyone still there. As we drove away from the campsite, I felt like I'd left a piece of my heart behind, but that was OK because it was safe with Noah. After driving in silence for a while, my mum spoke up.

"So, it was a good summer?" she asked. I paused for a minute and then replied.

"You have no idea." I told her and with a smile I looked out the window, thinking back on everything that had made this summer so great.

Epilogue: One year later.

Since the summer that had changed my life, me and Noah had enjoyed almost one whole year of couple bliss. I'd soon realised that my worries were silly. Noah made the journey whenever he could to come and see me, and I realised that thirty minutes really isn't that far. Then again, even if it was three hours or three days, I'd make the effort for him because he made me so senselessly happy.

Noah met my family, and my parents and friends loved him. Obviously, he met my dad at a different time to the rest of the family, but dad seemed to like him, and Noah made sure that it wasn't odd or awkward. He'd played with Bradley and Hailey, and they would jump all over him. Jake even seemed to like him quite a lot and talked to him about uni and what he was going to do. They joke around too. Noah just seemed to fit in naturally with my large crazy family.

Lexi, of course, grilled Noah- excessively- about his intentions and all the mad cliché stuff, but he handled it so well and they really liked him. They're so similar, so I wasn't surprised. Connie chatted to him a bit, which was good, and Noah asked about her art, listening intently as she explained each of her works. Even Lottie, while remaining her usual quiet self, still seemed pretty comfortable around him.

Now, don't get me wrong, they didn't get on as well as Emma got on with Dean, but I was glad about that. I didn't want another one of those situations! I still talked to Dean and Emma, and we'd really become a great group of four, with the boys getting along fine, now they weren't battling for the same girl!

I'd met Noah's family too. His parents were so sweet, and from what Noah had told me, they seemed to really like me. I was surprised that I felt so comfortable when I was there, thinking that meeting the parents was supposed to be this grand and daunting moment. But I felt good. Noah's younger sister was so sweet too, and he was such a loving big brother. I mean, the first meeting was rather nerve-racking, but Noah held my hand and I got through it. I love going down there now!

It had been better at home too. Mum and Dad had decided to try counselling while they were separated. I don't think they ever stopped loving each other – that was never the problem – but they needed to sort some things out. They had some time apart this year and dad moved out, but with Noah by my side it was much more manageable. He strengthened me, and I got through it. Mum and dad thought therapy would be helpful, and it really was. They found ways of actually talking about things and expressing themselves and they managed to work it out! Of course, it isn't perfect, but I've realised that nothing is ever perfect. That's a crazy idea. But the main thing is that they're putting in the effort. I love my family so much, and they've shown me what it means to love truly and with your whole heart – and that you must fight for love. And I planned to!

We were heading back to camp next week and I couldn't be more excited. I'd get to spend the next month with my friends I hadn't seen in ages and my boyfriend – I couldn't ask for more! Soaking in the sun, sneaking away with Noah. Me and Noah were going together and he was driving us. It would be nice to have some time to ourselves on a little road trip before we arrived at camp. We'd have our one-year anniversary while we were at camp, and I was excited to see what we were going to do. I already had a few ideas, but knowing Noah, he'd probably already planned a grand celebration.

After an hour of driving, we were nearly at the campsite. When I saw the entrance, my excitement bubbled up. I was anxious to see Emma after so long. Yes, we talked nearly every day, but it had been months since I saw her, and I was just hoping it wasn't going to be weird.

Noah turned his car into the field and pulled up. I was out of the car before it had even fully stopped. I scanned the campsite, then I spotted Emma stepping out of her tent on the far side of the field. The same tent we had last year. As soon as I saw her, I was off, racing over to her. She looked up, and shock gave way to elation. As we got closer our arms opened and I hugged her as tight as I could. We collapsed to the floor with the force of the collision, and soon we were both lying on the ground in fits of laughter.

"Well, this is an interesting sight." I heard Dean's voice before I saw him. I grabbed his hand as he pulled me up and I gave him a friendly hug.

"Hey there stranger," I responded to him, "how are you?"

"I'm doing well, thanks. Glad to be back," he said.

Dean pulled Emma close to him with an arm around her shoulder and she looked lovingly up at him. They were right together, and it was so good to see them happy.

Soon Noah came up behind me.

"Hey man," he said, shaking Dean's hand before turning to Emma, "and hey to you too!"

Noah stepped back, placing his arm around my waist as I leant into his chest.

I just knew that this would be a great summer. But that's a story for another time....

Being with Noah made me realise something – I *had been* content with Dean, and that was good, but contentment wasn't always enough. With Noah, a storm raged in my chest and I couldn't fight it. His presence calmed me, and I felt safe when I was with him. He made me happy – I smiled as soon as I thought of him and knew that nothing could compare to what I had with him. I'd known Noah for barely one year, but it was the craziest and best time of my life. He lit something up in me that I couldn't describe. He made the world seem brighter, birds louder, the sun hotter. Noah had changed my life and saved me in more ways than I could list. This is what happiness felt like and this is what I'd been waiting for.

Lexi once asked me – if I could go back to the start of summer and just be with Noah when he first got to camp, would I? Without hesitation, I said no. Then I thought for a moment – yes, if I'd just stopped what I was starting with

Dean when I met Noah, then things would've been much simpler. But then, I don't think I would've gotten to know Dean or Noah in the same ways. I knew in my heart that I wouldn't change a single thing. Everything happens for a reason, and if the rest of the summer hadn't unfolded the way it did I may not have met people that have become some of my closest friends. Plus, the greatest thing about what I'd found with Noah is that we built it off a friendship. Maybe that was what went wrong with me and Dean, going straight into a relationship before we were friends. Me and Noah and Emma and Dean both got to build our foundations on friendship – that's why I know that this will last. I'd always been told that you can't have a rainbow without the rain, and now I understood what that meant. There had been some bad moments – but I had Noah.

I was always a hopeless romantic and now I knew why. It gave me hope. I'd gone from counting down days to taking every day as it comes and knowing that things can happen when you least expect them to. Noah had taught me that. I'd no idea what to expect when I saw him arrive at camp, but now I can't imagine my life without him. That summer had led me to Noah.

I'd found that summertime feeling. Sure, it wasn't the easiest route to take, but I still got there in the end. I found my person – and I wouldn't change a thing.